THE NOVEMBER MAN IS BACK, BETTER THAN EVER!

"The plot moves smoothly . . . Granger writes crisply . . . Devereaux provides a satisfactory ending."

—*San Antonio Express-News*

"Ingenious and engrossing . . . a uniquely satisfying reading experience . . . Granger has created intensely interesting continuing characters. . . . The November Man thrillers are invariably absorbing. In HENRY McGEE IS NOT DEAD, Granger again gives us solid suspense, tense action, and provocative ideas. Every reader will savor each word."

—*Florida Deltona Enterprise*

"All characters are vividly drawn, and you'll find yourself in a spin of nonstop intrigue. . . . Another page turner by Bill Granger with a neat twist at the finish."

—**Bill Sweeney, KSRO Radio, Redwood Empire Book Beat**

D0402558

BOOKS BY BILL GRANGER

THE NOVEMBER MAN NOVELS
The November Man*
Schism
The Shattered Eye
The British Cross
The Zurich Numbers
Hemingway's Notebook*
There Are No Spies*
The Infant of Prague*
Henry McGee Is Not Dead*

CHICAGO POLICE STORIES
Public Murders*
Priestly Murders
Newspaper Murders*
The El Murders*

Sweeps
Queen's Crossing
Time for Frankie Coolin

NONFICTION
Chicago Pieces
Fighting Jane (with Lori Granger)
The Magic Feather (with Lori Granger)
Lords of the Last Machine (with Lori Granger)

***Published by
WARNER BOOKS**

ATTENTION: SCHOOLS AND CORPORATIONS

WARNER books are available at quantity discounts with bulk purchase for educational, business, or sales promotional use. For information, please write to: SPECIAL SALES DEPARTMENT, WARNER BOOKS, 666 FIFTH AVENUE, NEW YORK, N.Y. 10103.

ARE THERE WARNER BOOKS
YOU WANT BUT CANNOT FIND IN YOUR LOCAL STORES?

You can get any WARNER BOOKS title in print. Simply send title and retail price, plus 50¢ per order and 50¢ per copy to cover mailing and handling costs for each book desired. New York State and California residents add applicable sales tax. Enclose check or money order only, no cash please, to: WARNER BOOKS, P.O. BOX 690, NEW YORK, N.Y. 10019.

HENRY McGEE IS NOT DEAD

A NOVEMBER MAN NOVEL

BILL GRANGER

WARNER BOOKS

A Warner Communications Company

WARNER BOOKS EDITION

Copyright © 1988 by Granger & Granger, Inc.
All rights reserved.

Cover illustration by Cliff Miller

Warner Books, Inc.
666 Fifth Avenue
New York, N.Y. 10103

 A Warner Communications Company

Printed in the United States of America

This book was originally published in hardcover by Warner Books.
First Printed in Paperback: December, 1989

10 9 8 7 6 5 4 3 2 1

*This is for Philippe Pelletier,
who knew only Alaskan winters.*

Here's a pretty state of things!
Here's a pretty how-de-do.

—W. S. GILBERT

Truth sits upon the lips of dying men.

—MATTHEW ARNOLD

ONE

Captain Holmes

Peewee waited, rocking back and forth on his sneakers, sometimes breaking into a little dance done to the sounds in his mind.

The fish stall was closed down. The boys had hosed down the counters and the floor and washed away the remains of the fish and the bits of shell. The only thing left was the faint and rotting smell of sea.

Peewee knew he was beautiful. Even the marks on his hands were beautiful. Girls look at those marks and look at the unmarked face with its deep, sad leopard eyes and they thought he was some kind of a man.

Peewee looked at his hands, at the new cut where the thin shucking knife had slipped along the seam of the oyster shell and tore into the thick protective glove on his left hand and bit the flesh underneath. Just a little cut, not like some of the other cuts.

How did you get cut?

He'd grin at them and shrug and make his eyes look sad. Wasn't going to say he got cut because that was his stupid fucking job, cleaning fish and cracking oyster shells for old man Hunzinger. Girls wanted mystery, all the time living in a dream world, talking about soap operas, for Christ's sake, like they were real.

Peewee stepped into the shadows of the shuttered stalls of the Pike Place Public Market and watched the prostitutes trotting out along First Street, like they were going somewhere.

Friday night was always like this in Seattle, always full of hustle and people moving into position and the feeling that something was going to happen, something worth waiting for.

Peewee had the blade in a sheath under his SeaHawks jacket. The top of the handle was just inside his jeans. He took care of his knife. He watched a fat girl cross against the light up the street and the motorcycle cop was on her case just like that, went over to her with his long boots and his jodhpurs, swaggering because he caught her jaywalking.

Fucking town, Peewee thought. Get you a piece of ass any color you want any way you want it, get you dope, gambling, any fucking thing you want and the cops want to write you up for jaywalking. It was comical if you thought about it. Peewee had a con's sense of irony.

He heard a sound in his memory and tried a step on the hosed-down floors of the public market. Killing time, waiting. Traffic climbed up Pike Street to the top of Seventh, which was the top of the long hill that started way down at the Puget Sound waterfront, on the street called Alaska Way.

Damn, I'm beautiful, Peewee thought because he was

thinking about girls, not himself, trying to figure out what it took to get girls seeing him the way he saw himself.

Some of the little girls came over from East Side, little Norwegian girls with their little round cans carved out in jeans, looking for the price—you'd be surprised how many amateur tricks were out there. Some of the nice-looking girls from East Side go right downtown, right down to the Westin Towers or someplace, pull their tricks out of Trader Vic's or someplace. Some of these girls dressed, Peewee thought. He thought about the kind of money it takes for a girl like that with silky underwear, the kind you want to feel under your hand.

Like Mai-Lin. Little Hong Kong girl, shops the market, kids around with Grecchi and Peewee but she's miles from them. Not snotty, you know, just business. Mai-Lin sits in the big lobby at the Olympic Hotel when it's cocktail time, just sits waiting for someone to buy her a drink. They play the piano in the big room and got little dainty things to eat and the girls who serve the drinks all got long legs and wear these high-collar satin dresses that make their boobs look big.

"Shit," Peewee said out loud, thinking about it, thinking about Mai-Lin.

He went down the corridor to the back of the public market, where the French restaurant was that looked over the hillside down at the waterfront. Behind the public market was a flight of stairs that dropped three stories to the level of the waterfront, to the railroad tracks that ran a hundred feet beneath the elevated freeway. There were one or two restaurants up here and a lot more down there on the dockside street called Alaska Way.

It was a working and playing waterfront, crammed with restaurants and souvenir sheds and long piers full of working ships and ferries. Down at Pier 48, the large blue Alaska Marine Highway ferry was getting ready to sail, its hold full of trucks and campers and the mix of old-timers and residents who found it the cheapest way north. The ferry would sail for most of a week up the string of islands that formed the Inside Passage. It was spring now and the volcanic islands were full of trees and shining white glaciers and the waters were deep and blue and still.

Peewee thought about Alaska sometimes, thought about making all that money up there that he had heard about all his life. Sometimes he dreamed about it.

Nobody on the steps, steps slick with remains of a light early evening rain.

Something has to happen, he thought. And then saw it.

The barman was leaning over the guy at the edge of the bar. The guy'd been sleeping. Guy woke up fast, shook his head, denied everything. Moving the guy out. Big man with a black mustache and a red whiskey face and that walk. That walk, the way they walk.

Peewee held his breath when he saw the roll.

The big guy with the black mustache pulled a twenty off the roll and the barman started to protest but said what the hell, not out loud but saying it with the way he shrugged. He took the twenty and the roll went right back into the wrong pocket, the right-hand jacket pocket, the pocket it was so easy to grab out of.

The barman led him to the door and held it open twenty dollars' worth and the big guy said something and then lurched out onto the wet floor of the empty market.

Peewee held his breath, waiting in the shadow between the bar and the street. Like no one else was in the world.

You can tell which ones are the longshoremen and which ones come from the ships. The sailors carry a roll off the ships and they roll when they walk, even if they've been on dry land for months. Even when they stumble down on the wet walks to the back of the public market. To the stairs. Down to Alaska Way, down to the darkness beneath the viaduct road, down to the fog and sounds of ferries steaming out in the night.

Peewee put his hand on his jacket, felt the handle of the knife, felt the sheath press against his flat belly. He looked toward First Street again, almost to the place where he had been waiting for Friday night to start and nobody was around.

The sea wind cut across the rumble of the elevated freeway. The fog crept through the silence of the covered market. The sailor was on the stairs, holding on to the rail, rolling down the steps. He stumbled once and then rested, gripping the banister, heaving like he was about to throw up.

Peewee stood on the top of the steps and decided about the thing.

He started down the steps, graceful, beautiful.

Went down the steps all the way, past the stumbling sailor, all the way down to the dark of the street below where the warehouses were in shadows. Stepped beneath the stairs, away from the single streetlamp. Felt the knife in the sheath and pulled it out and waited.

There was a way to do it.

Don't just go stick people, go around sticking people every time you roll them, even the pigs get off their jay-walking patrol and start looking for you. No. Be cool. Let them know about the knife, know they're this close, let them shit in their pants if they want to, and then let them go. They get grateful, in fact, for you letting them go.

Away from the warehouses, across the tracks, the bars

and restaurants along the waterfront were bright. Along the gutters across the way, Indians slumped dead drunk, propped against garbage baskets and lampposts, their bodies sprawled in abandoned positions as though they had been slaughtered. The ferry boat for Edmonds slipped away from the pier and sounded the horn across the water. Puget Sound did not sleep, even in fog, even in darkness.

Heard the sailor above on the steps. Heavy, uncertain footsteps.

Fucker is singing, Peewee thought. It made him smile.

He stepped into the light and drew the knife right across until it rested against the Adam's apple. Pushed his shoulder so the seaman felt the knife on the front of his throat. The sailor felt it all right. Sailor was dead still all of a sudden, without a song. Sailor stopped weaving, felt the knife's edge on the softness of his frightened flesh.

Peewee waited, pulled the knife a little until the flesh felt the sharp edge sink in just enough to make a thin line of blood. The sailor was positive about it. The only thing that ever worried Peewee was that the drunk would be so drunk he'd fall against the knife and cut his own goddamn throat through no fault of Peewee's.

This one knew.

Peewee felt the roll in the side pocket, pulled it out of the jacket pocket, held his breath, slipped the roll into the pocket of his SeaHawks jacket.

"Don't cut me, man," the sailor rumbled.

Big fucker and he was shitting, Peewee thought. Felt good the way Friday was turning out, first day of spring, felt good about thinking about Mai-Lin sitting over there in the lobby of the Olympic. What it was all about was money. Just as soon open those pretty Hong Kong legs for Peewee as some fat-ass tourist with a Seattle duck on a T-shirt and an American Express card. Shit, yeah.

"You just put your hands out on the railing, hold them there five minutes, motherfucker, five fucking minutes and then you be alive for the rest of your life. You dig?"

The sailor gurgled something. It was hard to talk, feeling the blade across your throat.

Felt good making the sailor afraid.

Peewee drew the knife slowly away from the flesh and then put the point on the cloth of the jacket.

"Feel that?"

"Yes," the sailor said.

"You hold that rail. Just hold it. You don't know when I'm going, you just count five minutes."

The sailor held.

Peewee pulled the knife back.

The sailor turned with a wide swing and hit nothing but air. Smashed his body into the stair rail. Stumbled and rose, this time with something shiny in his big hand.

Peewee backed up, held his ground, looked at the strange knife. It was crescent shaped, with a bone handle on the back of the crescent. Peewee smiled at the knife, at the red-eyed sailor. Fucker was so drunk he could barely stand up. What was he going to do with a knife like that? Shave himself?

The sailor surprised Peewee.

He made a quick lunge and brought the funny-looking knife down and out and the blade flashed in the single streetlamp. Peewee felt the blade bite at his left hand and felt the slice. He looked down and saw blood in a curved line smiling at him from the back of his left hand. He didn't think the sailor had got so close.

The move had been quick and sure and sober. But now the sailor was drunk again, overwhelming the adrenaline. The funny-looking knife was over his head and then he brought it down. He wasn't even close this time.

The sailor took a step, lurched, stumbled on a broken piece of concrete and went down hard on hands and knees.

Peewee stomped the back of his hand twice and heard the yell. Stomped again.

"Leggo the fuckin' blade," Peewee said. Stomped again and heard the shout of pain and the crescent knife was kicked free.

Peewee saw his own blood on his hand.

Peewee's eyes took on that funny look. Grecchi knew that look when they were working in the stalls and old man Hunzinger came down on Peewee about this or that. The look was cold in leopard eyes. Peewee learned to do that look doing two years in Angola on the way west from New Orleans. Learned the look to survive inside, survive the old cons looking at him like he was a girl.

Peewee knew he was going to cut this dude. That's what you had to do, inside or outside: Don't take no shit, don't give them two times at you.

Knelt over the prostrate sailor and brought the thin-bladed knife down in the easy, practiced arc, the way you slice open a big salmon from head to belly without damaging the precious fillet.

The arc never finished.

He felt the blow a moment after it came. He rose, felt dizzy, hit his head on the steps. He held the knife and turned.

Where the hell did he come from?

He wasn't there a minute ago. This one had gray hair and gray eyes and a face just as cold as Peewee's leopard eyes. Some dude come into the play. Some fucking tourist hero come into the play he wasn't part of.

There was nothing to say. Peewee moved in, the knife fading back and forth in front of him, tracing an intricate pattern of threats on the night air.

The other waited. Just stood and waited. Stood like a flatfoot tourist, messing with something wasn't his business.

Peewee felt the anger coming through his eyes, putting fear on Gray Eyes.

"You a fucking hero, tourist? You come down to Sea City to be a fucking hero?"

Because the gray man had nothing in his hands. He was looking at the knife and he didn't have a fucking thing in his hands.

"Come on, hero," Peewee said. "You wanna fuck around so fuckin' bad, dad."

Slash across and down and it caught the hero's raincoat sleeve and Peewee stepped in, ready for the counterslash. But the crazy man was stepping in too, with nothing in his hands. Peewee realized he was too close. Too fucking close. He tried to pull his knife hand back and the other reached for his shoulder and pressed it.

All the feeling went out of his arm, from shoulder to hand.

He dropped the knife because he didn't even feel it.

And then, a moment later, felt the screaming pain up and down his dead arm. The hero stood there and made pain like that without hardly moving.

And then Peewee was moving except he wasn't doing any of it, swinging around like the end kid on crack-the-whip, the gray man pulling him fast and then Peewee saw the brick wall a moment before it crushed his nose. He felt broken teeth behind his lips and heard a terrible sound and then realized he had made it.

Was the guy going to kill him?

He had never thought about that possibility.

Swung out on the whip again, coming around fast and this time he closed his eyes so he wouldn't feel anything.

He thought of Mai-Lin, she said he was a pretty boy. Said it just so he knew wasn't nothing he could do about it with Mai-Lin.

Felt no pain again, except the thought that he wasn't pretty anymore.

Devereaux took the roll out of the SeaHawks jacket. He gave the sailor a hand and pulled him to his feet. The sailor blinked, looked down at the slumped skinny form of the mugger.

Devereaux gave him the roll and the sailor stared at it dumbly and then looked at Peewee on the ground. "Fucker was gonna kill me. Fucker practically broke my hand."

He looked at the other man then. "You kill him?"

"Probably not." The man said it as though it didn't matter. The sailor stared at him a moment, trying to figure this out. The man stood there very still, flat-footed, the large hands held easy at his sides. He had big shoulders when you studied him, but he didn't come off as a big man. The shoulders and arms and hands were all of a piece, coming down like the slouch of mountainside.

The sailor blinked again. His adrenaline-induced sobriety hurt. He kicked Peewee. "Ought to kill him."

"You tried once," Devereaux said. He said it flat but the sailor heard the contempt in his voice. The sailor stared at him.

"Captain Holmes. At least, it used to be 'Captain.' "
The sailor held out his hand. Why had he said that about being a captain? Why explain? But something in the gray eyes demanded the truth, knew the truth before he even said it.

Devereaux did not take his hand.

The sailor blinked again. It was all he could think to do. He dropped his hand and felt bad about extending it. He held the roll in his hand like a beggar's cup. His right hand was swelling fast.

"Who the hell are you?"

"The man who saved your life."

"So what do you want? You want money?"

Devereaux said nothing.

The air was full of city sounds but they were apart from it. No one had even seen the attack down here under the freeway, in the shadow of old brick warehouses. Holmes said, "What are you to me?"

"I saved your life. That makes you my responsibility," Devereaux said.

"That's Indian shit. You listen to Indian shit, you turn your brains inside out after a while."

"You lived with them," Devereaux said. "When you were in Alaska, working the Inside Passage."

"Fuck it, fuck you too," Holmes said. "Where's my fucking knife?" He found it, picked it up, held it in his left hand with the roll, the only hand he could use. He felt drunkenness coming back on a wave of nausea. It would overwhelm him in a moment.

"Jesus Christ, I feel terrible, I was gonna die," Holmes said.

Devereaux did not move, did not speak.

"What the hell do you want? I give you a hundred dollars you get me to my room all right. Pacific Plaza Hotel right up—"

"I know," Devereaux said.

"What the hell do you want, man?" And Holmes felt the same edge of fear he had felt when the knife was at his throat. He looked at the knife in his hand and looked at the gray man across from him. "Answer me, you sonofabitch." He was afraid and it made him shout.

"Henry McGee," Devereaux said at last. "I want to talk to you about Henry McGee."

Holmes took a step back. "I dunno nothing—"

"We'll talk about Henry McGee until you remember everything," Devereaux said.

And Holmes shivered then as if the knife was being drawn across his throat.

TWO

Henry McGee

Nels Nelsen met Henry McGee the year before in Anchorage. It was exactly a year ago, first day of spring, and everyone waiting for breakup.

Nels had cleaned and repaired his trapline and he didn't have the dogs anymore for company so he had taken a ride into Nome, sixty miles west of his cabin, and flown down to Anchorage. He had a few good days of drinking behind him when he met Henry McGee in the Polar Bar down on Fourth Avenue. One thing led to another and they talked about trapping. Trapping wasn't what it was; hell, Nels even took some welfare aid from time to time, just like a goddamn Indian. It wasn't like it was all right, Nels Nelsen complained, but he had enough to drink and enough to fly down to Anchorage when the winter made him crazy and waiting for breakup was never going to end.

Henry McGee was a good listener and never said a word when it wasn't needed. He was also a gifted talker. He could hold the whole bar in his hand so that the fat woman on the boards behind the bar turned down the television set to better listen to him. She had heard everything twice but Henry surprised her with his stories.

It was spring and bright and cold and everyone edgy waiting for breakup. That's the way March and April are, empty bright months of waiting. But Henry McGee took the edge off.

The days were long now, starting around three in the morning and lasting until after nine at night. The mountains were white and some of the glacier passes would stay white and frozen all during the bright summer. But in some of the streams, the water was moving beneath the ice and the fish were flowing with the water and the whole thing was breaking up, cracking winter and sliding down to the sea.

Henry McGee said he went out with an Eskimo flotilla one year to hunt the seals off Little Diomede and damned near ended up riding the floes across to Siberia and what the hell would he have done then?

As it was, Henry McGee said, they got a couple of Siberian dogs that got trapped out on the ice. He spun the story along, talking about the differences between Siberian dogs and the bigger and stronger Alaskan dogs and the whole bar became quiet and they could actually see it after a while, see the butchering of the seals on the floes and the Russian boat that came out from Big Diomede in the straits, coming right after them. . . .

Good stories and good company and Nels Nelsen felt better than he had all winter. The dogs were gone, all sold off or killed a long time, and you can't talk to a snow-go machine. He had the radio but it made you sick after a while, talking about things you didn't have and didn't need and telling you how much you really needed them so that you got to the point where you thought you really did need them. He was an old trapper, doing things mostly in the old ways, and in the dark months when the sun barely lifted to a dull line of red glow in the southern sky, he talked to himself and heard the wolves speak in tongues. He read the Bible for company and also John D. MacDonald.

Henry McGee was mysterious in a good-natured way. He talked about his past in terms of stories but the stories all had ends. The spaces between the stories were kept black. It was all right with Nels Nelsen.

Nels thought it was Henry who had brought it up but it had been on Nels' mind as well. The trapping was thin but it was a lot of work and maybe they could make more of a go of it by doubling the labor and doing more hunting. Maybe Henry suggested it and maybe not. They talked about it and they thought they both could get along with each other.

" 'Sides," Henry said. "I'd just as soon go into the bush for a while, maybe a year or two, hunker down a little, get away from places." It was the closest he had come to talking about the blank spaces between his careful stories. Nels did not press him; everyone in Alaska had a past and a lot of them never wanted to talk about it.

Breakup came in little separate explosions.

First it was the Yukon River, here and there along its ice-choked spine; and then the Kobuk and the other rivers and the thousand little unnamed lakes; and then the sea itself in early May, the wide and shallow Bering shuddering and cracking and opening itself all the way to the straits between the tip of Alaska and the tip of Siberia.

The ice began to retreat a little on the North Slope and the race was on, up from the Pacific toward the Beaufort Sea.

It was a time of frantic activity when the supply ships and fishing boats from Seattle raced north and fanned out from Haines to Anchorage, from Dutch Harbor in the Aleutians through the straits to Deadhorse and Barrow. The top-heavy ships raced along the shallow, freezing northern waters with washing machine parts and snowmobiles and tanks of gasoline and kerosene and hydraulic drilling machinery and the thousands of things the North wanted to survive the next winter. The ships came low in the water because of all the things people wanted to make next winter more civilized.

After breakup was the time for fishing salmon and the other creatures of the northern seas. The salmon season was very short because there were fewer and fewer salmon but the flotilla of fishing boats struggled up from Seattle and Vancouver and from Japan and the Soviet port at Vladivostok.

The ancient Bering Sea was alive with fishermen and supply boats and factory trawlers from the Soviet Union that sucked up all the fish from the smaller boats and processed them in bloody machines right on board. Everything must be done fast, against the clock, against the brief window of bright summer between the breakup and the freeze-up.

Henry McGee and Nels Nelsen went back to the traplines and the cabin and lost themselves in the wide wilderness.

The Alaskan bush stretched around them for hundreds of miles in all directions. The bush was full of silence so that they sometimes could hear nothing but the loud knocking sounds of their own hearts. They fished the Yukon and salted the cache and sold some of it and ate their fill. The summer stretched twenty-four hours a day and the dusty brown tundra began to turn a light, hesitant green. At the end of the brief, bright summer, they would go out and kill the caribou, which went up to the mountains again. They would kill the caribou easily because the caribou were stupid and ran in a brown river, thousands and thousands and thousands. Caribou was the meat for the winter and when they had skinned the beasts and divided the meat, they would put it in the meat cache on the roof of the cabin.

They worked hand in glove. Henry and Nels had silences between them and that was company as well. They listened to the same good music on the radio. Nels talked about his father coming from Norway. Henry just told stories and never filled in the black spots between the end of one story and the beginning of another.

It seemed Henry could turn his hand to any task. He sewed and cooked—cooked better than Nels had ever tasted—and he played a mandolin sometimes and sang old songs they both knew. Henry was a rangy man with wide shoulders and modest eyes. He knew how to laugh. They went into Nome now and then to get their supplies off the lighters from the big boats waiting out in the shallow harbor. They got drunk at the Board of Trade bar and they picked up a couple of Indian girls there and had a good night with them. They walked along the stony breakwater that was over the old beach where the gold rush had started a long time ago. Henry told him a little about gold and he seemed to know what he was talking about.

"Gold is not real to me," Nels said. "I never had enough of it to make it real to me."

"It isn't even real when you find it," Henry agreed. "It's like the oil business but only more useless."

"You worked the pipeline—"

"One hell of a year. And there's gonna be another pipeline too, in our time, coming out of the east of Alaska. And gold. There's still a lot of gold in the country, but it doesn't mean nothing because the getting of it makes it not real. The old-timers hit the Klondike and then went on to Nome and they were shoveling the gold dust into their pokes and for what? Go to town and pay ten dollars for a caribou steak and a hundred for a woman when the Eskimo would share his wife with you for friendship? Everything you read about it, you wonder where the hell the gold went. And then you realize, the gold was never real."

"You spend your life looking for gold, you end up not finding any, then what the hell did you do in your life?"

"Looking for something that wasn't there," Henry said. "Everybody does that. Not just about gold."

"I'm satisfied," Nels said.

"Yes. I saw that the minute I laid eyes on you in that bar down to Anchorage," Henry McGee said. It was like a compliment.

"You looking for gold still?" Nels said.

They had been very drunk, sitting in the midnight sun on the breakwater of the Bering Sea that runs behind the main street in Nome. They drank out of the whiskey bottle and felt the wind. The wind never let up, even when it was warm.

"Stopped looking," Henry said in a soft voice. Nels could hardly hear him. "What is worse than looking for something you can't find? Finding something you didn't want to find. You look for gold long enough, you never really want to find it.''

"That's crazy," Nels said.

Henry had looked at him. "Yeah. I guess you're right.'' And the story was over—if it had been a story—and the blank spot was reached and Henry had nothing more to say until the next story began.

The cold started suddenly that year. It snowed in Nome on September third. The supply boats raced across the Arctic Ocean—across the Beaufort Sea and the Chukchi —for the Bering Straits, trying to beat the ice back south. The sun dropped in the southern sky and was less and less each day. As suddenly as spring light had pierced the black heart of the Arctic winter, the fall fell back to blackness. The ice crossed from the Soviet Union to the tip of the Seward Peninsula. The summer roads shut down. The ships that had not made it were locked in ice and the supply barges were beached along the barren wilderness of the North Slope. The glaciers in the mountains crept between the peaks, and the snow came and the wind and the cold and, last of all, the darkness.

The darkness came over the northern sky and reached to put out the last of the sun in the southern sky.

Nels worked the west traplines and Henry worked the north. They would be gone for four days a week, out of each other's company. Henry killed two wolves the first time out and the trapping for martens went better as a result. They had plenty of food and when they met again on Friday night after all week apart, it was like a celebration.

First man back boiled snow in the black pot and threw in the meat from the frozen cache above the cabin. But it was Henry who did the delicate cooking touches. Nels loved to eat a meal made by Henry McGee, and sometimes on the trail, in the dark silence of snow and black sky, he would think about the weekend meals to come.

And the talk.

The stories took on richer ornaments. Henry would tell him about the commonplace things that had happened that week on the trail, and they were the same things that had happened to Nels but Nels had never really seen them. Henry could observe things and made them different and new. On those Friday nights in the darkness, in the dancing light of the kerosene lamps, Henry McGee made his stories and sometimes they went on all night long.

On Christmas Day, Henry played Christmas songs on his mandolin and they decided to go to Nome and find women. They got drunk in Nome for three days and then sobered up and went back to the cabin.

Like all of the bush rats, they did not curse winter or darkness or wind or snow or wolf or bear. They feared fire, dying alone and nothing else.

Then one morning, the southern sky was purple for a moment. They saw it together—it was a Saturday—and they drank to the purple. And the next day and the next day, the light came a little more and then it was as though the light was racing north. There were illusions in the sky, formed by ice and light and snow and the sheer, blinding clearness of the air.

Everyone north knew of the illusions. Sometimes, on a clear morning in Anchorage down at the spit of land in Cook's Inlet, a person might stand on Fifth Avenue and look north and see the slouching power of the Denali Range of mountains seem to loom over the town, though they were more than a hundred miles north. The face of Mount McKinley—an amiable, ugly huge mountain with a long skyline—might seem to appear right behind the Captain Cook Hotel. The illusions formed in the northern lights that scraped the sky above the Arctic Circle. The illusions were magic and the Indians and Eskimos and whites all agreed on this; the magic was so powerful that it could not be spoken of, merely witnessed.

The two old trappers worked hard together. With their crescent-shaped knives, they scraped skins clean of gristle and blood and sinew. The skins were stored in the cache. Two men could do more, even if they had to share.

Each day, through March and into April, the days stretched more and more and the southern light made other lights dance in the darker northern sky, reflected by clouds and ice.

On the first day of spring, Nels Nelsen returned to the cabin after a week at the trapline and put on the water and threw in the meat and waited for Henry McGee. They had known each other a whole year.

Nels puffed his pipe in the cabin and read a long chapter of a murder mystery set in a strange place called Miami Beach, Florida. He had been back to Norway once, to see the village of Tromso, where his father had been born, but he had never been to Florida and could scarcely imagine the place, though he had seen it on television in Nome.

On the second day of spring, Nels took down his rifle and the medical kit and drove the snow-go up the northern trapline to look for Henry.

The line extended out a hundred miles in the snow, along tundra and into the frozen river valley and into the stunted hills beyond. The roar of the snow machine made the silence more profound. The earth was covered with silence that was as immense as the sky. The day was flat and gray and there was no magic to see.

He found Henry sitting on a hill, looking down at his snow-go at the bottom of the hill.

Nels put the machine in neutral and climbed up the little hill.

Henry stared at him with his modest eyes and the small, crooked smile.

Nels got down on his knees and opened the parka and saw the blood, and all the while, Henry McGee seemed to be staring at him. Except he was dead.

Nels felt the immense and profound silence of earth and sky. The world was gray and white, without perspective. It was flat and it was also the depth of the universe.

Nels picked Henry up and carried him down the hill. Henry was frozen solid. He put Henry on the snow-go and tied him down. They rode off together back toward the cabin, just the way they had ridden off together to Nome at Christmastime.

In the cabin, Nels put on the water and put Henry McGee down on a wooden kitchen chair, at the table where he always sat and told his stories. Nels took his parka off and then took off Henry's and hung them up to dry. When the water was ready, Nels made tea. He put a mug in front of Henry.

"You want tea, Henry?" Nels said.

The silence had penetrated the cabin as surely as the cold. Nels felt very cold.

"You probably want whiskey but there ain't any whiskey left and I'm damned if I'll go sixty miles to Nome just to buy some whiskey for you," Nels said. He sipped his tea and found it good enough; but Henry wasn't drinking tea.

Nels stared at Henry awhile.

"Well, what held you up on the trail? How was it you didn't come last night? I put on the beef and waited for you all night."

Then Nels thought he heard the dogs howling outside the cabin. He went to the door and looked out. The wind was up and he thought he heard the dogs above the wind but he couldn't see them. It was still light outside and there wasn't a tree all the way to the horizon.

"Damned dogs," Nels said. "Get rid of the whole damned team and get me a snow-go."

He went into the cabin and closed the door. He looked at Henry just sitting there. And then he knew the dogs were all gone and that Henry was dead. It had just taken him a little while, as though it might have just been a mistake or a dream. He had to call up Nome on the shortwave and they'd get a plane in here from the state patrol.

"I love you, Henry, goddamn it to hell, why did you let yourself get shot out there?"

Henry didn't say a thing.

"Whiskey is what you want, Henry," Nels said. There were tears in his eyes but he was smiling. "All right, you want it, it's all right with me. We'll take a day and go down to Nome and get some women and whiskey. You liked that last time well enough, Henry. Just let me get a few things together and we'll close her down and be in Nome in two hours."

He dressed Henry up snug and tied him down in a sitting position on the snow-go. It was getting dark but he knew the trail. He felt the power of the machine whir and he was gone then, through the snow, with Henry sitting behind, swaying in the turns. The machine prowled the frozen Yukon River. As they got closer to Nome, Nels saw or heard other machines.

"Have a good time in Nome tonight," he told Henry. But Henry just held on through the turns and did not speak at all.

It was nearly nine o'clock at night on the second day of spring before the two men from the state patrol took charge of the body strapped to the seat of a snow-go parked in front of the Nugget saloon at the far end of Front Street. It was quite a sight, seeing a dead man frozen in a sitting position, and the Indians were gathered around and were telling jokes about it and about Nels sitting in the bar, drinking whiskey alone. The police ignored the Indians and they talked to Nels a long time and then they unstrapped the body of Henry McGee from the machine.

When they wrote the report, they called the dead man Otis D. Dobbins because that is who all the papers on him and in the cabin said he was. The state police checked the identity of the dead man with the FBI in Washington. The FBI had a small file on Otis Dobbins, confirmed by fingerprints and an old photograph. He had once served three years for robbing a small savings and loan in Oklahoma City. Nels Nelsen said it was his friend, Henry McGee, but the police saw that Nels had become disturbed by the death and was probably thinking of some other old partner.

Despite the certainty of the police, one of the officers noted the odd name in the report of the murder. In less than forty-eight hours, it became part of a permanent computer file, achieving a bureaucratic idea of immortality.

The ambitious state policeman even ran the name past the FBI. The FBI computers blinked. The name was sorted back and forth, and finally a fourth-rate bureaucrat named Tyler in the FBI headquarters on Pennsylvania Avenue said the name did not exist in FBI files. This was a lie.

Nels Nelsen was treated at a psychiatric hospital in Anchorage for several weeks after the murder of his partner. He finally stopped insisting that Henry McGee was Henry McGee. This seemed to satisfy the nurses and they stopped giving him those horrible hot baths that made his skin turn raw.

He was very nearly ready to return to his cabin when the man from Dutch Harbor came to see him that strange spring afternoon when the light lingered strong and sure. It was light now from the hour after midnight almost until eleven at night. The light was long but the cold was still longer and lingered in the broken ice fields in the sea and in the ice still surging down the rivers from the mountains.

The man from Dutch Harbor talked of Henry McGee and what Henry McGee had been like and Nels was off guard. He corrected the man from Dutch Harbor several times when he made mistakes about the character of Henry McGee.

Nels had had his share of dealing with authorities this spring, from the state cops in Nome to the strange people who ran the psychiatric hospital. He was careful of the stranger. The man from Dutch Harbor spoke to him patiently about the stories of Henry McGee. He seemed interested most in the stories.

Nels did not know that the stranger had also ordered that the body of Henry McGee/Otis Dobbins be exhumed. But it would not have surprised him because he thought he had seen everything twice in all the years he lived in Alaska.

THREE

Henry McGee Is Not Dead

He had lived nearly a year in the town house on Rhode Island Avenue in Washington. He had lived with Rita Macklin, a journalist with several regular clients.

Twice a week, Devereaux went to an apartment building in Alexandria and sat across a table from a man who was a professor of science at Georgetown University. They were both agents of R Section and they played a game between them that involved probabilities. It was called If. When the game was played out, the tapes of the game were delivered to the highest level inside Section and turned into transcripts called stories. The stories were studied by serious men and it was all taken very seriously, in the way that shamans once divined future events by studying the entrails of birds.

That was all the intrusion Section demanded of him for nearly a year.

He loved Rita Macklin. She was thirty-three and her hair was red. She had freckles on her nose when she had too much sun. Her skin was pale and delicate to the touch and Devereaux thought she always smelled sweet. When she woke in the morning, she would often find him lying next to her, leaning on his elbow, studying her.

The only bad thing between them was Section.

He was an agent and Hanley once said to him, "There is no such thing as a retired spy." There were retired spies of course, living on the west coast of Florida and in southern California and in certain approved foreign countries but, in a sense, no one ever retired from the trade.

Rita Macklin felt two fears in her life.

In the first, he would die.

In the second, he would love the trade too much. The second fear was more complicated in her and she sometimes could not explain it to herself. She hated the second fear even more than the first because it made Devereaux hateful in her eyes and it made her lose her love for him and it made her, sometimes, want to leave him. And she knew that if she left him, she would be lost for all her life.

They made love to each other as though swimming naked in a secret pool, hidden in a dense woods, perhaps hidden in a cave in the heart of the woods. The water was warm and dark and they sometimes could not see each other but they touched and found each other. They were wet and exhausted and all the crowded thoughts and feelings in their lovemaking were wet and warm and made them close their eyes to better see each other.

One afternoon in spring, a man from Section called on the phone. Devereaux said nothing except "What time?" He replaced the receiver. He was standing in the hall of the town house and she was in the living room, watching him. She saw what it was and she began to hate him again.

The cab made slow going down Pennsylvania Avenue toward Capitol Hill. It was not the most direct route to Union Station but Devereaux said nothing. The fares in the District were low because congressmen set them for their convenience, and Devereaux felt empathy for the old drivers in their soiled shirts and hopeless gray faces.

Besides, he wanted to be late. Nothing in the trade demanded this. Hanley was merely playing spy again, the bureaucrat yearning for the trappings of the real world.

Union Station was across from the Capitol and it had once been a train station and then something else and now it was a train station again, with marble columns and the sense of impending majesty that all great train stations share.

Hanley was waiting for him in the lounge, a suitcase at his feet. He had missed his usual dry-martini-and-cheeseburger lunch and it made him look more sour than usual. That and Devereaux's lateness.

"You didn't bring a bag," Hanley said.

"I travel light," Devereaux said.

"We are supposed to look like travelers. To blend in with the scenery."

Devereaux sighed and sat down. He ordered Finlandia, which the barman did not have. He settled for the American vodka and stirred the ice slowly when it came. He did not look at Hanley and Hanley stared at a television set at the end of the bar.

Hanley was director of Operations in Section. There was no R Section, of course, any more than there was a covert-operations intelligence directorate in the Department of State that arranged arms transfers to Afghan rebels. Any more than CIA sanctioned persons. Any more than there were spies. Everything in the trade could be explained as a figment of imagination, which is what the spies wished you to believe.

"You've had a good long rest. It's time to come back," Hanley said.

"I might choose not to," Devereaux said.

"You play If very well but we can always find players for If. I thought of you because I thought of the stories we make out of your If games."

Devereaux said nothing.

Hanley looked at him, a little smile at the edge of the dour mouth. He was small and bald and his eyes were absolutely cold. His voice was as flat as Nebraska, where he had been born.

"Aren't you curious?"

"It doesn't matter. You'll tell me anyway."

"It involves Henry McGee."

"I don't remember the name."

"You remember everything."

It was perfectly true. Sometimes the vodka made him forget but the vodka had its limits and then it would be time to remember again.

"Henry McGee disappeared four years ago."

"He went across?"

"We assumed so," Hanley said. "Quite a disappointment, our Henry. We had been running him for nearly ten years."

"And he was running you," Devereaux said.

Hanley stared at the martini glass. "We wanted him

badly. We chased him for nearly two years, every trail. Clues kept turning up. We weren't discouraged. We wanted to find him."

"To ask him why?"

"To ask him many things," Hanley said. "It became a continuing embarrassment. We found Henry McGees but they were never the right ones. We were intended to find them. Henry McGee was very clever at setting down trails. We had to follow the trails. We found a Henry McGee in Santa Cruz, California, drunk on a beach. Yes, he was Henry McGee but the trail had been forged. Henry McGee—the real one, the one we were interested in— was playing with us. He turned Operations upside down. It was very bad for a while. We began not to trust each other. That's a bad thing."

"Especially since you are so worthy of trust."

"We shut it down. We buried the files. We buried Henry McGee and did not admit we had made a mistake. We did the right thing."

Devereaux was not expected to say anything.

"Three weeks ago, our man in Dutch Harbor flew to Anchorage to investigate a little matter. A trapper, one of the old-timers in the bush, was found shot to death. He went by the name of Henry McGee. We had never known about him. His name was really Otis Dobbins. He was a storyteller."

"So Henry McGee decided to trigger your files," Devereaux said. "You should not have put in computers."

"Henry McGee is out there. He must be. There's no reason to spark a new trail for us. We had buried him. Here." He tapped the brown envelope on the bar top. It resembled the closed envelopes used by lawyers for their cases and was marked ULTRA.

"You aren't supposed to take that out of the building," Devereaux said.

"It's all we know about Henry McGee, the last four years. The stuff we buried. If Henry means to do us more harm, we have to find him. All the names are in here, all the contacts he had made. We went over them for two years."

"Why not rehire your original chasers?"

"Burned out. It's no good. One of them wanted to keep on with it when we closed the matter but we gave him Eurodesk in Paris. We can always give them Paris."

"I like things the way they are," Devereaux said. He pushed the empty glass to the bar tray and the barman came down. "I like the game of If, I might even be good at it."

"If becomes stories, our scenarios for the day after tomorrow. I thought about you right away. I would have made you a chaser four years ago but you were listed as dead then. It was your last chance to get out. Now you have to find Henry McGee."

"What did you call him?"

"Storyteller. That's why I thought of you."

"I saw him fifteen years ago."

"Fifteen years ago," Hanley repeated. "Henry was supposed to be a Siberian, coming across the ice bridge in the straits, leading a sorry pack of Siberian Eskimos. You did the initial questions."

Devereaux said, "I was in Kotzebue and you sent me to Little Diomede and I took Henry to Anchorage. Why was I in Kotzebue?"

"Some matter, not important."

Devereaux remembered it then. He remembered everything. Hanley was right; it was some matter that was not important. But he had been the closest man to the Siberian refugees and he had questioned Henry McGee. The other services got to them as well—especially the CIA and FBI—but Henry McGee belonged to Section.

"It was cold and depressing. The snow was piled up against the winter entryways and there weren't any windows in the grocery store. Kotzebue was just frozen and full of people who wanted to survive the winter. They walked across the ice from Siberia and they were all ragged and half starved, and the thing about Henry was his eyes. He called himself Chukchi. Then he told his stories. He was really Henry McGee and he had been in a fishing boat and it wrecked and he went ashore in Siberia, it was at Kivak. He lived with them for three years and convinced some of them to come across. He promised them snowmobiles, he said all the Eskimos had snowmobiles."

"There had been a wreck, a fishing boat was lost," Hanley said.

"All of Henry's stories were true. All of the stories could be proven," Devereaux said.

Hanley looked at the crystal ball in his drink.

Devereaux said, "What happened to the others? To the Siberian Eskimos?"

"They were studied. They began to miss their homeland. Someone came up with the idea of diverting them. We turned them over to the *National Geographic* for a while and they liked that."

"Did the women have to bare their breasts?"

"What has that got to do with it?"

"My subscription has lapsed; I wanted to see if traditions continued," Devereaux said.

They were silent in the dark lounge. The afternoon travelers straggled to the trains. The Metroliner for New York was nearly filled and the milk run from Boston was just coming in. The faces were tired, intent on travel, on getting home, on rest, on trail's end. Nobody paid any attention to them, even if Devereaux had no suitcase.

"You didn't believe him," Hanley said.

"No." He tasted the vodka. "I didn't believe him."

"You said he had too many stories."

"Too many stories, not enough secrets."

"He was a spy from the beginning."

"That's what you think," Devereaux said.

"He *is* coming back, that's why that old trapper was shot. Henry McGee had to die so that our records would be reactivated. It was a signal to us. Like the fox coming back to the hounds and barking at them. We have to chase him again."

"You have chasers. I don't want this. I want to play If with the professor and invent stories for your pleasure."

"You don't miss the field?"

The question was soft, almost sly.

Did he miss it? Not at all. The field had burned him out and now she was the only important thing. He thought of Rita Macklin's frown when he had put down the phone in the hall.

"You have to do this, you know," Hanley said.

"It's a free country," Devereaux said.

"Not really. Not in this case. You warned us about Henry and we took him in, he had so many good stories about the other side and he had contacts. We sent him into black three times to Siberia and he was very good, he worked out very well for us."

"Except he wasn't your man," Devereaux said.

"Kill him," Hanley said.

"I won't be your killer."

"Then bring him in and we will take care of it."

"You have wet men. I won't be your wet man."

"You belong to us, November." The use of the code name for the agent—the name in permanent file—was intended. It was more than a reminder of obligations.

"I can't," Devereaux said.

"But you must. You belong to Section," Hanley said.

It was not a matter of spelling it out. There were controls that operated all the puppets in the end. Rita Macklin, in one sense, was a control for Section; so was the boy, Philippe, who attended university now and whom Devereaux had rescued once from the hell of a Caribbean island. The cases of the agent called November might be parts of the control if it came to it.

"I can't do this," Devereaux said.

But they both knew he must.

She tried to sound concerned.

"Is it dangerous?"

"It's a little trip. A few questions. Very low stuff."

"That's a lie," Rita Macklin said.

"Yes."

"You said you'd never lie to me."

"Yes. Not about the things that count."

"I hate this. I hate the secrets outside me. You have me in this world and you still go outside me."

"It's a little business," he said. He put the extra pair of trousers in the bag and closed it. He did not show her the pistol, a nine-millimeter Browning automatic with a thirteen-round clip. It was the new issue of Section and despite Devereaux's aversion to automatics, it had been issued to him.

"Don't leave me."

"Two weeks. Or three."

"Don't leave me for this."

She put her body against him. She pressed her breasts against him and held him low against his back and pushed her pubis against him and buried her lips on his neck. He clung to her.

"Two weeks," he said. "Or three."

"You do it because you love it."

"It's dead in me," he said, "it's been dead for years."

"You won't say you love me."

"Words are for lies," he said. He kissed her wetly and she opened her mouth to him. For a moment, they might have been on the verge of making love.

She pushed him away.

He tried to see it in her eyes, without any words. He saw and it cut right down through his chest, into his guts, and he was bleeding all over. He saw it in her eyes.

"Two weeks," he said.

"I'm going to get rid of this place," she said.

"Do you want to?"

"I love you," she said.

Devereaux stared at her.

She was crying now; then she came to him and held him. He held her. Now they made love and when she was sleeping, naked, in the moonlight that streamed through the bedroom window, he put on his clothes and took the bag and his gun and went away.

FOUR

Kools

Kools heard the plane bank in the darkness. Kools knew the motions of the plane through its sounds. It was in the brief night of spring, a hundred miles above the Arctic Circle. It still snowed a little during the daylight, although it was spring. The clouds, sullen and gray during daylight, had blown in behind the snow front and stretched across the breadth of Kotzebue Sound, which was open now but still full of ice floes.

Kools put two red lanterns on the far shore of the nameless lake. The lanterns were fifty paces apart. The wind died and the cold rubbed against Kools' brown unsmiling face. His parka was damp already with his own odor and the smell of the animal skins. Kools put his mittened hands under his armpits and did a slow, shuffling dance on the frozen tundra to keep himself warm. He waited and listened to the plane's motor like a hunter listening to forest sounds.

The plane turned again and the motor dropped to an

indifferent growl. It was falling now and he still could not see it.

He stopped dancing, stood still, let the cold enfold him. The cold was nothing; it was part of him. The old ones in the settlement became like the whites, they listened to the radio for news of the weather and then they spoke of the weather all the time. It would drive you crazy. The weather comes and it goes and it is enough to know the cold can kill you softly. The old ones became more like the whites as they waited to die.

Then he saw it.

The plane dropped over the crest of the hills at the far end of the lake. The wingtips were mounted with blinking red lights and a powerful headlamp was slung under the motor. The Cessna, wearing water skis, touched the choppy surface of the lake, seemed to hesitate, seemed to rise and then settled down. The plane made a slow taxi across the water to the edge of the land.

There were no trees, no scale to the darkness or the light.

The cabin door opened and there was a brief stab of light from the plane. A figure formed against the light and descended to the ice along the shore. The slight figure was wrapped in a Seattle-made parka and mukluks. The pilot leaned over and dropped a bag on the ice and pulled the door shut.

The passenger picked up his duffel and trudged across the ice toward Kools. The plane turned at the far end of the lake and waited and then took off fast in a burst of throttle, climbing above the red lamps on the ice. In a moment, there was no sound again and the great silence penetrated them like the cold.

Kools went to the lamps, picked them up, and extinguished the flames. The other man followed his steps back up the ridge to the huts. There were three huts in the village. The cold was utterly silent and without dimension, like the tundra. In the winters, the drifts passed under the cabins built on stilts. None of the huts had more than a single, small window. They all had a winter entryway, a box with a door on it to serve as a weather chamber outside the main door. There was just a thin layer of snow and ice on the ground now, and in a little while, the brown tundra would show through and turn a slow, pale green as the summer waxed.

The hut was very warm. The passenger took off his parka. The warmth was infused with the mingled smells of animal skins, sweat, urine and the dampness of clothes and bodies turning from utter cold to utter warmth. The parkas were covered with frost already melting on the wooden floor. The kerosene stove made light and heat.

Away from the light was an old man scraping away at the caribou skin. He did not need the light because he was nearly blind. The crescent-shaped knife had caressed the skins of hundreds of caribous in his life and he knew the way.

Skins were piled on a ledge that was both bed and couch. The ledge was by the stove and the light was warm and low in the low, smoky room. Kools moved to the other side of the stove and cut down a piece of meat hanging from a rafter. He chewed the raw meat and looked at the thin white man. And at Narvak, his sister, who made a place for the man on the skins. Kools looked at Noah and his sister snuggling under the furs and knew the white man was touching his sister. Kools knew the places. He had touched her, long ago, in the cold nights when there is only shelter and darkness and the smell of human flesh next to you.

"Noah," she said, smiling, handing him a cup of warm soup. He looked at her pretty almond eyes while he drank. She waited for Noah, sitting with her hands on her hips, her jeans tight against her thighs, her flannel shirt open at the collar. She always waited for him, to speak or touch her or tell her what had to be done.

Kools finished chewing and belched. He lit a cigarette.

Noah opened the pack and took out the Johnny Walker Black. For the first time, Kools smiled at him.

"For you," he said, handing the bottle across.

"To share," Kools said. He squatted, twisted the cap. He drank from the neck. The warm, smoky whiskey taste filled his throat and his nostrils and made his eyes water in the half-light of the room.

There was more. There was always more. They all waited while Noah opened the clear envelope of powder. He passed it to Kools, who put his nose to the envelope and looked at his sister. But Narvak kept her glittering almond eyes on the passenger they called Noah.

"I only had room for two cartons," Noah said and handed over the mentholated cigarettes. Kools accepted them without acknowledgment; the cigarettes were his great weakness. Acquired from the whites during the two years he had spent in prison at Palmer. The cigarettes were the medium of exchange in prison and the common source of daytime pleasure. The daylight lasted twenty-two hours some months in the prison at Palmer. Palmer was so close, achingly close to the freedom of Anchorage. You could hear the trucks on the highway outside the prison. Everyone had someplace to go except the prisoner. On those hard summer months, without the comfort of darkness, Kools could only think about oblivion. It had been his refuge. He had thought of the cold and how it wrapped itself around your heart and allowed you to sleep. It made your heart still and you dreamed into a new life. The old ones—some of them—thought there was more beyond oblivion. This was the evil brought into the villages by the Baptists. The old would become afraid of life after life. But Kools was not afraid. Oblivion was his belief.

When he had been in prison on the blinding white days of summer, he knew that oblivion was whiteness. It would pluck all the color from him and from the prisoners and the color from the walls of the prison and the color from the warden and the color from the guards and the color from everything in the world and suck it into whiteness. They caught him staring at the sun one afternoon in the exercise yard and put him in the hospital for three months to observe him, to see if he had become mad.

In the hut, the old man had put down his knife and shuffled over to them and got his due. He lit one of the cigarettes and let the blue smoke fill his nose and mouth and lungs. His teeth were nearly gone and his skin was fine, like vellum.

The white man who called himself Noah smiled at Narvak. If he had brought her some gift, he would not show it to her now while her brother and the old man watched. Later, under the furs, when she was naked below her waist and opened her legs for him, he would tell her the gift. Kools knew this, knew all about the ways of Noah and Noah's way with his sister. Noah had small, precise, white teeth, like the teeth of a mink or marten. He had a thin red beard and his pale skin blotched in the cold. When he had been brought to the settlement by Narvak, Kools had distrusted him as he distrusted all whites. This one was no different. Except in the things he did.

Narvak had met an old dark-skinned man in Fairbanks who said he was Ulu. She had been amused by him, by his stories, by his glittering, shrewd eyes. She had asked him why he was Ulu, which was the name of the knife of the native Yup'ik people.

"Where does the *ulu* begin or end, little honey?" the dark-faced man had said. His teeth were bright and even in that dark face. "That's what you call a riddle. Like an *ulu* cuts east to west and back but rests right in the middle. The point is: Where's the middle?"

Narvak had gone to Fairbanks to work on the excursion trains that went down to Denali Park, where all the tourists took pictures of Mount McKinley and the grizzly bears. She slept with everyone. She was sixteen. She slept with the man who called himself Ulu. And then Ulu had given her this one—they called him Noah—and told her to take Noah back to the settlement with her and to learn from Noah what to do. She had liked sleeping with Noah, even more than the old man.

Noah looked at his black-faced watch. "Twenty-one minutes," he said.

"Can you be so sure?" Kools said. "The country takes its own time."

"We have to be precise on this," Noah said in his soft dry voice. He looked at Kools with that look that made Kools hate him sometimes. It was a white man's look, like he didn't stink but you did, or he was smart and you were as dumb as a dog eating shit in the snowhut. Kools opened the whiskey bottle again and drank from the lip.

"Why are you back here?" Kools said at last. He sat back against a ledge, the fur tickling the back of his neck.

"I thought you were waiting for after the Kobuk breaks up, we were going up the Kobuk to do hunting."

"Things changed," Noah said. He looked at Narvak and put his hand on her and she moved closer to him, to be within his possession.

"We go back across, one more time," Noah said.

"Breakup—" Kools began.

"Come on, brother," Noah said. He smiled at Kools because he thought Kools was a coward about going across. Kools was afraid of Siberia, of the Russian soldiers in their greatcoats, of the crude training quarters. When Noah realized this, he had power over Kools from that day. "We go right across the straits, take a little boat. Hell, we walked across in the winter, that was a lot harder than floating across."

It was true: The other side frightened Kools the way prison did. He had no fear of ice or cold and the people on the other side were like the people here. But everyone knew the story of the people who had gone across six years ago to visit relatives. They thought nothing of it because the relatives were just people "over there" and not of a country that was different.

The whites on the other side had taken them all away and they were never heard from again.

Kools hated Noah but not the dark-faced man named Ulu, who had come to the settlement twice. Ulu spoke the tongue of the people and this pleased them because even the Baptists had not mastered the careful, clicking sounds of the people's speech. The dark-faced man showed them magic and they took his magic and were delighted with it. One of the old men asked the dark man questions: Where did he come from? Where was his tribe? What was his name?

North, he replied, which was not possible.

East and West, he replied to the second question. The riddle intrigued the people, even Kools.

Ulu, he replied to the third question.

One old villager understood. The *ulu* rolls east to west to east, cutting all; its power comes from the handle, which is above the blade, which is the north.

The explanation of the old villager pleased everyone. It even pleased Ulu, who stayed five days with them and told them things and left some magic and went away. The second time he came, he took Narvak aside and told her to take a rifle and do a thing for him and tell no one. But he left magic for the others and Narvak's eyes had glittered at what he told her.

Some of the magic was in the white powder. Some in the trips to the other side. Some in this thing they were doing now, which Kools did not quite understand. There was money in the magic done and Kools wasn't a fool. He could love his "brother" if he had to. He had no feeling about his sister Narvak because women were not very important.

At least, the dark-faced visitor who came to the settlement from time to time and said he was Ulu had accepted old ways. This was important, oddly, even to Kools.

He tasted the whiskey again. The people of the other side had vodka and they always seemed drunk.

"Now it comes, do you feel it?" Noah said to Narvak. It was so much later. She placed her hand, long and quite beautiful, on the place between his legs. She rubbed his trousers.

He smiled at her, at the cocaine in his head. At Kools asleep on the floor under the furs. At the light. "Not that, the sound of it, the explosion."

"Do you think it happened?" Narvak said.

"Of course. Everything happened the way it was supposed to. The way a thing is done." He reached under the fur and she had removed her jeans. He touched her furry wetness to open her. She groaned.

"Do you think it makes a sound?" he said.

"What?"

"If there's an explosion and no one hears it, does it make a sound?"

"No," she said, slipping down on the furs.

She pulled him onto her and opened her lap.

"And what about Narvak?" he said softly in the drug-softened voice. "What did Narvak hear?"

She opened her almond eyes and smiled at his blue eyes and the softness above her, around her, floating like a dream. "Nothing," she said.

And he penetrated her.

She made another sound.

"What did Narvak hear?"

She saw it as her gift to him. Smiled and kissed him. "Two shots only." Smiled wider and wider in the darkness, beneath the furs. "Whip-cracks on the dogs. Crack. Crack." She was thinking of the rifle and the thing that Ulu had sent her to do. Noah did not understand.

"It was done," he said, stopping a moment.

"Yes," she said. "Yes, yes, yes." Noah had been told; the dark man called Ulu had told Noah and it was so good that he should know it, know her power.

"How did you leave him?"

"It was a week ago. I followed him on his traplines and he never saw me until I wanted him to see me. Crack, crack! He sat down, he stared at me, he looked puzzled. He was dead all right but he was sitting there, staring at me. He didn't believe it. He did not believe I had killed him. His name was Henry McGee." She lifted her belly. "Deeper," she said. She moaned.

She had killed the old trapper a week before. She saw the death and felt him in her. She liked the mingling of the thought and what she did now.

"Do you hear it?" Noah said.

Yes, she thought. Yes, I can hear and feel it exploding in me, around me, collapsing on me. Yes, yes, she said in the sounds that were not words.

At that moment, 487 miles east and one degree north of the settlement of three huts on the nameless lake in the land north of Kotzebue Sound, twenty one pounds of plastic explosive blew a gaping sixteen-foot-wide hole in the pipeline below pump station three. The warm oil spilled out like black blood on the frozen tundra.

Twelve minutes later, the oil flow ceased. The line had been shut down.

Sixteen minutes after that, the helicopter blades broke the silence again. They were coming down from Point Barrow, following the pipeline to the rupture. The pipeline would be shut down for less than two hours before the go-around line kicked in. The sabotage had been cunning, sophisticated and futile; the public information officer on duty saw to it that not a word of the minor disaster was reported.

He had called former Senator Malcolm Crowder, who had arranged the media silence that followed the explosion. He made telephone calls to his friends and the secret was kept. The line was too important to call attention to itself. The line carried the black oil down the spine of Alaska from the Arctic sea to the warm port at Valdez, where it was shipped out in tankers throughout the world. The line had brought riches to Alaska, even greater riches to all the companies and suppliers along the line. Senator Malcolm Crowder was an important man because he knew the value of silences and secrets and not one word of the explosion got out. Not this explosion, not the other explosions.

He was one of the few men in the world who knew that the pipeline had been under continuous terrorist harassment for sixteen months.

FIVE

Denisov

D enisov dreamed of Moscow still.

He expected the dreams every night of his life but he never knew when they would come.

The dreams were set pieces, full of commonplaces, almost without stories. But they made him very sad when he finally awoke to the foggy chill morning of Santa Barbara and recalled the restless night spent dreaming.

In the old life, he had not dreamed of Moscow, even when he lived in other places in the world. He felt glad to be out of Moscow in the old life; perhaps because he could always return there. He had been part of the rigid operation that is the Committee for State Security, the KGB. Like his compatriots in the field, he had found his way around the rigid regulations and the constant watch on his movements.

Now he was living in California. Every six or seven or eight weeks—they notified him by postcard—the man from

R Section came to see him. They would sit for an afternoon and talk of the world. Sometimes, they would look at photographs and Denisov would be expected to make some comment on them into the tape recorder. Sometimes they played If. The man from the government who came six or seven times a year was his only reminder of imprisonment and exile.

Once a month, like the old-age pensioners, he got a green check printed on rigid paper from the United States government.

When the Moscow dreams came on him, they always focused on the little cluttered apartment they had shared off the Lenin Prospekt. In the best—yet most poignant— of the dreams, the apartment would be empty and it would be afternoon. His wife would be gone to the shops, and his son to skate and drink in Gorky Park. He would be alone, listening to the music of Gilbert and Sullivan operettas on the records he had smuggled in by courier from London.

On sad mornings in Santa Barbara, the white fog came down from the tree-lined hills above the town. It filled the streets and lay over the red tiles of the houses and it gradually fell down the hillside to the harbor. The white fog made streaks in the water and surrounded each of the oil-drilling platforms offshore. The long beach was empty this early in the morning and even the stream of traffic along Highway 101 was muted. The fog made everything silent. Sometimes Denisov broke the silence by singing in his deep, flat voice. He sang the songs of *The Mikado* as he bathed.

The words were sad and he sang them in a sad voice. He sang the song of the minstrel with great tenderness and none of the irony Gilbert intended.

A wandering minstrel, I
A thing of shreds and patches,
Of ballads, songs and
snatches
Of dreamy lullabies. . . .

Once a day, he walked down through the town along Pacific Street or Figueroa to the sea. It was a long walk down the gentle hillside of the pretty town. He always had to wait at the stoplights where Highway 101 slashed a wide scar of roadway through the middle of the city. Highway 101 was a river of cars and trucks night and day, flowing between Los Angeles and San Francisco, impervious to the delicate beauty of the city or the soft hills above the bay. Except that every six minutes, a thin picket of red lights parted the river and the walkers continued across from the upper town to the lower.

Denisov always thought of Devereaux after the Moscow dreams. He thought of the gray-eyed man on the beach in Florida that night, telling him that the game was ended and that he had lost. Telling him he would be an exile to the United States for the rest of his days. Devereaux had given him this jail and this comfortable California prison of beach and ocean and pretty houses on a pretty hillside. He would never forget that.

He had money, quite a lot of it, stolen from the KGB when he was active, secreted in Zurich bank accounts, augmented by his shrewd trade in a secret world. The world wanted things that it was not supposed to have; he supplied part of that want, the part that was interested in cases of arms, ammunition, rockets and other ways of death.

He had been very careful in the beginning to hide his enterprise. He did not have to bother. The government knew about the arms trade. The government also used the arms traders when it was convenient to do so. It had taken Denisov a while to understand why the government did not interfere with his trade. He was useful to the government in the way all men without voice or status can be useful.

The fog began to burn off as the sun pushed over the hills and filled the streets with watery light.

Denisov always rested on a bench at the wharf that pushed out into the gentle harbor. He would watch the gulls strut on the wooden walkways or watch them dive along the shallow waters at the edge of the beach. He thought of nothing when he watched the birds; he felt rested, contemplating their graceful, unceasing activity.

What was wrong with this life?

He frowned, stood up, brushed his trousers. He started down the path along the beach again, as though he had someplace to go.

And for the second time that morning, he saw the same man.

This time the man was sitting at a café table across the street, watching him through an open window.

Yes, he was watching; he did not try to disguise it.

Denisov turned, felt strangely humiliated by the stranger's stare.

There was no expression on his face. The stranger had a blank look behind wire-rimmed glasses. His eyes were wide, his face stolid and the color of gray putty. He wore a suit and a tie.

Denisov turned again and walked away, not quickly, but in his usual, ponderous way, along the sidewalk that led into the parkway and past a soccer field. He walked all the way to the Fess Parker Hotel and pushed into the sleek circular lobby. He found a pay phone and picked up the receiver.

There was sweat on his upper lip, the same line of sweat he felt in the mornings after the Moscow dream.

The same man watched him. He saw the man twice.

The man knew he had been seen.

Denisov blinked at the buttons on the telephone box He tried to think through that. His eyes were blue and clear, without secrets or menace; the eyes of a saint. The saint stared at the plastic buttons on the telephone box as though they might have a message.

A long time ago, when the exile began, they had explained to him about the vastness of America and the way they could hide people in America. They could change his face and his voice and the color of his eyes; they could change his name; they could give him an occupation or not; they were the magicians and they could do magic and make people disappear.

Until one bad, foggy morning in Santa Barbara when a stranger began to watch him.

He punched eleven numbers and waited for the tone and punched fourteen more numbers.

He turned away from the telephone box and surveyed the lobby. He expected to see the stranger but there were only the ladies of morning in their careful daytime clothes, pressed smooth against their aging skin and expensive sun-bathed wrinkles. The men were never around hotel lobbies in the mornings, only their women.

"Redbird," he said. It was his code, drawn from a computer. His code changed every eighteen months.

The woman's voice said he would be contacted in five

minutes. He gave her the number on the telephone box. He replaced the receiver and rested his hand on the metal counter beneath the green box.

The telephone rang once two minutes later.

Again he said, "Redbird."

"What's the problem?" The man's voice was not the same. Denisov thought the agency kept changing personnel. In fact, it was the same man but his voice was altered every week by an adjustment in the telephone computer.

Denisov told him.

There was a long silence when he finished.

"Do you want a baby-sitter?" the voice finally asked.

"Of course. Unless it is one of your people who—"

"We'll check on that. We can have someone there this afternoon. At the apartment."

The connection was broken. Denisov replaced the receiver. The number he called was in the San Francisco area but it was unlisted.

He wondered if he should get his pistol out of the safe in his apartment.

In the end, he had not wished to alter his face; it was the only familiar thing in the strange world of exile. They had said it was his choice. He had changed very little over the years, from the time he had been KGB, in that section of counterintelligence called the Committee for External Observation and Resolution. He had been in Asia, in Spain, in Ireland, and finally, unexpectedly, he had been on a beach in Florida one night with the agent from the other side who had betrayed him into this exile. Suddenly, in one night, Moscow became a dream he would never see again. It was an ache in him when he dreamed of Moscow; it was a flash of pain when he thought of

Moscow while reading through some news dispatch from there. Moscow was more real now that he could never return there.

He touched his chin. His face had betrayed him twice this morning to a stranger who did not try to hide himself.

The old feeling of fear—so long buried under endless California days and nights—began to gnaw at him again. He could run—he could be on the first plane to Switzerland—but what was he running from?

He left the phones and walked into the lobby again. The place was large and cheerful and pink. The sunlight seemed part of the staging.

He crossed the lobby to the rotunda entrance and pushed through the glass door.

And the face was very close now.

He stared at the stranger coming toward him. He had no weapon, the stranger carried an umbrella. Yet there was no chance of rain today. They had used an umbrella in London in 1980 to place poison in the skin of an anti-Soviet radio broadcaster. The broadcaster had been a defector, just as Denisov was. Just the tip of the umbrella, an accidental brush—

Denisov waited with the solidity of a martyr: This time, this day, this place, they had found him after all those years. It was almost a release. It would be over in a moment—the Moscow dreams, the gnawing endless hatred for the man who had pushed him into this false exile, the vague yearning for the part of his life that had been amputated.

"Ivan Ilyich," the man said in mocking, perfect English, a slow smile on his face. "What a pleasure to see you again."

* * *

Wagner thought about it for a couple of minutes after hanging up on Redbird. He pulled out the file and looked at the photographs of the dull Russian face pictured in profile and full front.

The trouble was that everything was recorded. The government of secrets wanted to have no secrets itself. Wagner had to be damned careful all the time.

He pushed a button on his desk and waited.

The woman pushed open the door and took a step inside. The office was small. There was only one chair in front of the government metal-gray desk. Wagner nodded at the chair.

She sat down and kept her knees together. She had the standard businesswoman's suit: slate gray skirt, white blouse, a loose bow tie of gray silk. Wagner almost smiled. There was something vaguely absurd about Karen O'Hare. She was very beautiful, with ice blue eyes and black hair and flawless pale skin. Her body was generous and yet she clothed it with extreme conservatism, as though ignoring the obvious. The absurdities in her extended to her extreme seriousness about everything. He thought about the way she would look naked; he thought about that too often to make himself comfortable with her in the office. She didn't understand she was just a cute piece of ass.

Too young and too close for Wagner but he knew the others talked about her as if she had possibilities. Some women you have to take seriously, even if they're beautiful and much better suited to being a piece of ass. And then there were people like Karen O'Hare.

She insisted on ''Ms. O'Hare'' and getting to work on time and taking exactly forty-five minutes for lunch and changing into gym shoes at night for the long walk home.

She wore her black hair with bangs and she was always sending off for government publications that explained exotic things and she went to night school three quarters a year.

Absolutely great tits, everyone agreed. A great can and legs up to there. And she acted as if she wasn't beautiful at all. How could you figure her?

And then someone would tell about the time she was changing paper in the Xerox machine and dumped a cup of coffee into it by accident and insisted on turning herself in and offering restitution for accidental destruction of government property.

Wagner realized he was grinning and Karen was not. He let the grin fade and pushed the file of Redbird across his desk.

"Field check," he said.

Below the window, traffic pounded up and down Powell Street. All the charming old streets of the charming old city were always full of traffic now. The charm was seeping out of the place day by day. San Francisco was covered with white clouds and felt chill with the damp. A cable car clanged beneath their third-floor window. Wagner glanced at it: Full of tourists, the whole fucking city was full of tourists all the time, you couldn't eat or drink without rubbing asses with a bunch of fucking tourists. He counted himself as a native, though he had lived there only five years.

"We got a call from Redbird. He says he's spotted a watcher. Make the agency sweeps and make sure no one else is poaching our witness and then go down and hold his hand."

Karen O'Hare couldn't let the excitement stay out of her face. She thought Wagner was doing her a favor.

Karen was grinning like the girl who wins the poetry prize in eighth grade. It warmed Wagner despite himself. Wagner wanted to grin again but held it in.

"This is a great chance for me," she said. Her voice was soft, full of gee-whiz enthusiasm. Who could believe someone like her in this day and age? Wagner thought again. Her ice blue eyes were as wide as a doll's.

"Redbird is a little paranoid like a lot of them, he sees ghosts. He saw a ghost a year ago and sometimes he just needs someone to pat his hand and tell him everything is going to be all right."

"And if it isn't a ghost?"

Honey, how would you know the difference? The eager-beaver GS-7, reading all the government bulletins and all the agency rulebooks and playing it so hard on the square that it was painful to watch sometimes. She hadn't missed a day of work in three years. She lived with her aunt. She dated a proctologist who was nearly as dumb as she was.

Wagner knew she was perfect for it. She couldn't screw it up for him if she tried; she didn't have a clue. So Uncle could listen in on his recordings and see that Bob Wagner, GS-13 in charge of the San Francisco office of the United States Witness Relocation Program, had done his job, taken the threat seriously, sent out a perfectly qualified GS-7 to do her duty.

And if everything went all right, she wouldn't be hurt at all.

The rust-streaked hull heaved on the bulging gray sea, settled in a trough between waves, heaved again.

Devereaux had never expected to see the waters again. There had been a little matter fifteen years ago involving the smuggling of very high-tech pieces from Dutch Harbor in the Aleutians up through the straits into the hands waiting at Big Diomede. The Russians owned that piece of rock and the Americans watched them from four miles east on Little Diomede. The matter was cleared and a mark was put in a file someplace.

Devereaux had expected to be cleared out of Alaska when a second matter intervened. A dark-faced man led a tribe across the ice from Siberia and it was Devereaux's last Alaska job to interview them. And now, after fifteen years, Devereaux was on the trail again of the dark-faced man, who had decided to call himself Henry McGee.

Four weeks ago, a computer in Section read the name as a mark when it had been circulated through the various intelligence agencies from the morgue. Henry McGee, the computer read, and it looked in memory and found buried files and signaled the director of Computer Analysis.

And now Devereaux was on a cargo ship on the Bering Sea. He was tired. His eyes were gray and cold, like the sea, and he thought of the lie of weeks, two going to three, three going to four. Could he ever stop the lies?

"It's flattening out," Holmes said. Devereaux turned to him, a chipped mug of coffee in hand. Holmes had changed. His red face was a more normal color and his eyes looked peacefully at the churning sea. His right hand was bandaged and swollen from the mugging in Seattle. There would have been no berth for him on the ship without the telephone call to the freight line from an important man in Washington.

"How can you tell?"

Holmes grinned. "The clouds, the smells, the way the water changes colors. Bering is very shallow, all the way through the straits, you can see the colors change all the way to bottom."

"I don't see the bottom," Devereaux said.

"Henry McGee taught me that. You can see the bottom the way you see the light on the water. I thought it was a trick and maybe it is. Taught me a lot of things I thought I already knew. He was like a magic man, a shaman or something."

"And got you to lose your ship," Devereaux said.

For a moment, Holmes' face flushed again and he licked his lips. It had not been very easy for either of them.

They had left the kid in the alley beneath the public market steps and they had not gone back to Holmes' hotel. Holmes had not wanted to talk about McGee and the trouble McGee caused him in the end because it made Holmes look stupid and because he still admired the sonofabitch and couldn't deny it.

Devereaux persuaded him.

He showed him words and then alternatives to words.

Holmes had said it was like being in fucking Russia.

Devereaux had said it was, in a way.

When Holmes understood the way it was, it went easier for both of them. And now they were making the long climb north toward the breakup of the ice on the straits.

Devereaux followed Holmes below to the cabin and they both sat down at the Formica-topped table. Holmes picked up the coffee pot. Devereaux shook his head. Holmes poured himself another cup and sat down on a bench. Every day there was this time: Holmes sighed, waiting to get it over with.

Devereaux took out the photographs again. He put them face up on the table.

"I told you six days ago I was sure," he said. "That ain't Henry McGee. That ain't even close."

Otis Dobbins' eyes were closed in the photographs and his hands reposed on his naked belly. He was in the morgue in Fairbanks and the photographs were in Polaroid color. He was very pale because the blood had been siphoned out of his body.

"He called himself Henry McGee for nearly two years. He convinced a lot of people, both in Nome and in Anchorage. Why would he use that name, tell those stories that matched with things the real Henry McGee knew?"

Holmes had thought about that on the trip north. He wanted to get this man off his case, he wanted to forget about the little Indian prick who tried to knife him in Sea City, wanted to be left alone for a while. Henry McGee was a long time ago.

"I was thinking and I guess it was Henry did it, made the guy up. I mean, he took a guy and convinced him to be Henry."

Devereaux stared at him. The ship groaned against the sea. There was a clammy feeling inside the cabin. Tomorrow they would be in Norton Sound, crossing north toward Nome.

"Could Henry do that?"

Holmes began to smile. The G-man didn't understand about a man like that. G-man, whatever his name, was just a government man and that means he wore blinders. Holmes let the smile get big enough to show all his discolored teeth. He got up and went to the locker on the bulkhead and opened it with a clang. He took out a bottle of Jack Daniel's and splashed some in the coffee cup and looked at Devereaux. Devereaux shook his head.

"Henry McGee could do anything he wanted. Which is why I figure he was doing something for you or you wanted him to do something for you, which is why you're looking for him now."

"Don't figure too much," Devereaux said.

"Why is Henry McGee important to the government? To you?"

Devereaux could scarcely remember the face of Henry McGee as he had been fifteen years ago. Just a man who told stories, and Devereaux took them down and made his report. His conclusion had seemed too cynical to the people in Section. *Do not trust him*, Devereaux had finally written. *He has no secrets, only endless stories*. The argument against Henry McGee was buried in those words and no one in Section chose to dig under the words. They had decided fifteen years ago that Henry McGee was bona fide and that he would be a useful man because of his years in Siberia and his skill at insinuating himself with native groups.

"You're in a different country now," Holmes said. "All that is outside and now you're coming inside. This is a different country and different rules."

Devereaux let his fingers rest on the photographs of a dead man. It could have been Henry McGee, he thought. He could not form a clear picture of the man, even when it had been offered him from the files before the hunt began. Henry McGee was an illusion, a trick of ice and light and snow. Maybe Henry was dead and none of this mattered.

"See, Henry was an expert on everything. He knows

all about the Eskimos, all about everything. He even went over there a couple of times.''

Holmes waved his arm carelessly but the direction was west and they both knew where he meant. Henry went to Siberia for R Section—it was called going into black— and he had gotten drunk one time or another and told an equally drunken seaman. It was incredible. He broke every rule of the careful agent and he survived.

"I think he was a spy," Holmes said. His voice was low and there was a touch of awe to it. He sipped the whiskey and coffee with reverence.

"Why do you think he was an agent?"

"A spy," Holmes said. "If he wasn't, why else would he be going over there?"

"You said that one too many times, didn't you?"

Holmes made a face. He put down the cup. "How do I know it was Henry did it to me, put Canadian customs on me? Could've been some of you? Some of you people."

"We don't do things like that."

"Canucks stop me in Victoria and unload me and say I'm smuggling heroin from Sri Lanka. Jesus Christ, I come off fifteen thousand miles of ocean and get a kick like that. They just seized it finally but there was this hearing and I lost my license—"

"I know," Devereaux said. He had read all the scripts and notes and the 201 file on Henry McGee and it was like fog on a California morning, everything in the file obscured everything else. There was a paper trail for Henry McGee, a scenic and winding paper trail that led up and down the mountains and turned in on itself and never seemed to get anywhere, like the road followed in a bad dream. It had never occurred to anyone in Section to find out where the trail led because of the beautiful scenery of the stories along the way. "That was a setup. You knew Henry did it."

"I thought I knew. I saw him in Seattle two months later and we had a few drinks and I was feeling down because I couldn't get a ship and Henry said, 'You shouldn't talk so damned much.' That's when I knew he did it. I was going to kill him but you don't know Henry, the way he looks, he looked right through me. I asked him for a chance. He said there was a supply ship going up to Dead-horse and he'd get me a berth on it and he was as good as his word. And when I came back, he was gone. He could do any damned thing he wanted."

Holmes said this with awe. Holmes' ugly face was breaking out in blotches of sweat. He felt the gray eyes on him and tried to look defiant. "I told you every damned thing. You been on me eight days. Over and over and over, we look at the photographs and I tell you the same damned things."

"That's the way it's done," Devereaux said. He had not moved. The ship shifted in the water, back and forth, up and down. The fluorescent lights made both men ugly in the closed, damp room. There were others on the ship, boots up and down the ladderways, voices. This room was set aside for the government man to talk to Holmes.

"You get me back my rank," Holmes said.

"It can be done. Everything can," Devereaux said.

"Do I got to beg for it?"

"What else have you been doing for eight days?" Devereaux said.

"You're a bastard, like Henry. But I liked Henry. He was real, he had a voice and he was real. You're a fucking ghost."

"Tell me about the trips across," Devereaux said.

"I told you a hundred times. Henry told me when he was drunk. He was drunk and laughing about it and I didn't see harm in telling no one, not if Henry told me, but I wasn't supposed to and that's why Henry got me in trouble."

"Henry talked too much."

"Stories and stories. Like he lived on telling stories, like he couldn't even breathe if he couldn't tell stories. He had this story about this Eskimo fisherman was out by the Diomedes and he runs into these relations from the other side and they have a camp and kill seals and talk and drink and he falls for this girl, this Eskimo from Russia. Well, the camp breaks up and everyone goes back home, and all winter, the fisherman can't get her out of his head. He's got a woman already and two kids but that other woman must of been some beauty. So—Henry can really tell the story so you see it—and the fisherman decides what he is going to do, so that he can have the girl and win the respect of her people and somehow get the Russians to let him into the country. You know what he does? He goes out—this time in summer, the following summer—and takes the kayak to Little Diomede and he scuttles it. He's wearing bear grease all over his body and he jumps into the fucking water and he swims over to Russia. Well, to the big island, that is. What is it, four miles? It's summer but that water is like freezing cold but he gets over and he gets on shore and he finds the people in their camp and—you know what happens?"

It was a new story. Devereaux waited. Scraping the essence of Henry McGee out of Holmes, out of Nels Nelsen, out of the others was like squeezing water out of ice. You had to wait to make it melt.

"The Russians never saw it. Got a big installation on that island according to Henry but they're looking for big things, like submarines or shipping, not one little guy swimming across. They never picked up a blip on him. And the girl was in love with the fisherman too, so the family arranged it and they're living over there now, on the other side, and Henry said he's got three kids, raising them all to be nice little Communists. Henry was so drunk when he told that story, I thought he'd fall off the bar stool, we were in the white people's bar in Kotzebue then.''

"Why did Henry tell you stories? Why did he get mad when you repeated his stories?''

"Henry said the story proved that true love conquers all. We laughed about that because Henry didn't have an ounce of love in his body, he was just a good man to be with, to be drinking with. Then he said something I never did forget. He said all the spies and watchers in the world are always looking for the wrong thing. Like a little kayak going across to Siberia would get across because nobody was looking for it. He said people were looking for what they believed in instead of what was. I was drunk when he said it and I swear to God, I understood it then but I don't now.''

Devereaux said nothing. Stories and chance remarks. Philosophies and jokes. Henry talked and talked and broke the rules and got away with it.

Holmes stared at the empty cup, thought about whiskey again, thought about getting back his pilot's license. He hated Henry McGee from time to time, and at other times he wished Henry was back.

"Henry was crazy. Is crazy. Crazy lonely. He had to make a friend. I was his friend but he had lots of friends. It was like he was coming down off something. He'd go away for six months and come back looking like he'd been run over by a herd of caribou, looked like shit, all beat

SEVEN
Denisov's Choice

"The matter is simple," the agent said.

Denisov spread his hands. He waited.

The agent said he was Karpov. It didn't matter because Denisov did not believe him. Karpov had followed him down the beach, back to Figueroa and the strip of coffee shops and bars near the pier. They had talked as the fog lifted on the bay and they could clearly see the oil platforms squatting in the water. The sun was rising over the hill above the town and the day was warmer. Karpov had a line of sweat on his lip and another line of sweat on his narrow, high forehead, but he still wore his topcoat and hat. The complete spy, Denisov thought, packaged by Moscow.

"If we intended to eliminate you, it could have been done simply," Karpov said.

"The umbrella touch," Denisov said.

"That. Or the simple way."

"No, I do not think so." Both men spoke in the drawled accents of Moscow Russian, which is as snobbish a dialect as Parisian French. "You want two things: First, me. And second, you do not want the American agencies to understand how you have penetrated their Witness Protection Program."

Karpov smiled. "Then you understand."

"Because it is not a simple matter," Denisov said. He stopped at the same café where the Soviet agent had sat that morning, watching him. He hesitated because he thought of the call he had made to the San Francisco number. Should he cancel the call now? Was the danger past?

Denisov sat down at the table by the window. He ordered coffee and Karpov did the same.

"This is what they call coffee. Everything in this country tastes the same. Perhaps it all is the same," Karpov said. His face was very narrow and his eyes were very large. He wore wire-rimmed glasses, as did Denisov.

"You have been in America long. It is the custom to complain about the coffee. It is very subtle of you." Denisov did not raise his voice. "I drank coffee in Moscow that was leavened with sawdust. Is such coffee no longer served? Is coffee so free now? And tea, I do not miss the tea very much. I do not know what I miss at all."

"Return to your homeland, Ivan Ilyich."

"Do you remember the saying 'A man with two countries has no country at all'? Perhaps it is true, Karpov. Perhaps there is no home."

"A great deal of effort was made—" Karpov began in a low, angry voice.

Denisov tore open a packet and poured sugar in the coffee. "Yes. You tell me this is a simple matter. I am a simple man. Perhaps you must explain to me why this simple matter requires so much effort. I have been gone from service for six years. It is too long to care. I am not important, not to you, not to Gorki." "Gorki" was the permanent code name of the man in charge of the Committee for External Observation and Resolution in the apparatus of espionage in Moscow. Its headquarters were not on Dzherzhinski Square, where the KGB was; like all departments of the state, it was both centralized and chaotic in structure. Denisov had been its agent until Devereaux had arranged his unwilling defection in Florida on a warm January night.

"You will be told in time."

"I do not think so." Denisov made the words precise. Moscow-television Russian, the language without misunderstanding.

"You will not come back? Your wife is in Gorki." Karpov meant the city this time, the traditional place of exile.

Denisov did not think of her. He stared at the spoon in the black coffee and stirred while he did not think of his wife and did not remember how she looked and smelled and sounded and how she slept next to him all those years. No, he did not think of her.

"It is impossible. You cannot fool another Russian, you know."

Karpov sat in silence for a moment. Denisov looked at him with soft contempt. Had he appeared so clumsy in America years ago? Karpov's clothes did not fit very well and his large, dark hat was ill-suited to the climate.

Denisov looked around him. The café was filled with ferns and light wood panels. The menus were large and colorful bits of plastic, describing cute salads and hamburgers for vegetarians. What did it all look like to a drone like Karpov?

"*Glasnost*," began Karpov.

Denisov held up his hand. "I can read. I know what *glasnost* is, even if you tell me it is something else. If you tell me the truth, then I will know it is the truth. Believe me, Karpov, you are too subtle for your own good."

"You have been found, damn you. You're no longer free to decide."

Denisov felt a great sense of calm. For the first time in months, he thought of Alexa, who lived in Los Angeles now and was the friend of a man who made motion pictures. Alexa had been an agent as well. How many others were there in the vastness of the country, living with disguised faces and new names and the green government check in the mail once a month?

"I made a call this morning, before you introduced yourself. It is a telephone number we can use when we feel we are threatened. Already, there is an alert." Denisov said this in a flat voice, drawling out Moscowese again. "Why do you threaten me in the middle of the morning in this café in California? Do you think we are in the basement of Lubyanka?"

Karpov glared at him with large hazel eyes, and when the glare brought no response, he put his small hands on the table. He said nothing. He swallowed and cleared his throat. His voice was softer now.

"I am authorized to light all the candles in the church," he said.

Denisov understood the term.

"There is a man called November."

"That is not a name."

"November," repeated Karpov.

Denisov waited.

"November, who defected you." He said this in English because the Russian is too clumsy, too ambiguous.

"Yes," Denisov said.

The rock music blared from loudspeakers in the bright, California café but the room was silent for both of them.

"He has gone to Alaska. In a little while, he will want to go to Siberia. To the district of the Far East, to be exact."

"How do you know this?"

"Because we have arranged it," Karpov said.

"Why?"

"An important man to the Soviet peoples wishes to arrange his disappearance. No, I do not intend to say that; I mean, to arrange his acceptance in the Soviet Socialist Republics. To do this thing, he will need a guide. He will have a guide."

"He will not call me," Denisov began. "Besides, I would refuse him. I have no contact with him."

"As you refused in Chicago last year? As you refused in the matter in Zurich?"

"What do you know of me?" But Denisov felt afraid now. The background music in the café seemed louder and it penetrated his fears.

"Everything, Ivan Ilyich. I tried to tell you."

Fear was cold in his belly. It was like a large, round stone in his belly. It was making everything in his body cold. In a little while, he would be so cold that he would have to shiver.

Denisov was not a believer, even if he had the eyes of

a saint. He saw the imperfections of systems from the first; it was the reason he had become a rich man, even while an agent for the committee. But perhaps he had really believed in his sanctuary in California. Perhaps all the fern-filled cafés and the women with perfect bodies had convinced him of this system and his safety, leaving only the dreams of Moscow for night and sleep.

The system had betrayed him. It was the only way they had found him after all these years.

"You want to know, don't you?" Karpov said.

"Yes."

"Alexa," Karpov said.

Denisov's heart seemed to stop. Alexa was beautiful, voracious, a fellow exile, a former assassin for the committee. She had been trapped in the spiderweb of America as well. She had once opened her bed to Denisov but it was more in friendship than deep love. Alexa's beauty and the depth of her feeling made her precisely right for the motion picture business in Los Angeles. He saw Alexa in his mind and realized that she could have done everything Karpov said.

He could not speak for a moment and could not let Karpov see this. He had the flat expression of the perfect agent. He waved to the waitress—a girl whose hair was layered in strikingly different colors—and she poured him more coffee with a pretty pout on her face. Karpov took the coffee as well. He was smiling at his cup because he knew he had scored on Denisov.

"So I am betrayed twice," Denisov began.

"Do not speak of betrayal—"

"By the program, by Alexa."

"Perhaps by Alexa both times."

"Impossible."

"She wishes to come home."

"Impossible. She has Hollywood."

"It is not relevant."

"Why will November call me?"

"He will see he needs you."

"Why do you want him? What is he? An old agent, such as myself. What do we know about anything? We have no knowledge you do not have now."

"Perhaps," Karpov said.

"*Glasnost*?" Denisov referred again to the ambiguous Russian term that could mean "openness" in one context, something else in another. "You have the *Washington Post* for *glasnost*, you have books, spies who never stop talking, corruptible congressmen. . . . Is there a part of the American apparatus you do not understand yet?"

"A friend of the Soviet Union—"

"Who is he?"

"That, I cannot tell you."

"You wish me to guide November? If he really does call upon me? To betray him?"

"Of course."

"For what?"

"For your life."

"I have that."

"That is not certain."

Denisov paused.

"I told you we are not in the bowels of Lubyanka. You may kill me here or not but I live now and the odds are against you. Put your umbrella away, Karpov; it is no threat. It never rains in California."

Karpov did not blush. He just became more pale.

"Here is the threat, comrade." Just clear, deep, bureaucratic Russian now, the kind used for orders and threats and pronouncement of sentences.

And he took out the photographs.

In the photographs, Denisov saw Alexa sitting in the straight-backed chair of some typical American motel room, facing the camera, her hands holding the movie clapboard in front of her chest. She was naked and her eyes were very wide, as though she were frightened.

On the clapboard was written, in Russian, "Denisov kills Alexa."

In the second photograph, Alexa was sprawled on the bed in the motel room. Her hands were tied to the posts of the bed and she was naked. She wore a gag in her mouth.

In the third color photograph, there was a scarf around her throat and her face was very pale, even though the outline of the perpetual suntan could still be seen. The gag had been removed. Her cheeks were puffed out and her eyes seemed to protrude.

"Dead," he said.

Karpov smiled.

"Not at all."

Denisov was very pale, very cold. The stone thing would never leave his belly. He would have to carry it in his belly all his life.

"Not at all," Karpov repeated. He took out a fourth photograph. Alexa sat on the bed but now she was dressed in her jeans and halter and she still looked frightened. She was holding up a photograph.

"Take this. Our eyes fail us in middle age."

It was a small looking glass.

Denisov examined the photograph.

Alexa was holding the third photograph, the one that showed her dead. She was not smiling.

He knew Alexa. He had slept with her. They were exiles. He saw the dull fear in her eyes in the photograph.

"If Alexa were to be murdered, perhaps even more horribly than in the photograph, then it would be you who killed her. Perhaps you did not do it but we could convince certain people that you had killed her. What would the Americans do to you?"

Denisov said nothing.

"Perhaps they would kill you. Perhaps they would want to know how you had compromised their famous program. Whatever would happen, Ivan Ilyich, you would not be a man with a choice."

"She did not call you, then," Denisov said. His voice was very dull, very tired. It was eleven in the morning on a rare spring day in Santa Barbara when you can see all the way to the tops of the wooded hills above the town.

"As I told you, Ivan Ilyich," Karpov said.

"I have no guarantee."

"None."

"But if you wished to kill me, you could do so now. Or kill Alexa."

Karpov permitted a small smile.

"Why is November important? To your important friend?"

"I don't know. I am only the messenger, Ivan Ilyich."

Had Denisov said that before to others? He had been the messenger, the watcher, the assassin in his time, moving in the cogs of some vast machine, blind and deaf, moving his little part of the great mechanism because he had to do it.

He saw the truth in Karpov then.

on the wrong man and until the committee had decided to resolve her.

Alexa was Russian beautiful, which meant she had deep and wild dark eyes and black hair and an intense, almost religiously beautiful face. She was very dangerous and that made her attractive as well. Roger liked her accent, her beauty and the way she made love. Roger craved the danger in her. She knew she made love as no woman—even no man—had made love to Roger before.

Roger's new deal was putting together Burt Reynolds, Paul Newman and Sally Fields in an updated remake of *Animal Crackers*, with Sally Fields in the Chico Marx role. Everyone was intrigued with the idea. Roger was trying to convince the producer to convince Newman's agent to convince Newman that there was a lot of dignity in the Harpo role. The whole thing sounded absurd on the face of it, which is why everyone took it seriously. Even if the picture was never made, Roger would make a million dollars on the deal. The deal was more important than any movie.

What could Roger have done? Alexa thought.

She had been very afraid. She could count the times in her life she had been afraid and they were not many.

Alexa ran along the beach. Los Angeles was full of haze. A weak sun tried to poke through the brown air. The boys were on the beach already, showing their tanned good looks to passersby of both sexes. The faint odor of corruption came from the sea and there were dead fish on the sand. Alexa ran along the beach with strong strides, her legs flashing beneath her shorts with the sureness of tailor's scissors. She ran until she was utterly exhausted, until she wanted to sob. She had run this way every day since the incident and she had not told Roger about it. Deep in her, she knew that all of Roger's power and his world and his wealth were illusions. Roger could do nothing, Roger would have been afraid and that would have shattered the illusion for Alexa.

They awakened her at four in the morning in her bed. There were two of them. They had small automatic pistols and one had injected her with something even before she could speak. When she awoke, she had been in a hotel room and they had taken her nightgown off. She spoke to them in English.

And then she spoke to them in Russian.

They had smiled when she spoke Russian; they had understood her.

She did as they told her to do. When the second one knotted the scarf around her neck, she thought they intended to kill her.

"No, you little whore," he had said in a mild voice. "Not yet your time. Perhaps tomorrow or never. Now put this cotton in your mouth and fill your cheeks and stick out your tongue as though you have been strangled. If you are a very good actress, you little whore, you won't be killed. We have no instruction to kill you unless you are not convincing and we have to strangle you to produce the desired effect."

She had tried to be a good actress.

When they were satisfied, one of them threw her a pair of jeans and a top taken from her closet and she put them on. They gave her the last photograph to hold in her hand. She had looked at her strangled self in the photograph. She saw herself dead.

She felt the sobbing pain as she ran. Soon, she would

be at the end of running and the pain would be all in her chest and her muscles would twitch and even her knees would hurt.

She realized how alone she really was. Roger was her illusion. To involve him in the real world would be to destroy him. Everything was gossamer.

She fell to the sand, gasping for breath. One of the boys on the beach looked at her and thought about coming over. She rose to one knee, heaving for breath, staring at the flat ocean and the dull brown sky and the weak sun.

What frightened her most in the days since the incident was knowing that they knew. She had been debriefed by the Americans and treated very well. She had not forgotten her old life but her new life had suited her. She never thought badly about killing people because it was what she had been trained for, like a soldier. Now she did not have to kill anyone. Roger said once, "Wouldn't you ever like to kill someone, just to see what it was like?" It was one of the strange things Roger would say when he was drunk or when he had taken too much cocaine.

Alexa had responded, "But it's like nothing, Roger."

"What's not like nothing?"

"To kill someone," she had said. "It is like killing a chicken. They are alive and then they are dead, all to some purpose. To kill someone for purpose is to feel nothing."

Roger had known then that she had killed someone. It had thrilled him even more than the cocaine and he had made love to her. Sometimes, when he was on top of her, taking his own pleasure, demanding that she give him pleasure, Alexa could close her eyes and feel helpless and that pleased her, even stirred her more than the pleasure of the flesh. But that feeling of helplessness was only an illusion. When she had been helpless and naked in the hotel room and held the signboard in front of her and read what it said—Denisov kills Alexa—she had felt only hollowness. There was no pleasure, after all, in being helpless.

She must confront this.

She walked slowly back up the beach, her breath returning, streaming with sweat. Her hair was wet with sweat and glistened. She wore white shorts and a light green top and was barefoot. She was tall and dark and so striking in appearance that Roger said she should be a movie star except it would bore her to tears to be a movie star.

Alexa opened the door of her car—Roger let her drive the older of the two Porsches—and slipped onto the leather seat. It would be warm again in Los Angeles without satisfaction. The sun would not burn off the smog and the bowl of the city would be filled with brown air and endless cars on endless roads. She loved Roger and films and parties in Malibu but this other part she did not like at all.

Denisov kills Alexa.

But what was it all about? They had explained nothing. They had dumped her in front of her apartment and threw her nightgown after her and drove off in a small, black Chevrolet. Four photographs, taken with a Polaroid camera in an anonymous motel room. For what purpose?

Alexa kills Denisov.

She thought about it. She could not be afraid all the time. She would get a gun and go north to find Denisov

NINE

Karen's Cleverness

"**M**y name is Karen," she said.

Denisov stared at the young girl. This was ridiculous.

She opened her notebook and held a pen in her left hand. Her black hair was in bangs, her shrewd blue eyes waited.

"How old are you?" Denisov said.

She blinked. She looked at the blank sheet and then at him. "Twenty-six."

Denisov said something in Russian.

"I didn't catch that?"

"It is nothing."

Denisov stood at the window of his living room and looked down at the lush vegetation on the side street. He lived on the third floor of an apartment building halfway up the hill from the beach. He had lived there all his years in exile. Where would he live now?

He thought again of the little apartment in Moscow, his wife rattling pots and pans in the kitchen, the constant bickering between his son and his sister over bathroom rights. He wanted only peace. He wanted afternoons alone in the apartment on winter days when all were gone, afternoons of Gilbert and Sullivan and drinking vodka in warm apple juice, afternoons of thought and dreams. He could do that now, dismiss this child, await his call back from exile. Karpov had showed him the way it was: If they had wanted to kill him, they would have killed him. He must show he is redeemed. He must bring November across.

"What did he look like?"

"Who?" Denisov turned from the window and looked at her sitting very businesslike on a straight chair at his little dining table. He thought she looked too young for this business. Perhaps they had not taken him seriously, that was why they had sent this child.

"Mr. Raspoff—"

It was his American name, the one on his driver's license and Social Security card and his Blue Cross card and his American Express card. How clever everyone was, to give him a new identity, to suggest that cosmetic surgery could be ordered up, to give him this safe place of exile.

Why not an American name, he had asked long ago. Mr. Gilbert. Mr. Sullivan. But the man in charge of such things had smirked. "No one would believe an Irishman with a Russian accent," he had explained. So much for disguises.

When he had undergone the long debriefing in the place where they did these things outside of Washington, he had felt utter despair. The babble of English around him, the cold-eyed men who stripped his soul and memory, the thought of living forever in this utterly foreign country— he thought to kill himself for the first time in his life. He had sat in his bare, clean room in the middle of the Maryland mountains, sipping a glass of vodka, and he had thought of killing himself because the loneliness was driving him mad.

Perhaps they knew this.

Perhaps that is why they had permitted Devereaux to visit him.

Devereaux had brought a very good phonograph and a collection of albums. *The Mikado* and *Pirates of Penzance* and *HMS Pinafore* and *Iolanthe* and *Yeoman of the Guard*. . . . He had sat with Denisov that single afternoon and Denisov had played the first of the recordings and listened to the English words even as he had done in his Moscow apartment on winter afternoons.

"The man who lives in two countries has none," he said aloud.

Karen O'Hare started to write it down and stopped. She said, "What did you say?"

"I saw a man twice in the past two days." He described the man who ran the cleaning shop down the street. "He stared at me as though he knew me. This upsets me."

"Which is why I'm here. It upsets us as well."

"Who is us, Miss O'Hare?" The voice was not kind.

"You know as well as I do."

"I do not know. Is possible they know me now? Is possible they find me after years like these?" His English was good but in moments of stress, he dropped words, reversed syntax, became the stage Russian.

"No, Mr. Raspoff. It is not possible. No one has ever been located who was put in the program."

"I am touched by your faith in the program. I am not so sure of it. You see, I am doubter and you are believer. If possible, it can be done."

"Now you're the believer," Karen O'Hare said. She was young, damnit, but it wasn't her fault. She wasn't stupid, even if Wagner back in the office thought she was just someone with big boobs.

Denisov blinked at that and came over to the table and sat down across from her. She was beautiful, he thought. And, without meaning to, he thought of Alexa, naked, holding a chalkboard with Russian words that read: "Denisov kills Alexa."

"I am the paranoid," he said softly. "I am seeing ghosts and have bad dreams. I know this. This was told to me before. But sometimes, it is that I need to say these things to someone."

"Yes," she said. She put down the pen. "We checked all the agencies. No one has a mark on you. Believe me, nothing has happened for six years, why would anything happen now?"

He had asked Karpov the same question.

Karpov had said it had nothing to do with Denisov, it had to do with getting November into the Soviet Union.

"Perhaps you are right."

Karen stared at him.

Denisov tried a smile.

"Perhaps I am just alone."

Karen felt a deep blush inside her and struggled to keep it off her skin.

"I am seeing the ghost," he said.

What was this?

"No, Mr. Raspoff," Karen said. She stared into his mild saint's eyes. "You have had experience, I looked up your 201, I don't have access to it, just to the précis, just to know who you are. I know who you are. You've been around the block."

"Block?"

"A way of speaking," she said. Her voice had lost its gee-whiz quality. It would have surprised Wagner, surprised everyone back in the office on Powell Street.

"I took down this description and I'm going to be around for a day or two, looking into this thing. I'm staying down at the beach—I'll give you a number—and I'm going to call in a few people on this thing. If the program has been compromised—and I don't think it has but something has been done to arouse your suspicions—then I want to know about it and my superiors want to know about it."

"It is all right," Denisov began.

"It is not all right. Besides, I can take you to dinner on the expense account and it's legitimate—"

"It is all right," Denisov began again.

"I'm sure it is." She drew back from the table a little, let him look at her. "You've had a fascinating life. The little I saw in your 201. Not that everyone has access to your 201, don't get me wrong. It's just that I had an NTK—"

"Is what?"

"Need to know." He was looking at her but he didn't look happy. Karen O'Hare knew how she looked to men. There was something wrong.

"We can have dinner, we can talk, maybe I can listen

to your stories.'' Her eyes got dreamy, the way she intended. She had learned a few tricks in her adolescence, only the most instinctive. She had watched other girls at school and this is what they did to make men do what they wanted. It had horrified her when she first discovered the trick, but she had learned it in the same mechanical way she learned the twelve-times tables.

He stared at her and saw the face of Karpov. He felt like a dying man invited to a party full of lively people. She wouldn't understand. Twenty-six years old. He saw Alexa naked on the bed, strangled, her tongue lolling from her puffed face. Would they invite Alexa back as well? A reunion in Moscow of all the exiles, reluctant and not, who had returned?

''Please, it is well that you came but I think about this too much and I think it is not what it was when I call the number in San Francisco.''

''I don't think so either, Mr. Raspoff. Just checking it out. I want to be sure I closed all the doors and locked them. That's just a way of talking. I want to be sure that you're reassured. Besides, it's nice to be in Santa Barbara, it's a nice time of year, maybe I can get some sun, you never saw a suntan on a San Franciscan.''

The words were too fast for him. He merely blinked again.

She smiled. It was a smile she knew that made men like her. She had learned that much from watching the other girls at school practice their pouts and their dreamy looks and their little coquetries. She knew all about herself, the way a pretty woman knows about herself. At least, that is what she thought.

Still he looked miserable.

* * *

She called from the motel room. Wagner answered.

"I'm staying down."

There was a silence on the line.

"Is there a reason?"

"Something's wrong. I talked to him and he doesn't want to talk. He gave me a glib description, not like someone describing someone he's afraid of, but like someone describing the elevator operator. I get the feeling he wants me to go away. Something happened between the time Redbird called and I got here. Something that's clammed him up. He looks terrible."

Another silence on the line.

"Mr. Wagner?"

"I was just thinking, Karen."

"Thinking along my lines?"

"No, not really." Another pause. "Thinking maybe you should come back to Powell Street, maybe we should buck this up higher, talk to someone else about it, get feedback and input."

She closed her eyes to hear the conversation better. She could even see Wagner in the office. She knew the patterns in his speech when he got nervous. The trouble with her was she was too goddamn bright. Her father had said that once and it was true. She did terribly in school, barely passed her first civil service exam. And yet she was too goddamn bright. She saw that something was wrong now, wrong at both ends. The Russian was afraid; Wagner sounded afraid.

"I think I should stay here. For a day or two. Just look into this a little, try to loosen our client up."

"How you gonna loosen him up, Karen?" But said with absolutely no leer to the voice. Not at all like Wagner, who spent all their time together staring at her breasts. He was nervous and afraid and obviously thinking about something else. She kept her eyes shut tight to concentrate on seeing the voice.

"I'm going to talk to him some more. There's something wrong here and I can't put it down on paper yet. Let me have a day or two."

Wagner paused. Four hundred miles north of Karen, Wagner was thinking about the tapes that recorded all the conversations on all the telephones in the office on Powell Street.

"Well, I just don't know," Wagner began. "You wouldn't just be exercising Uncle's expense account?"

It was a stupid thing for him to say. "That isn't even worth an answer, Mr. Wagner," Karen O'Hare said. They both knew it.

"I didn't mean it that way, I was kidding. You don't kid easy, Karen, you got to learn to take a joke."

She said nothing but she opened her eyes. She had seen enough of his voice in her mind.

"A day or two," he said.

"That's all. Just to make sure. To get something I can put down on paper."

"A day or two," he said.

"There's no point in sending someone down and then pulling them right back with nothing to show for it but a vague feeling that something is wrong."

"No." Pause. "I suppose you're right, Karen. I guess you're calling it."

They broke the conversation without pleasantries. Karen put the receiver back on the phone and sat on the edge of her bed for a long time, listening to her voices. There was Raspoff's voice and Wagner's voice and another voice.

She listened to the third voice for a long time and she understood it was her own.

The third voice was very clear about one thing: Something was wrong, worse than she had imagined a moment before.

TEN

To End the Trail

Norton Sound was gray. The low silhouette of the Nome Peninsula lay below the northern sky. The sun was quite bright but there was no cheer in the day. The lighter carried lumber, machine parts, two new Chevrolet trucks and a gray man, the sort of anonymous visitor who sits in airport lobbies or train stations or at sidewalk cafés and is never seen. The sea was too shallow to take the heavy cargo ship all the way into port. The sea route to Nome had always been too shallow and the Army Corps of Engineers was spending a fortune to reverse a million years of nature. The dredgers were at work in the sound, some to scoop the sand and rocks containing gold bits, some to shove the sand somewhere else so the ships could dock easily at the port. Captain Holmes, still not a captain, was aboard the cargo ship, glad to be rid of the G-man and his insistence on learning the stories of Henry McGee.

It had been important to stay with Holmes because Holmes had to be scraped clean of memory. He had been closer to Henry McGee for a time than any man. It had been a good time from the point of view of those on the trail. That is what Devereaux told himself to keep the idea of a trail fresh in his mind. He had never felt so far away from Henry McGee, the ghost he had seen fifteen years ago, the man of too many stories.

What had he accomplished in three weeks? Stories, the kind of stories they invented in the If game in Alexandria.

The trail was now cold. He had sent the wire from the cargo ship to the safe house in San Francisco and it had been passed along from there to Hanley in Washington. The message was not in plainspeak but the words were clear.

Devereaux had dreamed in his bunk on the ship the night before. In the dream, he had gone home to Rita and the house was gone. Not sold but gone. A vacant lot remained. He found Philippe sitting on the curb. He asked where she had gone. Philippe said, "Just gone." In the dream, he had gone to Hanley to find her and Hanley had winked at him and said, "She is just gone. She took the house with her."

He could not find her in the dream. When he woke, he was sweating and it was four in the morning. The worst time in life was four in the morning with a bad dream behind you.

He had to end this thing. He had all the tape transcripts of his interviews to turn into stories and he would work on Nels Nelsen in Nome for one more day and that would be it: End of the trail. There is no Henry McGee, there is no trick, the thing is over.

He had done the things expected of the careful agent.

He had followed the false trails again to see if the chasers had missed anything. He had gone to the Polar Bar in Anchorage to talk to the regulars about their remembrances of "Henry McGee," the man named Otis Dobbins who had met Nels Nelsen there. He had awakened nearly every morning in a strange room in a strange town and wondered where he was. He dreamed of Rita Macklin every night, and each time, the dream became worse. One night, Rita was pregnant and said she was going to marry the father of the child in her belly. It was not Devereaux. Another night, Rita said she did not love him anymore. The dreams became real as the search for Henry McGee stopped becoming real.

The lighter was very close to the rocky shoreline now and hands for and aft readied the lines. The lighter bumped gently against the dock and nudged it with its iron hull. The lines snapped out in the cold air and fell heavily on the dock. Devereaux picked up his bag and went down the steep inside ladder to the deck below. Devereaux stepped uncertainly down the ramp. It felt very strange to be on firm land after eight days in a choppy sea. He imagined he was walking with a rolling gait as he moved along the dock to the land.

The trail would be buried here in a day or two and then he would fly back to Anchorage and take the nonstop to Washington. He would call at Anchorage to say he was coming home.

Would the telephone ring in an empty house?

He shook his head to get rid of the thought and then he saw her. The woman was at the end of the dock, standing next to an ancient Thunderbird with a battered side door. She was wearing a fur coat and looked absurdly young to be in furs. She was pretty and her eyes glittered, even in the ugly light of the sullen morning.

He memorized her face because it was a trick he knew how to do. He thought her eyes were too bright for the middle of an ordinary morning.

He started to cross her path and she raised her hand. She smiled at him. Her teeth were bright in a wide, pretty mouth. "Nels," she said. "You must be the man, you're the only man coming off the lighter. I mean, Nels was drinking in town at the Nugget and he kept talking about how he had to meet the lighter because there was a passenger coming off it. So I said I had a car and I was tired of drinking. I said I wanted to meet someone different anyway. So I'm meeting you to take you into Nome. You wouldn't mind me giving you a ride?"

He understood the last words and the smile and shook his head. He didn't mind. She had a hushed voice and spoke English in the odd way Indians and Eskimos did. Her fur coat was open and she wore very tight jeans. Her black hair was long and tied back from her oval, almond face.

Devereaux moved to the other side of the car and opened the door. He threw his canvas bag on the backseat, next to a pile of beer cans. He slid onto the leatherette seat of the old T-Bird. The motor was running and the car was warm.

"You want a beer?"

"Sure," he said.

She fished two cans off the backseat. They were barely cold. They opened the cans and took a swallow and she put the car in gear and started down the road.

"My name is Narvak," she said. "My native name. I

am also called Catherine, you can call me anything you like."

Said this, smiled, turned to him, opened her mouth to him.

Devereaux thought she might be sixteen or seventeen years old. He tried to keep that in mind while feelings stirred his belly. She had brown breasts and they strained against her bright shirt. She had the shirt partially opened and she knew it; she knew everything she was doing.

When the dark-faced man had sent her to Nome again, this time to find out about the government man, she said she would do anything for him. Ulu had said she should fuck him. She had said he might be ugly or fat. Ulu had said to fuck him anyway.

But he wasn't ugly or fat and maybe it would be a pleasure.

"Are you looking at me?" she said.

"Obviously," he said.

"Do I look good?"

He tried to remember something. "Are you eighteen?"

"I'm as old as hell," she said.

"I suppose."

"Would you like me to stop the car?"

"How long did you know Nels?"

"Not long. I meet him in town. I seen him around. Him and his partner, but his partner got killed a couple of weeks ago. Something like that."

"Who was his partner?"

"Guy named Henry McGee. You come to find out about it?"

"Why would I want to find out about it?"

She didn't like this. She stopped the car on a gravel road that ran away from the town. She turned to look at him. "Nobody can see us," she said. She opened her mouth again. She licked her lips in an exaggerated way, perhaps in the way she had seen women in movies do.

"Did Nels tell you about me?"

She put her hand on his crotch.

"He said you were from some government agency about the traplines or something like that, about endangered species or crap like that." She made him hard and she reached for the zipper on his trousers and felt his hand on her hand.

"What do you know about Henry McGee?"

He felt the little bird hand flutter beneath his grip. Until that moment, he was not certain. But the little bird was trying to escape.

"You just want to talk, you don't want to fuck."

"Did you fuck Henry McGee?"

"That man? Hell, no. He smelled bad."

"What do you know about Henry McGee?"

"Leggo my hand, you want to hurt me?"

"Maybe," Devereaux said.

"I don't let nobody hurt me. You want to hurt someone, I know this one in town but she's fat, you have to like a fat one, but you can hurt her, you never see her without a black eye or something. But I don't let no one hurt me."

He released her hand. She pulled it back to the wheel. She was coiled now beneath the furs and there was no good feeling between them.

"You got wolf eyes. You got eyes like wolves but you can see deeper into your eyes. Wolf has flat eyes. You still look good to me. But you don't hurt me."

"I don't hurt you."

"You want me to suck you?"

"No," Devereaux said.

"You got it hard down there."

"No," Devereaux said.

"Well, you look good to me. I just want you to know that."

And Devereaux knew, staring at the wild young creature behind the wheel, that the trail had not ended. One more day and it would have been buried. But she had scratched into the rock and opened up a new way. A new and dangerous path to Henry McGee.

water and the new turbines made almost no sound. Congress was upset and threats were made against Japanese imports.

Given the political atmosphere at the time, the Japanese company bowed low and fired its director. This seemed to confuse and mollify Congress. Quietly, the Japanese conglomerate continued to ship its small, light cars to the United States market. It had sold 106,514 the year before. It also made and sold video cassette recorders, personal word processors and motor scooters, not to mention cordless electric toothbrushes.

The submarine was 110 feet beneath the restless surface of the sea. The pack ice was broken into floes in the cold spring, groaning and cracking here and there, waking the way a sleeper awakes from a deep, disturbing dream. The floes were so many swift moving islands in an invisible stream against the gray of the water and sky.

The passengers had boarded the submarine at Akaki in Siberia, seventy-five miles directly west of Wales, the village on the tip of the Seward Peninsula in Alaska. There was a military airfield at Akaki and a small harbor. The submarine was still undergoing tests. Now it was spring and the pack ice was all broken and the sub was testing the American sonar in the open, chill waters of the Bering. The tests were going well. The submarine had slipped up the Bering Sea to the straits, which was the narrowest water between the Soviet Union and the extreme western edge of the Seward Peninsula. Now it quietly treaded the four-mile gap of water between Big Diomede and Little Diomede. It was exactly on the international dateline with half the ship in Tuesday and the other half in Monday.

The ship was silent; the crew spoke in whispers; the sonar men adjusted the amber screens back and forth, trying to detect the Americans trying to detect them. The Americans sat on the rock of Little Diomede, which bristled with radar and sonar, and stared like blind dogs across the ice to the Soviets on the other rock. The submarine crawled slowly north and west, into the American sea, and still it was thought that no one saw the vessel beneath the water. The submarine crossed to the narrow waters of Kotzebue Sound, above the Arctic Circle.

Just like jail, Kools thought as the seaman led him along the narrow, clammy passageway toward the galley. The seaman had said nothing. Probably didn't even understand English, Kools thought. The seaman had a flat, Asiatic face, he and Kools might have been related. Ten thousand years ago.

The seaman had nodded at Kools. Noah had been staring at the pages of a Russian reader—he was trying to learn Russian, for Christ's sake—and looked up and saw the seaman signal and almost started to get up from his bunk. But the seaman had taken Kools' arm and led him into the passage and closed the hatchway with a curtain.

Like being in jail, Kools thought. Maybe worse. Ain't gonna drown in jail. Ain't gonna have all the water in the world crush you down, get in your mouth, ears, nose. . . . It wasn't worth thinking about but it was hard for Kools to put it out of his mind.

Kools and Noah had undergone the training at the tight Soviet compound. They had apple juice at night at first, until the spirit of *glasnost* unthawed enough for a few smuggled bottles of vodka. They were kept apart from the native village a half kilometer east of the frozen concrete compound, but Kools had made it out on the second night. He had visited with the people and it had been all right. They knew what he was, but he was a cousin to them, related over ten millennia. He nearly didn't make it back to the compound that first night.

The Soviets trained hard, without subtlety. Kools understood it from the days in prison at Palmer, understood it from all his life. He worked quietly, not like Noah. Noah liked to talk. Noah liked to be in charge, which was just like a white man.

Kools didn't see the point of it, but sometimes that was just the point: It was pointless, like the guards in Palmer waking you up sometimes at 3:00 A.M., just to fuck you around, just because they felt like it.

The seaman opened another curtain and there was the old man in a small cubicle, just as bare and sweaty cold as the one he had just left.

They hadn't known the old man was on the sub.

Kools had an instinct. You had it or you didn't. He had sharpened it in Anchorage, sharpened it in prison at Palmer.

He sat down on the single chair and watched the old man on the bunk. The old man sat cross-legged. He had very dark skin, as though he had been in desert sun all his life, and his eyes were bright, quick, steady. The old man nodded when Kools took out his cigarette pack.

"You like submarines," the old man said.

Kools said nothing.

"Ever think about all that cold water up there?" He touched the bulkhead. "But I guess I can't scare you none."

"You brought me here to scare me?" Kools' voice was a natural tenor, very flat and playing it cool. He blew out smoke that filled the compartment a moment before the passive air-ducts began moving it to wherever it was taken.

"Watching you two boys," the dark man said. He said it slow, in good humor, the way he had talked the native tongue those five days he had spent in the settlement with them, when he had brought his stories and his magic to the old people and convinced Kools to work with him. Kools knew that his sister, Narvak, would do anything for the dark man.

"What you watching for?" Kools said.

"Don't know. Know it when I see it. But I don't have a whole lot more time to waste on this. You like life at B43?" It was the code name of the camp where they took their training.

"Remind me of Palmer. 'Cept you could get out of B43."

"That's what I was looking for, I guess," the old man said. "You got out the second night, went and got yourself Siberian nookie. You had a few parties."

"I had parties," Kools said. Damn. They really did have eyes in the back of their heads.

"Why you think you were brought across? Given that final bit of training?"

Kools looked at the browning end of his filter cigarette. He hadn't expected the old man. The dark-faced old man with eyes like oil pools had come into the settlement two years ago. He had known all about Kools. The only thing was, they didn't know anything about the old man except that he was in charge of something. Maybe he was in charge of them. He told them how to set up ULU, the name he gave to the native terrorist movement. He had money for the settlement and he showed Kools and Noah how to get the plastique, how to make a bomb, how to bomb the pipeline. He never got around to telling them why, except for the usual crap about fighting for their own land and the environment. It didn't bother Noah, who invented his own why. Noah was a believer in causes. He had gone to university in Fairbanks. He studied the native cultures. He took his name—it wasn't his real name—from the Biblical character who had saved the earth in the flood. He tried to speak the native tongue. He screwed a native girl, Kools' sister. The whole thing had only bothered Kools, who didn't believe a damned thing the old man said. Or anything that the silence was supposed to imply.

"You don't answer a lot of questions," the old man said. He made a frown, made the dark eyes deeper.

"I ain't got a lot of answers," Kools said. "You keep yourself better that way. I notice you got the trick too."

The old man let himself smile. His teeth were white and even in that dark, burned face. "You ask me a question, maybe I'll tell you."

"Who are you?"

"Is that it? Jesus Christ, that's easy. Ask me something harder."

"You didn't answer it."

"The man your sister shot."

Kools didn't let it show. He put out the cigarette in the tin ashtray on the stand next to the bunk. The windowless cubicle was gray on gray. Everything was too cold and there was sweat on the bulkhead.

"Well, she didn't exactly," the man continued. "She shot someone, a trapper, down in Nome. She's got guts. I thought for a while it was going to have to be her, if you two boys didn't work out." The old man let the words sink in.

"Work out what? What about Narvak?"

"She's got another errand. She won't be there to meet you when you get back. I'm starting to move and I had to decide about you two boys. I decided, I guess, on you.

Noah is useful still and he makes your sister happy." The old man grinned and yet it wasn't a smile. "Noah believes in all this shit but I figure you're too smart a con to do that. Figured that from the beginning. Believers got their place. I used believers before. You don't have to tell a believer too much, just enough to keep the candles burning. But you don't believe in it, do you? So if it turned out you weren't smart enough, I'd have to get rid of you."

"I don't believe you, if that's what you mean."

"You believe I'm gonna shut down the pipeline?"

Kools thought about it, staring at the old man in the coffin of the submarine. He thought about going across three times, getting supplies and training. About the sneaking around they did in the polar dark, blowing up sections of the line.

"No," Kools said.

"You might be wrong."

"You stir them up," Kools said. "You get us to take the chance, you get this stuff out about the ULU movement. Ain't no ULU movement."

"Thing is, Koolie, you see it from the inside. That's the wrong side to see things from. See it from their side. They hear the talk, they see the natives getting restless, they think every damned Yup'ik is part of the thing. They know they got no business being there."

"You start to sound like Noah."

For a moment, the old man's eyes went dead. "I ought to sound like him. I gave him his words."

"You did that," Kool said.

"You get too sure of yourself, Kools, I'll drop you in a crevice."

Kools let his face go passive. He had a good, round face with flat eyes that looked steadily at you. He was very thin, which was part of the Indian blood that had gotten mixed in with the Yup'ik Eskimo over the generations. His body was hard and now he let his face lose all expression. It was the trick you learned in prison when the big ones decided you were going to be their Mary for the night and you knew you'd have to convince them it wasn't going to be that way. Never give them an edge. Wait quiet until they got close enough and stick the knife right into their gut. Maybe they'd live and maybe they'd die but the next one would think about the price of loving.

The old man let the silence hold.

They could not hear the engines, only feel the movement. It was an act of faith to let yourself be entombed on a ship beneath the icy sea for thirty-six hours, crawling slowly toward the top of the world in utter silence. She was rigged for silent running and all their nerves—especially those who waited—were on edge.

"Noah knows everything now about explosives," the old man said at last. "Took six months training in the army at Indianhead EOD school. Plus what we give him on the Siberian side." The old man spoke in a curious, rolled flat accent, like that of a Kansas farmer. The words were clipped off oddly, the tense changed for emphasis. "Could put an atom bomb on the line. Talk about an oil spill, Koolie, you'd make the news for months, make Chernobyl look like a Boy Scout bonfire."

"You gonna do that?"

"I think, Koolie; you do."

"I ain't gonna put no atom bomb on the line."

"But Noah is."

"Noah is crazy."

"But I know that and you know that. You figure we got them thinking that now? I mean, the other side?"

Kools made his eyes narrow now, not passive as they had been a moment before. "What's the other side, man?"

The old man grinned.

"Good, Koolie. Maybe I got what I was looking for. The question is the right question, Koolie. I need an outside man and an inside man. Can even use your sister, she proved she got a lot of guts."

"How'd she prove that?"

"Killed me," the old man said. "I told you that. Down in Nome. Put two bullets in me. Crack, crack, just like that, killed me dead and never thought another thing about it."

Kools saw the way it was and lit another cigarette.

"You ain't gonna really blow up anything."

"Don't bet on it."

"Is that what it has to be? A bet?"

"You want two hundred thousand dollars?"

Kools said, "Sure. Who do I have to kill?"

"Eventually, Noah."

Kools thought about it. He thought about Noah screwing his sister. That didn't matter but it was one more thing to put on the other side if he needed to make an accounting to get himself ready to kill Noah. But he already knew it didn't matter. He would find enough things to kill Noah for two hundred large.

"Why I gotta kill Noah?"

"Because there's a hundred apiece for you boys. Just a simple little job and you don't even have to blow up anything unless things turn out different. You know what this is?"

The old man reached under the bunk and pulled out the suitcase. He snapped it open. It was a cheap vinyl hard-sided suitcase. He opened it and there was a Westclox quartz alarm clock and a number of wires and two containers joined to a third container. The containers were rounded metal of different sizes, as though one container might contain something that triggered another container and then both went into a third.

"A bomb," Kools said. "We worked on those. You gonna leave it in the Fairbanks terminal? Gonna ship it on the Alaska ferry south to Juneau?" Kools was trying not to smile. The old man didn't need anyone special for this; this was kid's stuff. Hire anyone to take a suitcase into a terminal and leave it. Blow up some mothers and their kids waiting for the train south at Denali. That was so easy it was contemptible. Like rolling drunks instead of sticking up a gas station. That's what Kools had done. He had done hard time and he kept reminding himself not to think about it.

The old man said, "There's bombs and bombs, Koolie. Cartoonist named Herblock, which you never heard of, used to do cartoons drawing this fellow as a big guy with a bullet head who needed a shave, was supposed to be the H-bomb. But now we get all our best ideas from Japan. Like the turbines make this ship so quiet. Like very small things that go bump in the night. Like an atomic device, Koolie."

Kools stared at it. He couldn't get the passive look back. He had to look impressed because he was. He stared at the thirty-six- by thirty-inch case on the bunk with quartz alarm clock attached.

"Gonna blow up the line," he said.

The old man watched Kools' eyes, saw them staring straight down into the depth of the bomb. It was an atomic device, no fooling about that. The whole thing was tricky but you couldn't have fooling around to start with.

"You put it here," the old man said. He opened a map of the line that snaked down across eastern Alaska from the oil fields in the ice on the North Slope down through mountains and immense barren valleys full of wild creatures, down to the port of Valdez on the southern coast. His finger rested on a small red x.

"All right," Kools said.

The old man looked at him. "You'll do it?"

"What do we get?"

"Good, Koolie. Noah would salute and carry on but you want to know what you get."

"Yeah."

"You get to save your people. To save the land of the north. To save the old ways. To save the immense treasury of wildlife—"

"That's bullshit."

"Sure it is."

"Then what is it?"

"I got a hundred thousand for Noah and another hundred large for you. You put it down in exactly three days. You put the clock on eighteen hours. And then you get the hell out of there. The next place I see you is in Seattle. You just get a room in the Pacific Plaza and you wait there. Don't go off bragging, don't get drunk and don't get picked up by the cops."

"What does Noah do?"

"Noah is the beard. He takes the credit. He makes the noise. And he meets you in a week in the same hotel."

"What happens then?"

"What happens then is up here," the old man said. He tapped his head with his forefinger. "You got any questions?"

"One."

The man waited.

"Who are you?"

The old man smiled again. "You always ask the dumb questions, the ones that don't matter."

"I like to know, if I'm setting a bomb like this."

"I told you: The man your sister killed last fall down in the Seward Peninsula. One hell of a girl, Koolie. Shot me dead just like that, without even thinking about it. Admire a girl like that."

The prow of the submarine broke the thin ice in Kotzebue Sound beneath Tikizat. The ice barely groaned at the pressure of the hull and gave way and the crackling sound of the ice startled a trio of polar bears prowling on the sea ice in the darkness. The ice was very thin, just a skin that had built up over two cold days. It was an hour until the first red band of light would come across the southeastern sky. It was just after midnight and the days were already twenty-two hours long. The water fell away from the black hull in sheets and clattered on the surface of the Chukchi Sea. The endless polar wind moaned across the ice and blew grains of icy snow against the bulkhead. The beast of the submarine was above the water and there were only a few lights in the immense blackness.

The hatch opened and two men clambered out and two sailors came after them with packs and a box like a suitcase. First, they lowered the inflatable raft over the side and then put the packs and suitcase down in the raft and then helped the two men down the steel ladder cast over the side of the hull. The submarine seemed to shudder as it held the position and when Kools reached the raft, he fell into it.

The night was pitch black beneath the northern stars.

Lights seemed to flash from time to time against the blackness. The north was a land of endless illusions. Monsters and mountains could be seen where there was nothing but ice and snow, and the end of the world was in the stars.

Kools and Noah paddled across the inlet to the land that was Cape Krusensterm. A kilometer inland sat an immense lake and the settlement of Talikoot on the other side. The plane would land on the lake just after dawn, before the patrols began. Unless the American sonar men had spotted the submarine breaking the surface of the sea.

The two men climbed the little ridge and then trekked down to the shore of the lake and did not speak. Their breath was palpable and their eyes were encased in goggles to cut the tearing wind.

While they waited, sitting on their packs, in their parkas and flannels and Danskin underwear, Kools began to tell Noah what the old man had told him. He only left out a couple of the parts. Noah listened and asked some questions. Kools knew that Noah was smelling around at what Kools told him. Noah was a believer but not that much of a fool. Noah wasn't sure what he was supposed to think about things.

"Why tell you and not tell me?"

"He told me why. After." Kools stared at his mukluks. "I'm the one he wasn't sure of," Kools said. "He said he had to lay it out to me, and if it wasn't going to work with me, I wasn't going to be able to tell you. I would've gone back with the sub."

"He wasn't sure of you?"

"That's it," Kools said. "I didn't know that, I figured he wasn't sure of you, but that wasn't what it was. He had to be sure of me, so he told me."

"He's sure of you?"

"I guess so. I don't know. He's crazy, that old man. He's got so many ideas in his head that I can't believe he remembers from one idea to the next what's really going on. I ask him who he is and you know what he says to me? He says he's the man my sister killed down in Seward. He said that twice. What was I supposed to say? And then he says my sister is doing some business for him now in Nome."

"Narvak wasn't part of him," Noah said, almost jealous.

Kools was smiling but Noah couldn't see it because of the masks over their faces. Noah was taking it all, the way the fish take the line to their guts and then deny it. Three days to a bombing, he thought, and he wondered what an atom bomb going off in the middle of Alaska would look like.

And Noah, deep in thought, was thinking about the man Narvak had been sent to kill. A man named Henry McGee. She had told him that night, beneath the furs, as he made love to her. She had shared the secret of Ulu because she thought he knew all about it. Henry McGee was dead; this other Henry McGee was not dead. He tried to sort out the puzzle while they waited for the first light of the Arctic morning.

TWELVE

Wagner's Problem

Wagner walked in the Fairmont Hotel bar as if he belonged there. He made $41,765 a year as a servant of the government in the U.S. Witness Relocation Program's Department of Liaison. The drinks in the bar were five bucks each. Someone else was paying.

He drank the first of three Stolys on the rocks thirstily. When the Russian vodka burned the back of his throat, he slowed it down enough not to get drunk right away.

The man who would pay joined him at exactly 5:31. The second man took a handful of peanuts and tasted them, one at a time. He looked at the barman for a moment as though wondering who he was and said, "Let me have a Beck's. Not in a chilled glass."

Wagner sipped the vodka and felt a little better.

The second man was six feet tall and wore a dark blue suit. He had blue eyes and blond hair and a long nose.

His eyes were narrow when he talked to people like Wagner.

The big ornate room was filling up with remnants of a Japanese tour group calling it a day. The small Oriental men in uniform dark-blue suits, white shirts, rep ties and identical Nikon cameras drank big glasses full of Johnny Walker Red Label and explained San Francisco to each other. The inevitable Muzak polluted the room and Wagner stood very close to Pell when he told him what was wrong.

"I sent down Karen O'Hare and she's fucking it up. She's staying down for a couple of days, which wouldn't worry me if she was just fucking off, but that isn't the way she works. She got a federal fucking wiretap order approved at ten this morning. She's tapping his fucking phone."

"You amaze me sometimes, how dumb you are," Pell said.

"I had to send someone to Redbird."

"So you send a Girl Scout."

"What is this about?"

"This is about ten thousand that you got on the first of the month and it's about nothing more than that as far as you're concerned."

"I want to get out of this."

"You are out of it. You were never in it."

"I know that. I appreciate that. So you people could let me get out of it because what do I know about anything? I know nothing about anything."

"What are you trying to tell me?"

"Just I want to get out of it."

"I already told you."

Wagner had thought about it all the way to the hotel. He wanted to catch the trolley on Powell on his way to the hotel but it was jammed with tourists as usual. The whole city was one gigantic adult amusement park and the residents had become backdrop providing local color. Wagner felt like the guy who wears the Goofy costume down at Disneyland. He got a cab instead and felt sick all the way up Nob Hill. It had started to rain as he walked into the Fairmont.

"You're out of it," Pell said. He poured the German beer out of the green glass bottle straight down the middle of the glass. The head formed as he poured and was exactly right when the glass was filled. Pell took a long swallow and had foam on his lips. He ate another peanut from the collection in the palm of his left hand. "I could even make a joke about how out of it you are. You just got to finish up and finish up means getting your girl to come home to San Francisco. Would make a song, don't you think?"

"I can't do it right away. I got my own restraints, you know. Everything is taped. They don't trust anybody, they tape everything. I wonder what the hell they do with all the tape, whether they reuse it or trash it or where they keep it. I even wonder who listens to it. Who is out there watching us? I wonder that sometimes."

"I know. You wouldn't be wired right now, would you?"

Wagner looked shocked. He hadn't even thought about it.

Pell saw the look. "It doesn't matter. When we get done here, you go to the men's room. There's a guy in there is gonna feel you up, to make sure you don't have any wires."

"I will not—"

"Sure you will," Pell said and popped another peanut in his mouth. He looked around the room, his back against the bar. "Fucking Japs and their cameras. What do you suppose they do with all the photos? I mean, they must have trillions of them by now, they been taking pictures like crazy people for the past forty years. You ever been to Tokyo? Very crowded city. I can't imagine where they put the photos."

"I don't give a shit about photos. I want to—"

Pell broke him off with a look. He held a peanut poised. "You got two days from this morning, which means one full day and two nights. That line is clear by Wednesday morning 9:00 A.M. or you are in the deepest shit you ever saw in your life."

Wagner didn't want to hear it. He shut his eyes a moment in lieu of plugging his ears.

"Go down to Santa Bee," Pell said in a more reasonable tone. "Talk to your girl, talk to Redbird, tell her you're making a field evaluation and then get her ass home and give her what-for about tapping that guy's phone."

"It's legal. She got an order. She'd never do anything illegal."

"I had a sister like that once. She could only afford to live like that because she lived in Iowa. She'd have been dead meat in L.A. in two days."

"I guess I gotta go down."

" 'I guess I gotta go down.' Fucking A you gotta go down."

"Pell," Wagner said in his miserable voice.

Pell looked at him. The peanuts were gone. So was the beer.

"I feel like shit," he said.

"You look it too," Pell said.

"When do I get out, really get out?"

Pell smiled. "You don't really get it, do you?" He looked for peanuts in the bowl but it was empty. "You were never in it, like I said. You ever want to become a larger part of the picture, you just fuck up. Then you will be very important. For about twenty-four hours or however long it takes to ice you. You are not part of anything right now. The next time we want something, I come to see you and give you money. You take the money and you give us what we ask for. You spend the money discreetly. No Porsches, no house in Pacifica. You be cool and we be cool, like the tutsones say.''

"I never should've started.''

"No. You were a lousy poker player and even worse at blackjack. You never should've started. But what the fuck. That's the fun of gambling. And now you can really afford it, not like before.''

The third Stoly just numbed him—tongue, throat, belly. He wasn't tasting a thing when he drank it.

"I'll go down," he said at last.

Pell tried out a small, blond smile. "Good. You better go down tonight before Redbird makes it deeper. All I know, Redbird has got his own scams going, make it harder to get Miss O'Hare to give this up and go home.''

"What is this about really? I mean, what do you want with this guy? Who wants him?''

"You're finished now. I'll take the check, Wagner. You might want to take a leak. Bathroom is down there. Don't be shy when the guy cops a feel. Like they tell the ladies, just lay back and relax.'' Pell wasn't smiling at all when he said it.

THIRTEEN
The Reality of Dreams

Rita Macklin sat at her vanity and brushed her hair. She was going to have dinner that night with Mac, her editor. It would be the usual thing—gossip about other journalists, and savage and funny observations on the politics of the city.

She was thirty-four years old today.

Her eyes were changing, she thought as she stared at herself in the vanity mirror in the bedroom. She stopped brushing her red hair and leaned forward to inspect her eyes in the soft light.

She wore a black slip and nothing else. Her skin was soft and warm from the bath and she smelled of flowers.

He always said she smelled like flowers, even when it wasn't true, when she knew she wore no perfume at all.

There were little wrinkles at the corners of her eyes. She would not have noticed them three years ago. Three years ago was the threshold of her thirties and things were still possible and everything could be accomplished in the future.

It was still possible to become pregnant at thirty-four.

She sat up straight on the bench and picked up her brush again. She stared very hard at her green eyes in the mirror.

Kaiser. She never thought of Kaiser anymore but she had loved that old man, her first mentor in Washington. Then Kaiser killed himself one day and the pain of it tore into her again and again for months. She dreamed of Kaiser and could hear his cigarette-rough voice and his endearing cynicism. He called her Little Rita and he had been as kind to her as her father.

In the end, you could stop dreaming about everyone. You could lose your brother and father and stop dreaming of them; and you could lose old Kaiser, the crusty editor of the two-bit news service who had hired her and trained her to the kind of bloody journalism that wins prizes, and in time, you would stop thinking of him or hearing his voice.

She stopped brushing her hair. She looked at herself. Why the hell love Devereaux?

He was not her first man. It wasn't that. He had used her once, betrayed her once, led her into danger more than once. He could not speak to her of the secret things in his life. He was a constant enigma, even to himself. He never said he loved her.

He never said it; he said words lied.

She was thirty-four today and alone. He had been gone three weeks. Another lie to explain. But he wouldn't even explain. Did he love the trade so much that he had to leave her from time to time and descend back into that maelstrom of secrets and spies and wash himself with brutality and deceit and all the things he said he despised?

She shivered suddenly.

The afternoon was cool and full of clouds, and pink light streamed through the bedroom window. She went to bed alone and wanted him next to her. He had left her before, packing the single bag, making certain that she did not see the pistol he always carried. Did he understand he was killing it between them, every time he went away?

That was it, she thought.

He was killing it. You could only stand so much of it. It was dying day by day. He might be dead or in Russia or in prison or back in Asia or merely a block away, listening at keyholes.

And when he came back to her, there might be a wound or not. Sometimes, she could guess at what it had been by the look in his eye. When it had been very bad, he tried to make his eyes stop seeing. Sometimes, literally, he would almost be blind for days. He would walk around in the house in the darkness of 3:00 A.M. and bump into furniture and never make a sound or curse.

He never told her. He might tell her where he had been but he would never tell her all of it because it was a secret.

Even when they swam together in love in a secret pool of their own, he had this other secret, tucked away in mind, never to be spoken of.

She looked at herself in the mirror and she was crying because it hurt her so much. She thought she would have to leave him, to have one final hurt and get rid of it. Cut the arm off and feel the pain and the absence of the limb but, in time, learn to live without it.

She was thirty-four today. When would it be dead between them? Would it take another three years? She would be thirty-seven. Would it last five more years? She would almost be forty. When would she be best able to start her life again with someone else or alone?

Damn him, she thought. She took a tissue and wiped her eyes. She was going to get good and drunk with Mac tonight, and if he made a pass at her, she would let him.

FOURTEEN

Narvak

The old man was waiting for her.

She came into the single-room cabin from the winter breezeway and took off her fur coat and hung it on a peg by the front door. The place was very warm because the old man had turned up the kerosene fire. It was true spring outside.

The spring was spectacular and it broke your heart. When you were certain the ice was permanent and the darkness was all there would ever be and the snow would finally-bury every living thing, then spring came. It was incredibly light and the sullen snow retreated and the ice cracked across the sea like thousands of pistol shots. The sun felt good all day long.

Now the old man looked at her. Narvak held out her hands at the stove and her back was to the old man.

"What did you do?"

"I tried to do what you said. I really did what you told me to do."

There was a moment of silence. The dark-faced man said, "So it didn't work."

"It worked in part. I talked to Nels Nelsen and he got drunk and I went down to the harbor to pick him the American. He was a good-looking man, not pretty to look at it, but he was a good-looking man. He was looking at me too, I could tell that."

"Everyone likes to look at you, honey. They like it almost as much as you do, you little tramp," he said.

She turned to him and looked annoyed. She rubbed her buttocks and pouted and stood in front of the stove. "You told me to fuck him."

"So did you?"

"I think he's a queer," she said.

"Honey, if he was a queer, I woulda sent him Noah, Noah'd take a dick up his ass for the cause." He was smiling at her and his teeth flashed in the darkness of his face. "What happened?"

"He asked me about Henry McGee. He wanted to know if I knew Henry McGee. He knows I killed him, I swear he does," Narvak said. She remembered the look of the gray man and the strength of his hand squeezing her hand.

"He said that?" the dark man said. "He asked you about Henry McGee just out of nowhere?"

"Well, he wanted to know how I knew Nels Nelsen. He wasn't very nice. He could've been nice."

"Why you think he asked you about Henry McGee?"

"Because that was who got killed. That's what this is about, isn't it?"

"Bless you, honey, that isn't what this is about at all.

You're a cute thing and you like to do it about as often as I do, but you don't really have a clue, Narvak, honey," the dark man said.

"This is about ULU, about the pipeline—"

"Not at all," the dark man said, still grinning. "Honey, I told you once you killed me and you couldn't figure it out from that. Why do you think this man comes up here to talk to Nels Nelsen? About a murder? Hell, he isn't interested in the murder of that fool Dobbins. Otis Dobbins and I were shipmates and he really thought all he had to do was to be Henry McGee for about a year and then I would give him the twenty-five thousand dollars. Hell, he did a good job, and if I didn't have to have him killed, I would've paid him. He was a good shipmate. Honey, I'm Henry McGee. I'm the guy he's come up here to find."

She really didn't understand. She stopped rubbing her buttocks. The dark man could scare the hell out of her sometimes. You get coke into you and your head is turning around and he's on top of you and then he says something or does something and you don't realize it at the time but later you figure out that he hurt you.

"Don't scare me," she said.

"Come over here, honey, and let me soothe you. So Devereaux turned you down, huh?"

"He said his name was Wilson."

"Wilson Shmilson. They sent the right man. It would have worked with someone else but I guessed it would be Devereaux."

"I don't understand."

"Bless you, honey, I know that. Take off your clothes and crawl in beside me," the dark man said.

She took off her jeans. She didn't wear underwear. She slipped in beside him. His hands were on her. She felt his warmth beneath the furs on the sleeping shelf. She closed her eyes and said, "Nels Nelsen was drunk when we got back to Nome and he wasn't going to be able to talk to him. He took Nels up to a bedroom in the Nugget and I helped him. I was going to try him again but I saw that look in his eyes, like he was looking through me. Who needs that shit? I still think he's a queer."

"Well, anything is possible but I don't recall that was his problem exactly. His problem is he's one cold sonofabitch, and when he decides he has to go outside, he don't try the door, he goes right through the wall. Only bastard I ran into who seemed to know what the hell he was doing. Admire that. Thought those dodos would finally decide to go with their strength when I tripped the signal."

"I don't understand any of this," she said.

"You only understand this," he said.

She made a sound.

"And this," he said.

"Yes," she said.

"That's the way you think," he said.

"Yes," she said.

"Thing I like is you killed Dobbins, didn't ask me why or twice. I like that, I like the way you show off too. This thing is over one way or another in a week or so and then I get rich."

"You buy me something then?"

"I buy you everything, honey."

"Where we go? To Anchorage?"

"Fuck Anchorage, fuck Alaska, fuck this cold. We go down to Tahiti to start with."

"Is that like Hawaii?"

"It's French Hawaii. You'll like Tahiti and then we go up to Hong Kong, buy you some shiny dresses. You'll show off well in Hong Kong. We'll sort of go around the rim, down to Shanghai, maybe Saigon. Have a good time, be warm all the time, make lots of fuck-fuck.''

"I be your girl."

"Soon as those two fuckups, your brother and that other fuckup, do their thing and I get to do my thing. In a little while, we see if this plays or not. Reminds me of this dumb beggar I picked up in a sailor's bar in San Fran, he thought I wanted to do a sexual act with him. Well, instead of that, I bought him and put him down in Santa Cruz for a year to fuck around and drink his brains out. He did too because he was waiting for the golden payoff at the end, which was twenty-five thousand dollars. The funny thing is, chump money never seems to inflate. You can still buy all the chumps you need for about twenty-five thousand. It's something about a chump's brain, it doesn't think much beyond twenty-five thousand dollars.''

"That's a lot of money."

"No, honey, three million is a lot of money. Three million buys you warm and it buys warm water to swim in and a private beach to be naked on."

"I can't think about that much money," she said.

Henry McGee smiled and the smile broke across his dark face like sunlight. "You don't have to think. You're just an action, honey."

"I be your girl," she said.

"You be my girl," he said, thinking about when he would have to kill her. Down the line a ways.

FIFTEEN
Call to a Spy

Karen O'Hare left the door of the motel room open. They could hear the beat of traffic on the boulevard beyond the courtyard. It was just seven in the morning and she wore a robe over her pajamas and Wagner looked as if he had not slept all night.

"I'm in charge here, Karen," he had begun.

She had left the door open and gone to the coffee machine in the courtyard and put in a dollar in change to get two cups of coffee, one ostensibly mixed with cream. It was paler than the other. She gave Wagner the cream and sipped at the black. She did not sit on the edge of the unmade bed.

"I don't understand how you can exceed your authority this way," he said. His face had a hangover and his nose was large and red. The cup shook in his hand. "A wiretap? What the hell do you think we are?"

"There's authorization for this. In the field manual. In

the event the agent feels the witness program has been compromised and—"

"You got the same case of paranoia Redbird has?"

"I'm being careful, Mr. Wagner," Karen O'Hare said. She put the coffee on the plastic nightstand. She sat on the straight chair that went with the Formica desk *cum* dresser. He sat in the vinyl easy chair with the broken arm. It was a crummy motel room for sixty-two bucks a night. Still, it was cheaper than staying up the way at the Fess Parker.

"I ordered the wiretap because there is something peculiar about this. Redbird is . . . well, he's morose. He seemed disappointed . . . in me. I mean, I think he was looking for more action from higher-ups. I thought he knew what was going on."

"What do you mean by that? We're not spies, Karen. We're ordinary civil servants in a very ordinary—"

"The program is not ordinary. It takes all kinds. Redbird was a Soviet agent."

How the hell did she know that?

"I asked for his précis on the computer before I came down—"

"You're not authorized," Wagner began again.

"I have an X clearance," she said. "I could only go to the level of X in getting information about Redbird. But it was enough to see that he had been a Soviet agent and defected seven years ago."

"You're not authorized," Wagner said and let it go. "The point is, I'm in charge here."

"You sound just like that general sounded when the president was shot," Karen O'Hare said. She said it without her gosh-whiz manner. She had somehow slipped her gosh-whiz manner on the trip down to Santa Barbara.

Wagner stared at her.

It had been a hard night after he left Pell in the bar of the Fairmont. There was the night flight south that turned out to be to Los Angeles because there was no plane available to Santa Barbara. He had rented a car and gotten lost on the freeway. At one point, he was headed for Disneyland.

The scenery of southern California, so vaguely unsettled in smog-ridden daylight, was a frightening experience in moonlight. The endless freeways climbed hills, descended into tinseled valleys of light, climbed again past silent fortress homes. Each new neighborhood resembling the neighborhood past, each new town exactly like the one left behind. It was nearly morning when he had limped along Highway 101 into the heart of Santa Barbara.

"All right, Karen," he started again. He was sure his voice was reasonable. "What about the tap? Learn anything?"

"Not at first."

"What does that mean?"

"He made two calls at night, both to the same number."

"How do you know that?"

"TouchTone," she said.

Wagner stared at her.

"Beep, beep, bop, beep," she said.

"Why not speak English?"

"I recorded the tones. I got a phone. I went through the combinations until I could match the numbers he called. It was the same number both times. Los Angeles area. I called directory and got an unlisted number so I pulled rank. The phone belongs to Karin Orgonov. I went back to our files and that's a name we have."

"Did you sleep? I mean, the bed looks used." He was

being sarcastic and they both knew it, which made it in-effective. Karen looked at him for a moment with those innocent blue eyes and waited for the sarcasm to leave the room.

"I checked her out in files. She's a Soviet defector. They know each other, don't you see that? Why does he call her when he's feeling paranoid or when he really has seen someone who scares him? He called her, the last person I would have expected him to have contact with. So I called her. I got hold of her around three this morning. She has a heavy accent. I told her who I was."

"You have no authorization—"

The cold blue eyes held the room and stopped his voice. "I told her the code she would have expected. She sounded relieved. I asked her some questions and then she put her guard up."

"You didn't tell her about Redbird."

"No, Mr. Wagner, I'm not an idiot."

"You're acting like one."

"Something is fishy," she said. She used phrases like that all the time, as though she had learned everyday speech from a book.

"So what were you going to do?"

She caught the tense. She blinked at him. "I'm going to find out who she is. Get a picture at least. Then I'm going to talk to our client again."

"You're going back," Wagner said.

"You're kidding."

"I didn't sit up in a plane and a car all night to make a joke. This thing has slipped up a notch or two in security terms. I'm taking over from you as of now."

"What are you talking about? I'm as cleared as you are."

"That isn't the point. I'm assistant director and you're a very novice operative and—"

"Jesus Christ, this is shitty," she said. He was surprised at the words and the tone of voice. Karen O'Hare sat very still and her face was dead white.

Wagner was sweating. He had been sweating all night. Pell made him sweat, the whole stinking bag he was in made him sweat. His wife was a honey blond with a Dallas accent and the skin of a peach. She was also as dumb as a board. What could he tell her about guys who stand around in bars eating peanuts. Or about this one sitting in her blue bathrobe, holding herself in as if she was a nun confronting Genghis Khan? He was under a deadline they wouldn't know anything about, even if he explained it to them. And the emphasis was on the word *dead*.

Wagner knew he wasn't a bad guy in this, it was just out of his hands and it had to be out of Karen O'Hare's hands by today.

Karen stared at him without a word.

"Look, honey," he started. He stopped when he saw the eyes turn from cold to ice. "Look, Karen, we've been together, what? A year? Year and two months? I've looked out for you at the program, I can see you've got what it takes, very bright, I've put you in for two commendations."

She really wasn't going to say anything to help him.

"I think this is just a . . . bit more complex than you realize, maybe more than any of us realize. . . . This wasn't just my idea." He thought of the lie, thought of how she could check it out back on Powell Street, decided she couldn't. "Got buzzed from NSC direct on this last night, they want my input. I do have contact with NSC, you know, I gave them liaison when I was with GAO in D.C."

He felt better with the alphabet jargon. He even smiled. "They asked me direct to look into it. I don't want to take your play but the point is: They know me, they don't know you."

"So I was right," she said. "There is something going on."

"It could be. Maybe it was your wiretap request that interested them. I think I would have handled that differently. The point is: You set off all kinds of bells when you start making requests like that, they get interested more in finding out what you want to know than in what is really out there. You see?"

Karen said nothing for a moment and then let out a long sigh. "I'm using a secure room at the local FBI office, the tape is set up there. I've got the only key."

She reached in the pocket of the robe for the key. He looked at her. She really did believe she had the only key. It was just another complication, he thought, but he supposed the local FBI types were more concerned with tracking down dangerous radicals set to blow up the oil drilling rigs in the harbor than with something like this. He was sure they listened to the wiretap when Karen was not there.

At least Karen said she was going back to San Fran.

SIXTEEN

The Hunter

Devereaux woke four hours after dawn and turned
on the light. It was 5:03 in the morning. He threw
his bare feet on the floor of the small old-fashioned
room on the second landing of the hotel. There were only
two hotels in Nome and neither was filled because the
white school buses that brought tourists in summer from
the airport were only just beginning to run for the season.
The rooms were very expensive and bare and clean.

Sometime in sleep he had begun to figure it out, from
all the stories.

He stared at the floor of the room and the worn carpet.
In the very thin yellow light of the single lamp, he saw
only his thoughts.

Nels Nelsen snored in the next room. He had been awake
when Nels came out of his drunken sleep around midnight.
Nels had only wanted another drink or two to get back to

sleep but Devereaux had forced him to stay awake a while longer.

There was only one question left for Nels in the long trail of questions that had started in the 201 file in Washington and led to the man called "Captain" Holmes in Seattle.

"I don't know where he came from" is the way Nels Nelsen had answered it. "Man from Dutch Harbor asked me the same question. I answered every damned question he gave me. I ain't trying to hold out on you, not on anyone. I wish to hell I never had met Henry McGee, he's given me a god-awful lot of trouble since he got himself killed."

"Did he know the traplines?"

Nels stared at him. Nels had a heavy face to start with. The last few weeks, since the death of his partner, had added weight to it. He had dried out in the psychiatric hospital where they had taken him after he brought Henry McGee's body into Nome. That had just made him thirstier. His nose was veined and his eyes were always bloodshot and he thought he was going to die nearly every morning when he woke up.

"What about Narvak?"

"Catherine? You mean the Indian girl?"

"Eskimo, I think."

"Native girl anyway. Yeah, I met her yesterday or the day before, I don't remember. Lots of them start coming around in summer, looking for the tourists and dredgers. Lots of money and not a lot to do. Same for the girls, I suppose. They're not all whores but a lot of them are. They just want something interesting to happen. She was a nice girl. I gave her a tumble, she has a nice little bottom on her, always working."

Devereaux waited, staring at the blotched face, at the small, red-soaked eyes.

"You always get lucky like that?"

Nels Nelsen stared at the government man. He would have told the government to go to hell ten years ago. That's what the country was all about. Would have said the same thing six months ago. Before Henry McGee got himself killed. But the psychiatric hospital had frightened him very much. They said the man he had lived with was Otis Dobbins. The man from Dutch Harbor had asked a lot of questions after that. He had seen the way it was, that he had to go along with them if he wanted to be left alone.

"I had my share of luck," Nels Nelsen said. He tried to say it with dignity.

Devereaux stared at him the way the wolf stares at the prey on the trail. There is no fear in the eyes of the wolf, only this vague chill hostile look that is the beginning of a question. The answer to the question is death, for one or the other.

"She surprised me," Nels said at last.

Devereaux said nothing.

"She's a good-looking thing. I wasn't throwing money around. Tell you the truth, by the time breakup comes, I'm usually getting along toward short. I got some furs to sell and that'll flush me out, but I haven't done it yet. So I was surprised she was so friendly. She picked you up all right down at the dock?"

"She mentioned Henry McGee?"

"Well, not in so many words. Maybe I brought it up, come to think of it. Everyone in Nome knows about the day I brought in poor Henry. I beg your pardon, this fellow Otis Dobbins what told me he was Henry. Someone in Nome probably told her—"

"She know a lot of people?"

"Pretty thing like that can get to know as many people as she wants to know."

"She know many people?"

"She kept to me."

"She came in and saw you and it was love at first sight."

Nels frowned at the outlander. He had the manner of the fellow from Dutch Harbor. They had soft voices and they didn't come across hardcase like the cops on Fourth Avenue in Anchorage when they wanted to wade into a bar and bust up a few Indians. They just sat there and waited and asked smart-ass questions.

"I didn't say nothing about love. You asked me a question."

"Who is she, then?"

"Well, ain't that what they pay you for?"

He had sent the message through the Dutch Harbor station house this time. The message to Hanley was not the one he had intended. He had wanted to say that the trail of Henry McGee was cold and dead and that he was coming home. But the girl in the car had changed that. Was it by accident or design? He began to feel trapped by the stories of Henry McGee, as though he might be nothing more than a flat folk character in one of them and Henry was deciding how the story would come out for him. He remembered her hand on his crotch and the way it had fluttered and struggled free when he mentioned Henry McGee. If she had not reacted, it would have been dead and over. Was McGee that clumsy, to send a girl to him? Or was it really very clever? He could not decide.

He stared at Nels Nelsen and plodded on: "Why do you go down to Anchorage? Why didn't you go to Fairbanks to blow off steam?"

"I know people in Anchorage. I knew people at the Elmendorf Air Base there. Worked in Anchorage a year after half the city slid down into Cook Inlet in the quake Easter Sunday 'sixty-four. Why the hell shouldn't I?"

"Otis Dobbins say he came into Anchorage to sell furs?"

"He did not. Wasn't the time to sell furs anyway."

"He didn't say what he did?"

"You know now what he did."

"We don't. That's why we ask."

"Man came out of nowhere."

"No. He came from someplace. We just don't know where."

"Why'd you come up here by ship? There's faster ways."

"I had to talk to a man. For a long while."

"About Henry."

"About Henry. He knew Henry in a past life."

"You talk like Henry is a ghost."

"What do you think?"

Nels thought about Henry McGee sitting on a little hill, sitting straight up with two bullets in him, frozen and smiling. Damn Henry McGee to hell.

Devereaux waited, large hands held together between his knees, his forearms resting on his thighs, leaning forward, watching.

"Ship, thinking of something just now when I asked you why you come by ship. Ship," the old trapper said once again.

"What ship?"

"No ship. Just a carving he did out of a caribou antler. Was Christmas that year we were in the bush and he give me a little ship. Wasn't an old-fashioned thing with sails but it was a ship and a smart piece of carving. Said to him what did he know about ships and he said he had seen it in a book and liked the look of it. I think I must of lost it. When I got . . . put away."

"Why would he carve a ship?"

"I just told you, didn't I? He saw a picture of it."

"Why didn't he carve something else?"

"Maybe a ship was easier."

"Lot of white men carve?"

"No. That's native stuff. Go down to the Board of Trade down Front Street, whole shop full of stuff. The Eskimos come down and they got a piece of ivory all carved into a polar bear or something, something like that go for two hundred dollars or more down in the outside but the guy down to the shop give them twenty bucks for it. Got a whole shop full of stuff. They carve on everything. Carve on whalebone, carve on walrus tusk, carve on each other when they get drunk enough." Nels smiled at that. "I sure would like a whiskey if you could."

Devereaux gave him the vodka bottle he had in the single canvas bag and Nels drank it like whiskey, made a face, and splashed water in it. Devereaux asked him more questions but there didn't seem to be any connections to the answers. All the stories about Henry McGee—the stories he had poured into the beach bum in Santa Cruz, into Captain Holmes, into Nels Nelsen through the bogus Otis Dobbins—the stories were vignettes that brightened the stage, played, and faded out. Where was the connection to Henry McGee?

And now, in the light of sullen, weak morning, Devereaux thought he saw it.

He went into the small, old-fashioned bathroom and turned on the shower. The water groaned in the pipes for a moment and then splashed down into the tub. He stepped into the shower and felt the warmth cover his body. Warmth was comfort in this country; it was sex and enough food and drink and the smell of flowers in a mountain meadow. Devereaux comforted himself beneath the water and saw what even Hanley had not seen the day Henry McGee triggered the files in the bowels of R Section in Washington.

Devereaux was the connection.

SEVENTEEN

The Second Connection

The telephone call and the written message came within ten minutes of each other.

The servant shook Malcolm Crowder's shoulder for a moment and he came instantly awake. He blinked in the dim light. The curtains on the French windows were drawn, but here and there, bright sunlight peeped through. It was long after dawn, which meant nothing in an Alaska spring when dawn comes so early. He could see Terry's form next to him on the vast bed, twisted beneath the covers, her blond hair arrayed on the pillows. The wind howled against the thick windows and moaned around the chimney. Everything was all right; everything was secure; Malcolm Crowder blinked again at James standing next to the bed.

He nodded to the servant to show he was awake and then lifted his legs from beneath the down comforter. Terry grunted in sleep and turned. It had been a long evening.

Terry was on the committee seeking to restore historic Anchorage. Some argued that Anchorage had very little past and almost none worth restoring, but that did not stop the cream of society from feting itself at luncheons and dinners in the Captain Cook Hotel while it sought ways to make its work meaningful to the people of the city. The ball had lasted until past midnight and Crowder had drunk too much. It was all damned nonsense but Terry was twenty-nine years younger than Malcolm Crowder and she was a nice, warm thing to have in your bed.

James was the odd name chosen by the native servant who now led Malcolm Crowder downstairs. James had attached himself to Malcolm in the old days, before power and money, and was the only living memento of Malcolm's past, which he had consistently reinvented over the last thirty years.

The large house was all paneling, braided rugs, bits of carved ivory and photographs of wildlife. The large fireplace was crowned by a giant moose head with antlers. It was a man's idea of a house and even Terry could not change it. Malcolm Crowder's first wife had grown tired of the house and of Malcolm, so she took a flight south one day and never came back. Now she lived very happily in Seattle with the lawyer who had filed her divorce papers. Malcolm could not imagine such a dull existence.

He padded on bare feet down the staircase, tying his robe around his pajamas.

The man in the kitchen was a cabdriver and his red-rimmed eyes told the time. Crowder looked at the kitchen clock: It was just after four in the morning.

"I told him," the driver began, waving at James' flat, staring face. "Package came in on Alaska Air and the steward said he had the instruction to hold on to it until now and that I was supposed to get it to you by four in the morning. No later than four-fifteen.''

"Jesus Christ,'' Malcolm Crowder said. He had light hazel eyes and rugged good looks of the kind portrayed in beer or cigarette advertising aimed at men who will never look that good. He turned the envelope over. It was a standard 8½- by 11-inch manila envelope sealed with a clasp. Malcolm Crowder looked at the cabdriver.

"Do I know you?''

"Not me but I know you, Senator. I voted for you.''

Crowder let the famous smile define the face for a moment. "How much?''

"How much?''

"How much did you get?''

"Ten bucks.''

"Bullshit,'' Malcolm Crowder said.

The cabdriver turned sullen. "The steward took care of me. I don't need no tip if that's what you're worried about.''

"I'm not worried about anything. Steward comes off an Alaska Air flight and gives you a package and tells you you're supposed to drop it off at someone's house at four in the morning.''

"We get packages all the time to deliver.''

"At four in the morning.''

The cabdriver blinked. He saw the point. "I don't want any trouble. The guy duked me forty bucks. Forty bucks is forty bucks just to wake somebody up. Maybe it was a joke. I don't know who's gonna spend forty bucks on a joke. I didn't know it was you, Senator, until just right now when I saw you, it dawned on me. I voted for you.''

"You told me,'' Crowder said. He put his forefinger in the little opening between the flap and the back of the envelope and tore it open.

He read the sheet of paper.

There were enough details to make it real for him. He didn't know his face was turning gray or that James was now watching him instead of the driver.

"You know who gave you this?"

"Steward, I dunno his name."

"Where was he coming from?"

"He said he was given the package at Nome. He was on the circle, Anchorage to Kotzebue, down to Nome and back."

"Who gave him this in Nome?"

"Hell, I don't know. Look, forty bucks is forty bucks. I'm sorry I woke you up but you don't get any action at four in the morning and forty bucks is forty bucks."

"James, get him twenty more. And get him a piece of paper. I want you to write down your name and phone number."

"I don't want any trouble out of this—"

Malcolm Crowder looked up from the sheet and tried the famous smile again but this time it looked ghastly in the gray drawn face. Crowder looked all of his fifty-nine years in that moment. "There's no trouble, friend. I just need your name in case I have a question later. Maybe ask you to identify that air steward for me."

"OK, just so there's no trouble. I mean, for forty bucks, I don't need a beef."

"No trouble," Crowder said again, turning from the driver, already absorbed again in the message.

The telephone rang exactly four minutes later while James was locking the front door behind the cabdriver. The big house on Hill Crest Avenue at the extreme western edge of Anchorage was so quiet that the shrill ring of the telephone seemed louder than it was.

"Yes," Malcolm Crowder said. He was in the study now, sitting at his desk. The nameplate read: U.S. SENATOR MALCOLM CROWDER. It was a memento, as were many things in the oak-paneled room. People like the cabdriver still called him "Senator" but that had been over eleven years ago.

"You received the envelope?" The voice was nearly as flat and noncommittal as Malcolm's "Yes."

"This is just an elaborate blackmail—"

"Of course. But there's a kernel of truth in it all. Rather a large truth about the bomb. A very small device, contained in a suitcase, which will vaporize a large number of caribou, wolves, grizzlies, moose and a one-mile section of the pipeline."

"How much time do I have?"

"The clock is running. Do you want the account number?"

"Yes."

The caller gave him the name of an account in the Hong Kong Bank of Commerce. He repeated the number and then made Malcolm Crowder repeat it. "You see, we make a call and they tell us the money is there and we call you and tell you where the device is."

"This is the crudest form of blackmail," Crowder said.

"Yes, it is. The wonderful thing about crudity is that it gets your attention so much better than subtlety. Like a full-blown fart in that crowd your wife screws around with. You must really be in love with her pussy to put up with people like that. You used to be some kind of a man, Mal."

No one had called him Mal since the years he was a bush pilot, hacking a living at the edges of the wilderness. Did he know that voice?

"This is impossible, you know. This can't be done the way you want it done."

"Look, everything is possible, including an atomic device blowing up the pipeline. You know it and so does security and the state patrol and even the fucking government."

The expletive was delivered in the same, flat voice and made it curiously more sinister.

"I don't have any connection with the people who might be willing to pay," Crowder said.

"That's not true, Mal," the voice said. "There isn't a deal that goes down in Alaska that you haven't put a finger in. You are a professional greaser and go-between, just as you were in your senator days. Politics made you a rich man, Mal, and now we want a little of the money. Not from you, of course; just from the people you can deal with."

"But what if this is all just—"

"That is the problem, Mal. To convince you it's real. We thought we could send you notes on all the bombs we've set on the line in the last sixteen months but we chose just to give you the dates, coordinates and times. You know they're right. If you don't know, you check with your people."

"There are a lot of people involved in the pipeline—"

"No history lessons now, Mal. Those explosions did not make the media because that's the way we keep confidence in the country. But you know and we know that ULU was responsible for those explosions and that in sixteen months, you have not the faintest idea where or what ULU consists of. Now it's payday. Three million dollars in the Hong Kong Bank of Commerce by 6:00 P.M. Alaskan standard time. That will give you exactly two hours to find the suitcase and deactivate the device. The time allotted is more than generous. By all means, stir up the troops. Call out the army at Fort Richardson, recruit every bush pilot at Merrill Field, tell it from the mountains. We assure you that you will not find a suitcase in eleven hundred miles of wilderness, the odds are simply against you.''

Malcolm Crowder, for one of the few times in his life, did not have any more words.

''Mal?''

''Yes.''

''Three million dollars is not a lot of money anymore unless you don't have it. It will cost ten times that in repairs and damage control from a bombing on the line. You know that and other people should know that.''

''The note said four million.''

''Good, Mal. You have a firm grasp of details. Who do you suppose will receive the other million?''

Malcolm thought about it. The thought began to work on him like the heat in his sauna or Terry rubbing his balls.

''It takes one to dance but two to tango. This is all a matter of timing. Your distinguished successor to the United States Senate is in Anchorage all this week. Fortunately, your successor shares your ideas on ethical conduct. You get ahold of the senator and convince the senator that a million split two ways is decent pay for a day's work.''

''I don't need anyone else.''

''Sure you do. Think of the possibilities, Mal, always think of the possibilities. A sitting U.S. senator and a former distinguished U.S. senator are so convinced that the threat is real that a deal is cut before the stock exchange in New York closes. Three million into one numbered account, one million into a joint account bearing the names of two distinguished political leaders from 'The Last Frontier' state.''

"I don't have an account."

"Take the number," said the voice. The second number surprised Malcolm. The caller was organized, he was a planner, he even had an account set up for the grease. A half-million dollars was a half-million dollars. Malcolm Crowder thought about money the way he sometimes thought about Terry, but money was always available to think about. Some people said Malcolm Crowder knew the price of every building in downtown Anchorage and could figure the grease cost needed to have the building erected. He knew the price of nearly every politician in the state legislature in Juneau, including the ones who said they could not be bought.

"You start paying blackmail and you never stop."

"How many atomic devices you think I got?"

Malcolm's eyes grew very wide. The voice took on shape in his mind. The word *I* had been used for the first time. For the first time, Malcolm saw form and substance. He knew the security forces both private and public on the pipeline had thrown nearly two million dollars into the search for ULU, whatever ULU was. Native settlements had been raided, the usual suspects rounded up, and it had all been for nothing.

Crowder said, "You're ULU."

"The thing is to get people's attention. It isn't that easy. Used to be you could threaten people and they'd pay up. You can't threaten corporations or governments that easily. You can do it, but not easily. Everyone's got their own agenda, Mal, just like I do, just like you do. It ain't your three million, Mal, it's just that you want to give the people the best advice you can and you want to be sure that you really do find an atomic bomb planted where I say it is once you put the money in that account in Hong Kong. Which reminds me: The transfer of funds is cash. No checks, no vouchers. Now back to your problem, Mal, I don't have much time. Do you really think I'm kidding, Mal? I put down the days and the times and all that, but maybe underneath it all, you think I'm kidding.''

"No. I think you're crazy but I don't think you're kidding. The problem is, it isn't enough to let you get away with it.''

The flat voice was laughing now, more form and substance to what had been ethereal. Malcolm closed his eyes to concentrate on the voice.

"I like you, Mal, because you're not a stupid man. I thought that one over myself. You need a setup and I need a way to block a comeback. I'm not worried about Hong Kong, Mal, that money will be traveling the minute it's in the account and you know that those wily Chinese are just about smarter at it than even the gnomes in Zurich. So what do you want?''

"You know what I want.''

"I can give you two turkeys, all trussed and ready for baking. The first turkey is called Noah but his name is something else. The second turkey is called Kools. The way it works, after the money is sent and the bomb is found, you get the message about Noah, who will probably be sitting on his can in Fairbanks. Told the other one to meet me in Seattle but I don't know, he might just hang around with the first one in Fairbanks. Whatever it is, you get two turkeys for the price of one, Mal. I call that pretty good.''

"What about you?''

"Me? They'll implicate me for sure but what the hell, I won't be anywhere you ever gonna find me. You and the Justice Department fumblebums and the crack Alaska State Police—hell. You haven't found me in sixteen months, try sixty sometime. People get found when they leave marks. I don't leave marks. Travel alone, pay cash, eat simple and have a bowel movement every day and you'll live a long life."

"What do I do?"

"Call the senator now. That's your first selling job but I'll make it easier on you. I'll call the senator and mention that you'll be calling right behind me. Then you two cook your deal, but remember, Mal, the clock is literally running on this. Hate to see an ecological disaster, especially when I planned this so careful. If it has to be, it has to be. I'm not playing, Mal, you figure that out by now?"

Malcolm nodded before he spoke. "I figured that out."

"Good, Mal. Good for you."

The connection was broken. Malcolm sat in the light of full morning streaming into the room and listened to the wind.

He called the senator shortly before five in the morning. The conversation lasted no longer than it had to.

"Do you believe him?"

Malcolm looked annoyed. He had changed into his jogging suit and sneakers and was working on a pot of coffee on the silver tray on his desk. James was still awake, lurking in dark corners of the large house, and Terry would sleep until the middle of the morning.

Eleven years before, Malcolm had no intention of resigning from the United States Senate and recommending to the governor that the attorney general take his seat.

Until the day Patricia Heath called him to her office in Juneau. It was a warm spring day in the panhandle and the air had smelled of pine trees and the fresh warm wind from Japan. Senator Malcolm Crowder was then forty-eight years old and had shed his first wife. He had a long-standing liaison with a very discreet blond secretary in his Washington office and was always on the prowl for money and women. Oddly, he was then attracted to powerful women. Patricia Heath had fallen into this category. Normally, a summons from a low-ranking official would have been snubbed; but on that warm spring day in the Alaska panhandle, Malcolm Crowder had pussy on his mind.

It took three minutes for Patricia Heath to ruin his day.

She had all the details in the thick packet of Xerox copies she had handed him. Of course, Patricia assured him, she had the originals.

The details were about money. Money leaves a trail, even when it's cash. There are bank receipts and statements of fund transfers and even the indiscreet purchase of several large pieces of real estate in Virginia that should not have been affordable to a man of modest means, only eight years in the Senate. Malcolm Crowder was a man of the people, the bush pilot who had saved a Yup'ik village in the North Slope borough from being wiped out during a smallpox epidemic in 1955. He had braved a winter storm in his twin-engine Cessna to deliver the vaccine and other medicines to the forsaken village and made certain the Anchorage and Fairbanks papers heard about it.

Patricia Heath had cored out the myth of Malcolm Crowder in the papers she gave him that warm spring day.

"You're a crook," she said. She was then just thirty-three, very bright and pretty. She wore conservative go-to-work clothes in a way that made men stare at her. There was a smell of flowers about her and she wore her hair short. She looked both vulnerable and cold at the same time. It was the eyes, she had Julie Andrews' eyes and they were used to good advantage. Like Julie Andrews' screen persona, she made men desire her without loving her.

"These are—"

"Tedious documents that prove what I say. Now sit down and shut up and let me tell you how this is going to play."

No woman had ever spoken to Malcolm Crowder like that. Few could.

In the next sixty-one minutes, Malcolm Crowder learned all he ever wanted to know about Patricia Heath. She was every bit as ambitious as Malcolm, just as ruthless and, in the final analysis, just as crooked. Six days after the interview, he announced his resignation from the Senate and four days later, the governor nominated the party's surprising woman to the office. It played well in Nome and Sitka and the places between. The newspapers said Patricia had "spunk." It was the sort of word Alaskans used when complimenting their women, who in many cases were far tougher than their men.

"You've stolen your share," Patricia Heath had said, smiling at him, on that wonderful day in Juneau with the birds calling across the pine forests and the immense glacier glistening in the sunlight. "It's my turn."

So it was. Patricia was the senator of large interests in the largest state. Money talked and she listened well. There was enough money to go around and Malcolm still got more of his share than he had thought possible. Once in office, Patricia Heath was generous to him. She gave him all the vouchers and money transfers and letters "of understanding'' in her thick file on him and never brought up the matter again. Malcolm sometimes wondered if he would have let her off that easily.

He stared at her now in the harsh early morning light. The sun was low in a clear sky but there were heavy clouds on the Chugach Mountains just east of the city. The wind had died a little. She wore a simple skirt and blouse, no jewelry or makeup, but she still carried the smell of flowers about her and filled the room with her extraordinary eyes.

"Do you believe it?" she said again.

"Everything is right, right down to the bank in Hong Kong. The problem is, how does this come back to us if this is a hoax?"

"I don't mind doing business with you, Malcolm, but I don't trust you. Any more than you trust me, but I've got more cause. I know your kind, Malcolm. You can't stay bought."

"A half million buys a lot," he said. "Everything this guy said was right. I do need you on this, just the way you need me. The eco-creeps are giving everyone a hard time about a second pipeline and the new drilling off Norton Sound, but what if a genuine full-scale Hollywood four-star disaster really hit the line? You think a bunch of ragged-ass natives are going to get the blame? The line will take the blame, just for being there."

"Where the hell does he get an atom bomb from?"

"I don't know, maybe they make them in high school now for all I know. I know you can get them, same as you know, I was on oversight committee for four years—"

"So what do we do?"

"There are maybe twelve people we have to be in touch

with. We work it in relays. We can work it out of here, I had the phones swept on Friday.''

"You say."

"Jesus, Pat, you think I'm working a private scam? I don't even know half this stuff in the note but I know some of it. I don't deal in terrorism, honey."

"Maybe it never paid this well before."

"You don't trust me."

"Not from day one."

He stared at her eyes. She was in the cold mood now, looking right through him. She was forty-four by the clock and there were small wrinkles at the corners of her eyes and at the edge of her mouth but they only made her look kindly. Except when her eyes were turned on to cobalt blue. They could laser through steel, the way they were now.

"I consult, I go-between, I grease deals. I'm in the business of making money, not cutting my own throat. Do you know how much I get out of the supply companies using the Haul Road? Do you want to know about trucking interests I'm involved in? The line has been very very good to me, like the black guy used to say on 'Saturday Night Live.' ''

"I know about your interests, Malcolm. I keep track of you in case you ever decide to keep track of me." She let it rest between them. He stared at her, thinking that he had once wanted nothing better than to screw her. Desire was all shriveled in him when she let the words fall that heavy.

"I want to figure your angle, Malcolm, and I can't unless it's all on the square as far as you're concerned. You could have set up ULU yourself but that's not really your style, to leave those kinds of marks and that much vulnerability. You make your hits a lot cleaner now that I showed you how." She shook her head. "Christ. An atom bomb. Is it the Russians?"

"Or the Chinese? Or the Indians? Or just some Middle East arms dealer? You want to play twenty questions? It's eight in the morning and twelve hours from now, if we don't play, we find out the hard way if we were calling a bluff."

She bit her lip. She was figuring something out. Malcolm couldn't help himself; his mood was swinging back and he loved the way her blouse formed itself around her. She commanded the room in that moment and everything in it. Terry was cute and even fun and a great lay but Patricia Heath had power. He thought about spreading the legs of power and it started to give him an erection.

"We do it," she said. "The way you said it was. We find a suitcase with a bomb in it by eight tonight or you're hanging, Malcolm. Not today or tomorrow but you're hanging. I've got four years until the next election and I can repair my damage but you won't have four years, Malcolm."

"Don't threaten me, Pat," he said. He was annoyed again. She made his emotions swing back and forth like a teenage boy caught in a bus full of girls.

"No threats, Malcolm." Soft now, a voice from a remembered weekend in Washington. "I just want to be careful and I want you to be careful too."

And he thought then that it was going to work.

EIGHTEEN

The Man Who Wasn't

The girl drove like a man. She rested her right hand on the top of the steering wheel and let her left arm ride the armrest. She kept her eyes on the road. She left her jacket unbuttoned because she wanted him to stare at her the way he had done yesterday.

Devereaux thought he understood and that is why he carried the pistol. It was the Browning automatic. He had tried it out in a shooting gallery in Santa Cruz and he liked the feel of it better than he wanted to admit. The action was fast and the recoil was reduced and he got to the point where he could put all thirteen rounds in a pattern inside the target most of the time. He thought he could kill with the pistol and so he could trust it; he wondered if he would kill anyone on this simple matter.

He thought of Rita Macklin as he stared at the young body of the girl. He thought of a matter that would take two or three weeks. That had turned out to be a lie. He lied to her all the time because he had to; but the one true thing in him could not speak to her.

He stared at Narvak as the car bumped over the unpaved road into the countryside north of Nome.

"This is the road to Teller but we pull in in a little while," she said. "You got plenty of sleep."

"Plenty," he said.

"I like you, you know. I told you that."

He said nothing.

She turned to look at him a moment and give him the deep-eyed look. She had a trick of wetting her eyes when she looked like that. He stared at her. She was a little girl and she played the game of vamp like a little girl. He remembered the little girls in Vietnam, wearing their microminis, their half-formed breasts straining against the cheesecloth sweaters. They were whores and they went through the paces as though they had copied their moves from old American movies. She was like them and it made him sad again, remembering the days in Vietnam when the world was coming to an end.

She had come into his room at the Nugget Inn as he lay naked on the bed. He had been waiting for something, a sound, the stirring of life downstairs at the front desk. When the hotel came awake, he still had been waiting, perhaps for Narvak to come to his room. If he had been right about Narvak, she would come for him; she was the purposeful link in the chain that might lead to Henry McGee. She had not surprised him any more than if Henry McGee had walked into the room or Rita Macklin or Colonel Ready. Ready had scared him once, almost to his own death, and in the night, he thought Colonel Ready was still alive.

She had smiled at his nakedness and began to take off her clothes.

He watched her take off her clothes, and when she was done, she slipped into the narrow bed and pressed herself against him. She opened her hand and touched him and held him there.

What stopped him? Perhaps the thought of the sad little girls turned into whores, working the streets of Saigon in those last years before the end of the world. Perhaps it was only his weariness. To end it, he had said, "Where is he?"

She had stared at him for a long time but the question lay between them now. She had let him go then and got up from the bed and put her clothes back on. He had dressed apart from her as though they might have been married for years.

"Do you know who he is?"

"I know his name," she had said.

She felt ashamed to have been naked and in bed with him and not to have fooled him. She felt she had failed the dark-faced man.

The cabin was at the end of a side road. She stopped the car and got out and walked up the slope to the door of the cabin. The logs were thick and roughly squared off and set into the mortar. The winter entryway door creaked open and Narvak opened the second door, which was made of planking bound with black metal.

Devereaux was behind her and he had the pistol in his hand when the door was opened.

The dark-faced man sat on the sleeping ledge in the windowless cabin. The room was lit by the kerosene lantern on the table and by the little glow from the heater. The cabin had no windows.

She started to speak to the dark-faced man but he was looking at Devereaux.

"Long time," Henry McGee finally said.

Devereaux stepped aside from the girl and she saw the gun and she said something in her native language.

The dark-faced man spoke to her in the same tongue. It was a language composed of small sounds, delivered in a low voice, with little clicks at the edges of the words.

"You should have stayed buried," Devereaux said. "You made a lot of people angry back home."

"So they sent you along."

"You killed the old trapper."

"Me? She did. Look at her, not even seventeen yet and she kills as good as any grown man. Don't you, Narvak?"

The girl balled her fists and glared at the old man and Devereaux saw it.

"Hell, that don't matter to him. He's not from the fucking state police, girl. Sit down, Devereaux."

Devereaux remained standing and the pistol was just as pointed in his hand.

"Suit yourself but I don't have any guns on me, if that's what you want, a fucking shoot-out. Country's changed some since you were up this way. Didja notice that parking meter on Front Street in Nome? Funny story about that. They were going to pave Front Street, make Nome look like it was a real city, and the guy who owned the paper said it was a waste of money, which it was, but who counts? So they paved the street anyway, despite the newspaper stirring up a fuss, and they get the bright idea of putting in a parking meter right in front of the newspaper office. Only fucking parking meter in the whole Seward Peninsula. I like that story, Devereaux, because it is instructive of the power of government. Government is about the only organization that can kill mosquitoes with a sledgehammer and get away with it."

"The problem is how to get you down," Devereaux said. "I suggest we start by going into Nome together. The girl stays here."

"Who the hell are—" she began.

"It's more complicated than that," the dark-faced man said. "Shut up, Narvak."

"We take the flight to Anchorage and we start with a fill. I really didn't expect to find you, Henry; I just wanted to close the file so I could go home."

"I found you, Devereaux, not the other way around."

Devereaux waited. It was what he had thought in the predawn darkness, standing in the shower, feeling the warmth overcome the cold in his belly. It was what he had been afraid of.

"Why?"

"Lots of reasons. Started with that fool Otis Dobbins. I picked him up two years ago and worked on him, you know the way I can. He had some talent and I told him the stories. Most of the stories. I told him about Henry McGee."

"Who were you then?"

"I forget. It was when I was working the first part of this plan, this great plan you have the honor of being part of. I suppose you went first to the guy down in Santa Cruz, went back over the trail to find out if the chasers had screwed up."

"How did you find those guys?"

"Seamen, Devereaux. I work the sea. Seamen are all brothers under the skin, all dreamers caught up in their own nightmares. You work the sea for weeks or months, you shit, shower and shave with those guys. You get close to them.''

"Otis Dobbins carved a ship," Devereaux remembered.

"Otis was calling himself Tandy Stevenson then. We all got different names if we have to have them. Carver? Yeah, lots of the fellas whiled away the time carving, just like the natives. Bet you carve, Narvak, don't you? Skin a caribou with your *ulu*?''

The girl blushed.

"Didja fuck her, Devereaux? I told her to go right ahead.''

"He can't do it, he's not much," she said to the old man, but she was staring at Devereaux.

Devereaux did not take his eyes off Henry McGee.

"Is that right, Devereaux? Turn down a free piece of ass?''

"I don't screw children," Devereaux said. The girl blushed again, this time in rage.

"Kill him," she said to Henry McGee.

Henry smiled at Devereaux, as though a child had said something clever. "Ain't she hell on wheels? Time she gets to be twenty-one, she'll be fucked out.''

"I hate you," the girl said.

"Shut up," Henry McGee said.

Devereaux broke in with a quiet, flat voice: "And you were Soviet all those years.''

"Me? Hell, I was born in Sitka, went to the Orthodox church, the one that burned down. I was Russian and English and grizzly bear. You think I figure it out like that, figure that today I'm a Communist and tomorrow I'm a capitalist? You're talking about ideas, Devereaux. Never let ideas get mixed up when you're thinking about real life. My friends on the other side of the water let me have a long lead because I've been very good for them. In many ways."

"Come on, Henry."

"Not yet, Devereaux. Sit down. Get some coffee going, girl."

"I thought—" the girl began and stopped. She saw that look in Henry's eyes.

"You don't think, Narvak, you're an action. Get some coffee right now and please shut up."

"Come on, Henry."

"Or what?"

Devereaux said, "They don't care if you're dead or alive, you know."

"But you don't shoot me dead. Not for nothing. Not till you figure out why it was you."

Devereaux thought about it. He never bluffed. A bluff is always called, usually by a fool who doesn't know any better. He was careful about what he said, about what he would do if it came to it.

He sat down at the table in the middle of the room and put his gun down and let his hand cover the gun. The girl went to the heater and took the empty coffeepot and went outside to the water cache.

Henry McGee said, "I'm nearly as dark as I was when you first came across me."

"That was a trick too, right, Henry?"

"Sure. You take a certain number of doses of this stuff and it turns you yellow or brown, whichever you prefer. Little while from now, I'm gonna be a white man again."

Devereaux waited.

"Take Captain Holmes. It's attention to detail that I'm very good at. Captain Holmes is a detail. When my little girl here wastes poor old Otis Dobbins, how long is it going to take to trigger the files in Comp An back in Section? That's a matter of timing. The name 'Henry McGee' sets the bells off and here you come out of the block because you and me had our first dealings with each other—what was it, fifteen years ago? I know you, Devereaux, I know the way you think. One room leads to another. Like watertight compartments on a submarine."

"You came back on a submarine."

Henry McGee grinned. "Quietest submarine in the world. The kind the Japanese made for the Russian navy. Want to know how many there are? What class? Want to know where they are? Let's start with Wrangell Island. Got a gulag there as well as a submarine base. I don't mind telling you that because the boys in naval intelligence think that's what's there already but they don't have any eye-witnesses or bona fides or even a storyteller like me to tell them they're right. They got their spy satellite and I suppose they think they see this and that but they can't see through solid rock yet and that's where the Russians keep them. I know a lot of things about a lot of things, Devereaux."

"Why me?"

"I needed someone who could follow a trail."

"Was it all intended?"

"Everything."

Devereaux felt ill. The cold thing in his belly chilled him again and he felt drained by it. Henry was right. He moved from box to box, room to room, watertight compartment to compartment. It was the way he thought about things. It had to do with mathematics and a cold way of calculating the human factor in everything. He was a very good watcher, which made him a good agent for Section because the watcher is reliable if he is cold enough. The watcher lies naked on a narrow bed in a room at the top of the world and waits for a girl to come to him to lead him to the next room and the next, and in all of it, the watcher fears that he is too logical or that a god is watching him for his own amusement.

Everything had been intended.

"What about Captain Holmes?"

"He was on the beach in Seattle, I had him where I wanted him, and he got signed on that freighter just when you found him. I wanted you to go north with him and meet up with Nels Nelsen. Christ, Devereaux, you know people. They have lives as slow and predictable as three-legged elephants. I could put my finger on Nels Nelsen and Captain Holmes and all the—"

He had to break the words. The words were starting to fill up the emptiness. He had to keep the emptiness because Henry McGee could talk and talk and when you were finally filled with him, you had nothing.

"Nobody is that good, Henry, even if you stack the house with sycophants like her."

The dark eyes narrowed a moment. There was just a hint of the hatred behind the childlike eyes. She had stripped, climbed into his bed, and he had rejected her. He was going to pay, all right.

"I want to show you something."

Devereaux picked up the pistol just as Henry pulled aside the blanket over his lap. He held a scatter-gun against his thigh with his finger curled on the trigger.

"Come here, honey," he said to Narvak.

Devereaux said, "Don't."

The sound filled the room. Narvak's face was covered in blood splattered up from the gaping wound in her chest. The force of the blast had blown her against the far wall and the wall was splattered with blood. She was completely flattened against the wall for a moment before she started a slow slide to the cabin floor. There was no sound in the aftermath of the shotgun blast. The sounds of wind ceased. The world lost its voice.

Then Henry McGee threw the scatter-gun on the floor. He got up slowly and looked at Devereaux to see the effect in Devereaux's eyes. Devereaux's face was the color of ashes. Henry McGee went to the body and picked it up easily, the way a young man heaves a sack. He had blood on his shirt. He took Narvak outside and propped her body against the wall of the cabin in a sitting position.

He reentered the cabin and poured himself a cup of coffee from the blue metal pot on the stove.

He sat down at the rough wooden table across from Devereaux.

"Narvak was going to be a problem. Not today or tomorrow but in a week or so and I told you I got to travel light. It's the way to go when you don't want to leave marks."

"Maybe you're crazy."

"Maybe I just don't give a shit."

Sound began to creep back into the world around them. Devereaux listened to the wind beyond the walls.

"Why did you kill her?"

"I wanted to get your attention." Henry McGee smiled.

"What's it about, Henry?"

"Five or six million dollars. You figure I want to end up on a Moscow pension? You figure I was gonna do better in D.C.? Send me down to Florida to that retirement village for elderly spooks? Shit, man."

"So what do you want?"

"Security in an insecure world." Henry smiled at that

and his teeth glared brightly in the darkness of his face. "You got to look to your future, Devereaux, because nobody else is going to do it."

Devereaux waited. Henry wanted to talk now.

Henry smiled. "Got your attention with that, didn't I?" He swept his hand to indicate the blood-splattered floor and wall. "Thing about women is they really can work themselves into thinking they're the only one. If you got a million dollars, you got any piece of ass that ever walked on the earth, male or female. That's the truth of things. Walk up to a virgin and give her money enough and she'll end up on her back, begging for it."

"Everyone isn't for sale."

"I hope you are."

"If you know about me, you know better."

"Everyone has a price."

"What's mine?"

"Girl named Rita Macklin."

Devereaux waited.

"Lives on Rhode Island Avenue, Northwest, in Washington. Journalist. This is a straight hit, nothing kinky about it. In fact, the hitter doesn't even know who his employer is."

"Who is it?"

"Employment officer is me and the setup was made three weeks ago in Seattle. Just before you came out to chat with Captain Holmes."

"Don't give me that booga-booga."

Henry smiled. "All right. Try another one. Old lady in Chicago named Melvina is your great aunt and she saved your life when you were a street kid growing up."

"She's old. People die when they get old."

"Narvak there didn't get old. All right, maybe you are

hard enough. Maybe I'm even bluffing but at least I took the time to do my homework on you. But there has to be some price because everyone has got a price.''

''This isn't real estate. Everything is not for sale.''

''Got two prize crooks for you for starters. One is a sitting senator, one is an ex-senator. The sitting senator is a prize pain in the ass in the making on the Senate Select Oversight Committee on Terrorism and Intelligence. Going to make Frank Church look like a Langley cheerleader. Ask Hanley what he might think about nailing those two.''

''On what?''

''Terrorism for starters. Terror for profit.''

''What do you want in return?''

''Little peace and quiet to work out spending my money. And your share is a mil, give or take.''

''You guess wrong.''

''All right. You get the two crooked politicians, no great loss there, and you get the go-between who is selling out Silicon Valley to the people in Moscow Center.''

Devereaux still heard the scatter-gun shot in his head. He felt the same cold ball in his belly. He listened to Henry and tried not to follow the dancing words, but Henry was filling him in the same quiet, quick, insistent voice.

''Who is it?''

Henry smiled. ''It's less important who it is than how he does it, right? And what he does. And how many more there are just like him.''

''You say less with more words,'' Devereaux said.

''Ivan Ilyich Denisov. You remember him? The retired millionaire in Santa Barbara?''

''Show me.''

It was very good, very complete. There was the transfer of funds to the account in Zurich, which would turn out to be Denisov's account. There was a bill of lading on a gross of Beluga caviar sent to the wrong address on purpose from a gentleman in Santa Barbara. There were six black-and-white photographs where the grain was very bad but the light was good. It was Denisov all right, at the Haupt-bahnhoff in Zurich, and the man next to him was handing him a package and it would probably turn out to be this or that Soviet courier operating in the neutral country. The package of photographs and copies of transcriptions and various money transfers was in a brown manila envelope and Henry waited while Devereaux went through it all.

"Denisov is one man. There are several others, kept at great government expense in your Witness Protection Program."

Devereaux stared at Henry McGee without speaking.

"The point is that I bullshit a lot and drink too much and tell a lot of stories. But the other point is that at the bottom of everything, I tell the truth. I defected one way once and defected another way back. But now I just want to get out of it all and I don't want anybody coming after me when it's ended."

"What about the Soviets?"

"I'm on a very clever mission now, that's why I took the risk to come over. The submarine picks me up in exactly one week. I can tell you the place. In fact, I will tell you the place when the time comes because I would like the navy—I'm talking the U.S. Navy this time—to be there to meet it."

"And they'll figure we have you."

"And I'll be very long gone. You'll have Denisov and a few others like him and I'll have—"

"Where's all the money coming from, Henry, that you're going to retire with?"

"Couple of places. This is a rich country, you lose sight of that when you don't see big cities and a lot of people. Everyone in the lower forty-eight equates rich with cities because that's where they see people living rich. I can tell you about a miner down in Nome didn't bathe all winter and had a beard halfway down his chest. Smelled just like a caribou. He wore caribou hide, he ate the meat, for all I know he fucked caribou when he wasn't fucking half the girls in the Board of Trade saloon. See, he had money. Gold. Still mining gold and still finding it like acres of clams. You look at him and you want to put him on welfare but he didn't need it, though he'd take it. Must have been worth three, four hundred thousand. He lived in New York City, he'd drive a Mercedes instead of that old GMC pickup he had and he'd live in a high-rise instead of a shack near the Teller Road. I guess I'm saying there's money here, Devereaux, but half the people are too blind to see it. Always has been for sharp-eyed creatures."

"We're going down to Nome, Henry."

The babble of words was stopped up just like that. Devereaux held the gun very still, his hand propped on the table. His eyes never left Henry's face.

Henry said, "You don't get it. I'm giving you what Section wants. Plugging your own leaks. You said yourself you came to close the file on me, just go through the paces and tell yourself you did all you could."

"So we're going to Nome, right to the airport, get a special plane to Anchorage if we have to."

"I told you the way it was: I plan on the details."

"I have the gun."

"Dead or alive, Devereaux?" Henry had tilted his head and was smiling.

Devereaux had considered it in the moments while Henry was talking. "Dead or alive, Henry."

"You wouldn't bluff me?"

Devereaux said nothing.

"No. I guess I take you seriously. It's a lot of money. Not to mention the bomb. Did I tell you about that? About the atomic device as they call it? Sitting out there on the Alaska oil pipeline even while we're talking. I'm full of surprises, ain't I? It's the way you hold your audience. I didn't tell you that part because you never let me tell you where the money was coming from."

"Come on, Henry. You can tell your stories in Anchorage when we get there." Devereaux got up and the eye of the muzzle on the automatic stared at Henry's chest.

"You think I'm bluffing too? About an atomic device? That's what you call a thing in a suitcase, right? Instead of sitting on a missile?"

"Maybe I don't give a shit," Devereaux said. He smiled because the annoyance showed in Henry's eyes. And something else.

Something else.

He saw Henry's eyes shift and he turned.

Devereaux turned too slowly.

Narvak brought the ax handle down hard on his right shoulder and the numbness reached up to his brain and down to his paralyzed gun hand. He stared at the ghost of Narvak covered with ghastly red blood that had burst from the wound in her chest. Narvak brought the ax handle down a second time and there was no pain, only a slight sense of falling away like an autumn maple leaf. Her eyes were bright in that almond face streaked with blood.

NINETEEN
Desperate Hours

WILLIAM SCHWENCK. APT. 402. 534 FIGUEROA. SANTA
   BARBARA, CA.
MESSAGE: NOME. POLARIS HOTEL. 1100 HOURS
   THURSDAY.
SIGNED: ARMISTICE DAY.

It was Wednesday morning. The baby-sitter from the protection program had disappeared as suddenly as she had appeared.

Karen O'Hare. She had been replaced very suddenly by a large whiskey-faced man who had shown him identification and had begun a long, disheartening interview. He had assured Denisov that no one could have penetrated the program to identify him. The man—his name was Wagner—assured Denisov that the program had never been penetrated in its history, unless the witness under protection bragged about the fact or otherwise betrayed himself.

Denisov listened to Wagner the way he had once listened to the bureaucrats—the apparatchniks—inside the committee. They spoke of life in the field as if they had experienced it themselves. They spoke of agents, moles, doubles and triples as though these men and women were nothing more than moves on a chessboard. They knew so much that they were functionally ignorant of reality. Their reality was in plans, quotas, tables of organization. If Denisov did such and such, such and such would result. But it rained that day in Berlin and the agent stayed home; but the plans were lost when the bus crashed on the autobahn; but, but, but. The explanations were left to the agents. Wagner was like this, Denisov thought. Wagner could never help him because Wagner would never believe Denisov. And what would happen when they killed Alexa and blamed it on Denisov? Would Wagner testify for him? Would Wagner say it was possible for the program to be breached?

Denisov stared at the Mailgram again. It had been sent from Alaska, there was no doubt of that, and mailed from Los Angeles.

Denisov sat at the kitchen table with his fingers framing the Mailgram message. "Armistice Day" was one of their jokes, a way of identifying themselves to each other. He was William Schwenck, the first two names of Gilbert; Devereaux was the eleventh hour of the eleventh day of the eleventh month—the time when World War I ended and was thereafter commemorated for nearly fifty years as Armistice Day. He was the eleventh man because he was the eleventh month—November.

Who would know the code but November?

Denisov was in shirt sleeves. He wore dark blue suspenders in the current fashion and dark trousers. The climate of California had changed in three days. The morning fog seemed sinister to him and the photograph of Alexa feigning death haunted the mists. He no longer walked by the sea. He spent long coffee mornings waiting for the message from November, the message assured by Karpov.

What must he do with the summons?

They wanted November in Moscow and they wanted Denisov to return home. Was it possible to give them November without returning home? Was it enough?

Denisov had called his broker on Tuesday morning and carefully liquidated every stock. The money would be transferred to the bank in Zurich in five working days. There was quite a lot of money.

He thought he could live on it if he had to disappear.

He could disappear to Switzerland where he knew a man named Krueger who knew how to make disappearances permanent. Exactly what the Americans had assured him seven years ago.

He had called Alexa twice and there had been no answer, only the stupid recording device telling him to leave his name and telephone number. He had thought about it: "Hello, this is Ivan Ilyich Denisov, your murderer and your former lover. Do you wish to call me in Santa Barbara or Moscow? Unfortunately, I do not know where I will be staying in Moscow."

He got up and carried the blue and white Mailgram to the kitchen sink. He took a book of matches from the counter and lit the end of the piece of paper. The paper flared into flames and he held the edge, letting the flames curl the pages into blackness. He dropped the black ball into the sink and flushed the bits of paper down the drain. He looked at the coffeepot and thought about making more. He felt sour and fretful.

The knock at the door surprised him.

The building was equipped with an outside locked door, which generally ensured that every visitor would ring the bell in the vestibule and be identified over the intercom. It was not a totally secure building—there had been a burglary in another apartment during the winter—but it was not usual to have someone knock at the door.

Denisov took the Walther PPK out of his right front pocket and snapped the safety off.

"Who is?" he said.

The day was all fog and drizzle beyond the front room windows. The day pressed against the windows, seeking to invade the colors of the rooms illuminated at midday by lamps.

"I," came the voice and he knew it. It was the last voice he had expected.

He opened the door quickly and stood aside, the pistol aimed at Alexa's chest.

Her hair was wet and her dark eyes glittered in the darkness of midday. She wore very dark, very tight slacks and boots and she might have been a romanticized Cossack princess in a child's book.

She stepped onto the carpet of the little hall and raindrops fell on the rug. The raindrops glistened on her black boots.

Denisov did not move for a moment and then he prodded her belly with the pistol.

She turned around and put her hands on the wall and opened her legs. Denisov reached down her legs and felt along the boots and up beneath her leather jacket to the silk coolness of her blouse. He took her purse and dumped it on the kitchen table. There was a long knife in an ivory case and he slipped it into his pocket.

"All right," he said.

She turned and went to the table and began to scoop up the contents into her purse.

"I have loved that knife, it was from my brother," she said to him, her eyes on the table.

"Touching," Denisov said. His voice was flat and he had not put the pistol away. He sat down across from her at the table. He pointed the pistol at the Mr. Coffeemaker and the pot. "There is enough for one cup."

"I do not drink caffeine," she said.

"You are too California now," he said in English.

She switched to Russian. "I was kidnapped six days ago for what purpose I do not know. But it involved you. I thought to kill you."

"It involved me against my wishes."

"Is this true?"

"Alexa Natasha, the program is broken. A man who is called Karpov came to me three days ago and he showed me pictures of you. I thought you were dead. The pictures are a demonstration for me. They want me to return."

"To return." She said the words like a person on drugs. Her eyes did not leave his face. She was very beautiful and the eyes were part of it, but they were also the cool, frightening part of her presence.

The rain drummed at the windows of the small warm apartment. The damp was seeping into the room despite the lamps and the gentle thump of the baseboard heater.

"The program is broken. They identify me, they identify you. There is only the possibility to understand how much they know and to plan an escape."

"Nureyev returned to Moscow last year to dance," she said.

Denisov's saintly eyes opened wide with contempt. "I

am not a ballet dancer, Alexa, and neither are you. Will you work for them again? Will you stay in California and sleep with your movie people and act the spy?" The Moscow accent was strong with sarcasm; it was the way Muscovites showed contempt for others, to play out words like a scenario that always ended absurdly for the other person.

"I don't know," she said.

"Alexa Natasha, they said you betrayed me."

"They said you betrayed me."

"I did not," Denisov said.

"I did not," Alexa said.

"Can we believe each other?"

"No," she said. "There is no trust."

"Do you want to escape?"

"I thought I was free," she said. "I thought the other life was a dream and this was real. It is not real, is it?"

"Did they speak of anyone else?"

"No."

"What about our conductor?"

She narrowed her eyes. "Him. They did not speak of him." She meant the man called November.

"What will you do?"

"I do not have any money that Roger has not given me."

"You cannot stay here."

"They wanted to change my face. I could not bear it."

"It doesn't matter, Alexa Natasha. If they penetrated the program, they would have penetrated your disguise. But I have a problem. You see, I do not necessarily believe anything we have experienced."

She said nothing.

"You think it is Moscow and I am made to think it is Moscow. The absurdity of it convinces us. The Americans keep us. They keep me for six years. They give me California. The conductor said to me once, 'Is it such a bad prison?' No, it is not so bad. We have had dealings, the conductor and I, over the years that you know nothing about. That no one knows about. Or so I assumed. Perhaps it was ordered, perhaps it was testing of me to see what I would do.''

"I don't understand."

"I killed people, my dear little one," Denisov said. He did not say it with disgust. "It is not in the rules and he uses me to step outside the rules. We both understand, my jailer and I, that there are no rules. The rules are the things that are made up to justify everything that has been done."

"What do you want me to understand?"

He stared at her for a very long moment, as though deciding about her. He had seen her naked, made love to her with Russian urgency and selfishness. Later, in the same bed, in the same room, as they both lay naked, she had shown him the other ways to make love which were patient and which made a virtue of hesitation. What could she not understand?

"The Americans have this program and it is to their advantage. Just as we have taken care of our own agents. Philby lived well in Moscow, far better than many high bureaucrats, and what was he but our British double agent? We make a public point to show that we take care of our own, that there is always a home in Moscow for the good soldier of Mother Russia, no matter what war he fights in or what nationality he is. The Americans have their useful icons as well, Alexa Natasha. They live in fine houses in eastern universities and they preach from time to time as the American government desires them to."

She got up from the table and poured herself a cup of coffee. She began to refill the pot with water.

"What are we, little one?"

"What?"

"What are we? If the Americans wish to make use of us, would they tell us? Are we important writers, dancers, poets? We are unwilling defectors. The man with two countries has none. What is your country, Alexa?"

She shook her head. "That is philosophy, I don't have anything to do with it."

"Your country is that place where they tell you to reside. It is nothing more. Do the Americans manipulate their own program to convince us to act? For what purpose? Was Karpov a Soviet agent—or merely an American agent who spoke Russian? What is the point of this if it is to get us to act in some manner?"

"You make me dizzy."

"Alexa, Alexa," he said. He got up suddenly and put the pistol in his right front pocket. He went to her in the small kitchen and put his large hands on her shoulders and pressed her back against the kitchen counter and stared into her deep, wet eyes. He stood close to her but he did not hold her, only resting his hands on her shoulders.

"I thought to come to kill you," she said. "But I did not understand this thing. I will tell you something I would not tell you ten minutes ago. I get a telephone call this morning, very early, before it was dawn."

He waited.

"A woman from the program. She asks me if I am all right. Is this not strange? She knows my program name. I do not know what she wishes. Then I think of you and I am afraid that this is more of you, that you are testing me. That I will have to kill you to have any peace. I just do not understand."

"I do not understand, either. Except the danger. Except we are now the fugitives again, you and I. The problem is to understand where we must run and who we must run from."

"Moscow," she said.

"Or not," he said.

"I don't understand it," she said again.

"So we wait for understanding. You had your passport in your purse."

"I am always afraid not to have it. It is a habit from . . . from what we were."

"We have to go now. If you wish to go with me. If we are together, the danger is lessened."

Her eyes narrowed again and she shrugged herself away from him and turned at the entry hall. "You propose one answer which may be true, that the Americans have done this thing for some purpose we do not know. Or perhaps it is Moscow. Perhaps, Ivan Ilyich, it is you and you wish to manipulate me for some reason."

He did not smile but he let admiration shine in his eyes. She was not so stupid, he thought. She understood just enough to make him careful.

"Yes, that is a possibility as well, though I cannot have expected you to come to see me on this miserable morning. And I would have been gone in two hours in any case."

She glanced around the room. "You leave this."

"This is nothing," he said. "I sent my recordings yesterday to a drop that I have used from time to time. They are the only things I wish to save. There is a small bag in the bedroom and you are free to see it. I leave because I am summoned and if I cannot understand which side to flee, then I must do as I am told until I can understand. The child is a student at school until the day he understands the ignorance of the teacher.''

For the first time, Alexa smiled. She did not smile very often because it is the Slavic nature not to smile, even when pleased. The smiling face is one of weakness or deceit. Laughter is more natural to the Slav than smiles.

Denisov said, "You are right, little one. I made up the aphorism but believe it in any case. I must know which way to jump and who to trust.''

"You cannot trust me,'' she said.

"No. Certainly not.''

She considered it. "I brought a bag as well. In the car. I can leave the car at the airport and let Roger know where to find it.''

"Roger does not need to know,'' he said. "You simply disappear.''

"I don't have any money.''

"I have enough.''

"What will I do?'' she said.

He gazed at her with astonishment in his eyes. "My dear little one, you will succeed in any world, you must believe that.''

She understood. Her face resumed the stoic calm she had learned by nature and training.

"What we must understand, Alexa Natasha, is what world it is we are going to,'' Denisov said.

The decisions came between 2:00 and 3:00 P.M., central daylight time, which was still late morning, Alaska time. The decisions were made by only a dozen people in two cities: Dallas and Chicago.

The Chicago people agreed to the transfer and the Dallas

people agreed, somewhat more reluctantly. There was no question of using the Justice Department or the FBI. The federal agencies would just screw it up. In case it was true.

The people in Chicago and Dallas were convinced it was true because their contact in Anchorage, an ex–U.S. senator named Malcolm Crowder, believed it was true and so did a ranking minority member of the U.S. Senate Select Oversight Committee on Terrorism and Intelligence named Patricia Heath.

The point was: Would a bomb on the pipeline help or hurt?

Clay Ashley in Chicago made the majority point. He was a large man with large appetites and $900 suits. His office took a corner of the sixty-seventh floor of the white marble building on Wacker Drive, just west of Michigan Avenue. Clay Ashley had started life as a driller in Texas; that was three wives ago. Clay Ashley said Chicago and Dallas might as well pay up, it was only money. He was one of the few men in the world who could get away with calling it "only money." He pointed out that oil conglomerates were accustomed to baksheesh, the ritual payment of bribes to governments in the Third World. It was the way business was done. So what was a little more baksheesh in the Arctic North but a change of geography? He carried the majority with his argument.

A minority in Chicago said it was irrelevant, that the pipeline would never be allowed to shut down.

A majority in Dallas, meeting inside the glittering blue skin of a glass skyscraper, argued over Cokes and Perrier that it was all too tricky to calculate, even if they had time to set up computer models. Nobody needed the oil at the moment—the world was awash for the time being in cheap oil. But if the eco-creeps got agitated, the whole thing— in the words of one very tall, very thin Texan—"would make acid rain look like a Disney movie."

At 4:00 P.M., the world's seventeenth largest bank— located on LaSalle Street in the financial district of Chicago's Loop—sent four million dollars to two accounts registered by the Hong Kong Bank of Commerce. The money, literally, did not change hands. It merely was an accounting entry that transferred funds from Wednesday in Chicago to Thursday in Hong Kong. It was money in the bank, in any case.

Because it was raining at Los Angeles International Airport, the Delta flight for Anchorage was delayed by twenty-five minutes as the line of planes lumbered up the taxiway to the working runway. Rain panics Angeleños the way a blizzard frightens Washingtonians.

The Boeing 757 finally began the long runway leap into the air at 5:15 P.M., Pacific daylight time, one hour ahead of Alaska time. The plane groaned under its full weight of fuel and became airborne as it pushed out over the spit of land at the end of the runway and over the gray, churning ocean. The lights of Catalina in the distance were being turned on as the plane began a slow turn to the north and west. Anchorage was 2,400 miles away, and Denisov, as always, sighed at the fact of flight. Alexa sat in the window seat and turned to look at the ocean and the clouds above. The plane passed through the clouds with a few bumps, and a baby in the back began to cry. Finally, the plane broke through the clouds and sunlight filled the world.

She had asked him only one question more: "Is it necessary?"

He had taken a long time to answer because he was searching his own conscience.

When he answered, he did it with all honesty: "Perhaps."

It was all he said.

TWENTY

The Listener and the Watcher

Security buzzed Hanley at 5:35 P.M., eastern daylight time, at approximately the moment cash was being transferred from a Chicago bank to one in Hong Kong. "Well," Hanley said, very annoyed. "Send her up with a runner and I'll meet you at the elevator bank."

The R Section offices were in parts of two Department of Agriculture buildings: The intelligence section had been first funded under subparagraph R of a funding bill for agriculture. The funds that established R Section were vaguely labeled as money for "agricultural crop estimates and international grain reportage," clumps of words intended to make legislative eyes glaze over.

Hanley was a small pale man with almost no hair and the annoyed look of a constipated rabbit. He rarely spoke and then only in the clichés of his trade and of the bureaucracy. He was director of Operations for Section, which meant he oversaw the lives of the agents "in the field" and was most directly concerned with both intelligence and counterespionage. Counterespionage, of course, did not exist because it was not part of the mission of Section. It was as intangible as the money sent that afternoon to a bank in Hong Kong.

Reality was in the form of the persistent intrusion of this person who was riding up to the eighth floor now in a special secure elevator. Reality was in the form of her delusions and fantasies and her persistence. Her damned persistence, Hanley thought. She had been ragging at him by telephone, computer and now in person for nearly two days.

The elevator door opened with a heavy whoosh and the runner was next to her, his badge and his large pistol on his belt. She seemed very small next to him and, for a moment, Hanley felt a wave of sympathy for her. He was the hidden bureaucrat, always behind closed doors, always out of reach. She was—what was she now exactly?

"Miss O'Hare, you are extremely . . . well . . . persistent," Hanley said. He did not offer his hand. He nodded to the runner, who retreated into the elevator. He took her down the immense corridor to the warren of offices in the back of the building that afforded a view of Fourteenth Street. It was early May in Washington and the smell of flowers was carried on every breath of wind from Maryland and Virginia. The cherry blossoms had bloomed on the trees around the Tidal Basin and the smell of the earth was sensuous.

"I know that I'm out of channels," she said.

He made a face as he led her past his outer office to the inner sanctum. It was his place and yet there was no sign that it had ever had a human occupant. There was a leather couch on one wall where he slept during the tense times of critical operations; a standard government-issue gunmetal desk sat in the middle of the room; two gunmetal chairs with vinyl gray seats and backs completed the furnishings.

Karen O'Hare looked very brave because she was frightened about everything she was doing. She had telephoned in sick this morning and taken the 9:00 A.M. flight to Chicago, transferring at O'Hare to a plane to Washington National Airport. She was exhausted and looked depressed by a day in the sky. Her face was white and even her cold blue eyes were rimmed with exhaustion.

She put the manila envelope on the desk but did not open it.

Hanley sat down and let his right hand grasp his left on the desk in front of him.

"We received a call from Redbird at 9:43 A.M., Pacific coast time, Monday morning and—"

"You have gone into all this, about this man, Wagner, relieving you and all that. What I want to know is what you have—"

"Mr. Wagner said he was sent down to take over the matter by R Section. I scarcely know R Section—"

"You're not supposed to," Hanley snapped.

"I'm sorry."

"Proceed."

"But how do you call down? Everything is recorded in the program. It's a double check on us to keep the thing secure. Wagner said he was contacted by R Section. By someone in R Section. To take the matter over. That's what he told me that morning in the motel in Santa Barbara."

"I am intrigued enough to listen to you. To see your bona fides." He gave nothing away.

She opened the envelope and took out the telephone contact sheet. The automatic device recorded incoming and outgoing calls but listed them only by telephone numbers and minutes of conversation. The actual transcripts were Code Ultra Secret and not available in any case to an employee of a witness field office.

Hanley barely glanced at the list.

"Do you suppose any call from Section, if Section made a call, would turn up on a contact sheet?"

"You have to call from somewhere," she said.

"We have safe places to make our calls."

"So you would logically call from Maryland or Virginia, from the area codes just over the district line or from Washington itself." Her voice was flat, automatic, relaying information like a computer screen. "There are sixteen calls registered in the three area codes here. Do you want to know those numbers?"

"If I must," Hanley said.

She read from a second list. She had called back every number. One was a woman named Millie Sangmeister who was the aunt of Sally Anne Sangmeister in the office. Millie lived in Alexandria and talked for six minutes with her niece. There were six calls from the Federal Bureau of Investigation on Pennsylvania Avenue.

"The FBI, I am happy to see, has nothing to hide," Hanley said.

Karen finished her lists and looked up. Her eyes were wide and she knew she looked too young to be taken seriously but she was getting angry. Did the old man across the desk understand what she was saying?

"None of these was R Section," she said.

"So you say."

"None of them."

"So you say."

"This is your man. Redbird was your witness. So was Nightingale, the woman in Los Angeles. They've both disappeared."

"Is that correct?"

"Did I waste my time?" Karen said.

"Tell me what else you know."

"Redbird."

"What about him?"

She had a third sheet of paper that contained handwritten notes. "I didn't have any authorization. Wagner came down and took over and it was so phony. I mean, he's phony—"

"I don't care about your particular bureaucratic infighting."

"We have a slush fund, you can hide some expenses for up to six weeks before accounting takes over. I had six hundred dollars with me. It was money from the program. I left Santa Barbara and hired a man to watch Redbird for three days, it was all the money I had."

"You hired a man? Do you mean a private investigator? You mean you hired a private investigator to watch someone in the program?" Hanley knew his voice was rising and he didn't care. "Didn't you breach security?"

"I said he was my uncle, I wanted—"

"Miss O'Hare, you are a fool," Hanley said. His face was pale. "You have compromised one of our clients. What do you know about private investigators? Did you pick him out of a phone book? Did he wear a trench coat?"

"His name was Orville C. Prendergast and he worked on divorce cases and he was fifty years old or so and he must have weighed two hundred fifty pounds. He wheezed a lot and chewed Life Savers."

Hanley stared at her. The room was white, lit with fluorescent lighting. The room was cold because Hanley wanted it cold.

"I called him when I got into National Airport this afternoon. He had left a message on my answering machine. He said my uncle left the apartment with a tall, dark, foreign-looking woman in the afternoon and they drove to Los Angeles Airport and they both booked on a Delta Airlines flight for Anchorage, Alaska. The plane is probably taking off about now. And the woman who was with Redbird—it has to be Nightingale. Both of them are your witnesses, sent into the program by R Section."

For a moment, Hanley only stared at her. She might have been a madwoman who had wandered into his office. He stared at her because the single word—*Alaska*—had triggered a sudden dread in him.

"This was Redbird," he repeated.

"I don't think there's any doubt of it, Mr. Hanley. My man is respected in the business. He knows how to identify people."

Hanley drummed his fingers slowly on the edge of his desk. The fingers went from left to right. The fingers made a small, almost unnoticeable rhythm.

"What are you going to do, Mr. Hanley?"

Hanley, for the first time, felt the chill of the room. He stopped drumming and stared at Miss Karen O'Hare, a civil servant in the San Francisco office of the Witness Protection Program. She had persistence. Now she had something else. If any of it was true, Denisov was going to a most unlikely place in the world, a place momentarily occupied by the least likely agent in R Section. And he was in the company of Alexa, a former assassin for the

KGB. Hanley did not believe in coincidence because the normal paranoia of the intelligence officer is compounded by intense logic. Some agents saw the poetry of the trade; some saw the prosaic and numbing prose in the day-to-day task; but all saw the overriding logic of deception. Denisov had been spotted by someone he feared one morning in Santa Barbara and turned to the program for help; when none came—when too little came—he proceeded to his next place of refuge. And it had to involve the agent called November.

"Was the tap kept on Redbird's phone?" he said.

"No."

"At whose direction?"

"I suppose it was Mr. Wagner's."

"All right," Hanley surrendered. His voice was almost a sigh. "All right. Can you give me the name of the plane and the number and when it departed?"

"Are you going to do something?"

He glared at her.

She gave him the flight number. The plane made an intermediate stop in Seattle on the leg north. It wouldn't arrive in Anchorage for nearly seven hours.

"Sit here," Hanley said. He got up and closed the door of his office. He went to his secretary's desk. He rang Security. "Put a camera on room 535," he said, bugging his own office. "This is Twenty-two," he said, identifying himself with the security number changed daily. "Hanley."

He put down his secretary's receiver, crossed to the door and headed down the corridor. He opened the closed door of Ops room.

"Where is Pierce?"

It was the name of the man in Dutch Harbor station.

One of the bright men scanned the computer. "On station."

Hanley gave him the flight number and description of Denisov. "Tell him not to lose him and report in constantly. If Redbird books a flight for Nome, let me know immediately. Now, the same flight touches down at Seattle-Tacoma International en route to Anchorage; I don't know the time. Can we round up anyone to make sure our client does not disembark there?"

Again, the computer screens changed. A map of the nation broke suddenly into a map of the northwest with flashing dots at various points. The operator touched the screen and the dot and map disappeared into a profile card.

"We have a watcher on station in Tacoma. Current status: Watch on a Soviet science exchange-student at the university, very interested in the workings of Boeing Aircraft."

"To hell with Boeing for the moment. Get him down to the airport." Hanley paused while the operator tapped out a telephone number on the screen and began to make contact with the watcher in Tacoma. Hanley turned to another of the bright young men. They all gazed at him expectantly: He was the master, the old man of Operations, he had once known John Kennedy and he had been with Section from the beginning. He was a piece of history to them. Hanley spoke in a soft voice: "Now, where is November?"

"Booked at the Nugget Inn at Nome overnight. He missed the standard report time. We contacted the hotel and they were puzzled, the woman said he had gone out about nine in the morning with a young woman and that his bag was still in his room. Also, the contact—Nels Nelsen—is still in the hotel.''

"Typical," Hanley said, speaking of November. He stood in the middle of the Ops room surrounded by the bright young men who moved agent activities by computer tracks across the globe. The computerization was Mrs. Neumann's idea as head of Section. She was computerizing all the operations. She did not believe in colorful tacks on Mercator-projection wall maps; she did not see the romance of the business. Hanley would not have thought himself a romantic either, merely a conservative accustomed to the old ways when agents were tacks and the world was flat on a wall.

What the hell was going on?

A defected Soviet agent living peacefully in Santa Barbara for years suddenly reports he is made by the Opposition. A baby-sitter goes down to hold his hand and she is preempted by her superior, who immediately cancels the assignment. Then the defected agent takes off for Alaska with a girlfriend—perhaps a second defector agent—without notifying or being noticed by the program. What the hell was going on?

Before Hanley went back to his office, he ordered Security to turn off the room scan and send up a baby-sitter. He opened the door and Miss O'Hare sat as though she had not moved in the last five minutes. Hanley realized it was irrational to be annoyed with her and yet he felt resentment because the routine had been broken and the channels had been breached. Inevitably, he thought, such lack of discipline had to involve November.

She turned to look at him with her cold eyes. She really was very tired and the fatigue made her look vulnerable.

"What I have to tell you is not pleasant, Miss O'Hare," Hanley began as he went to his side of the desk and sat down. He touched a button just below the surface of the desk.

"I'm afraid you're going to have to go back to San Francisco immediately and be at the workplace tomorrow."

She looked distraught.

Hanley shook his head. "It's not like that."

"You don't believe this means anything."

"No, you're wrong, Miss O'Hare. I have come to your belief in the last few minutes; you might say you have made your first convert. The problem is deeper, Miss O'-Hare, and I'm afraid we are going to need your help now because you are in the program, right in the same office."

"With whom?"

"With Mr. Wagner. It seems obvious that Mr. Wagner is involved in whatever is wrong, as you observed, Miss O'Hare. But what, exactly, is wrong? We don't know, except two witnesses in the program are acting in an extraordinary way. We need a watcher, Miss O'Hare, and you will have to be the watcher. Can you watch, Miss O'Hare?"

She blinked and said nothing.

"This is very deep," Hanley said. He tried not to be unkind. He saw now how very tired she must be. He had a problem when dealing with women: He could never get the tone right, he was either too harsh or too soft. Now he felt sorry for her. "We'll arrange transportation for you, baby-sit you to the airport, get you fed something before you leave. You should be back in your apartment well before morning."

The door opened and a baby-sitter from Security filled

the frame of the doorway. He was large and he wore an ordinary brown sports coat and the Browning automatic at his belt hardly made a bulge at all in the expanse of his coat.

Hanley instructed him in a clipped monotone. The agent nodded at the woman and she got up. She brushed at the wrinkles on her skirt and took the manila folder.

"Leave the folder, Miss O'Hare," Hanley said in the same soft voice he meant to be kind. "Thank you for your initiative." It wasn't good enough, he thought. "Your persistence."

"Is it going to be dangerous, Mr. Hanley?" she said.

"Would it matter?"

"I was going to make out a will. I have some savings and I wanted it to go to my mother and father," she said.

"It won't be like that," Hanley said.

"How can you tell?" Karen O'Hare said. He saw the depth in her eyes now and he knew she was not so very tired that he had to treat her this way. He nodded and took her arm and led her to the corridor, where he turned her over to the baby-sitter.

"I can't tell," he said, answering a question that had really been answered by the silence since she had asked it.

"It's all right," she said then. She smiled at him. "I'm not really afraid of anything, you know. I just like to know. To know what you think."

"Very very dangerous," he said then.

"Thank you," she answered and she did not say another word to him.

TWENTY-ONE
Reports

Henry McGee was about fifty years old, an elementary fact of his life that no one knew. He had a very hard body, and if he was a step slower than younger men and if his eyesight was not the keen hunter's eye it had been when he was twenty, experience had taught him how to overcome age.

He would have explained that to Narvak if he had felt garrulous tonight.

He felt something else instead.

What he did could not be called making love to Narvak. It was merely the explosion of energy that had to be satisfied. He was a bomb that changes the force field for a moment and vaporizes the atoms all around it.

She was afraid of him.

She clung to him.

They were on very soft sheets in a large suite of the Captain Cook Hotel, the tall brown building on the western edge of downtown Anchorage. If they had known what they were looking for when they looked out their window, they would have been able to see the roofline of the large home occupied by former Senator Malcolm Crowder on Hill Crest Avenue.

The transfer of funds was completed and the exact co-ordinates of the suitcase were given. It was still light on the former Haul Road, which paralleled the pipeline from Fairbanks to Barrow. The sun now rose at about two-thirty in the morning in Anchorage and did not set until almost ten at night. The sun was still setting as Henry McGee made frightening sexual contact with the girl who was a killer and was not yet seventeen.

"You hurt me," she said the second time.

"It makes you feel alive," Henry said. He was grinning like a devil, she thought. She had dreamed of devils once after the Baptists had come and been driven from the village for the ridiculous idea they had of everyone jumping into the water. Her brother Kools had shown her the book the Baptists left behind and there was a picture of a devil and she now thought that Henry McGee looked exactly like the devil in the picture.

He had hurt her and the pain was not a thing she had intended. Like the pain when he had shot her in the cabin. He told her it was a wad and that the wad contained animal blood and that she wouldn't feel a thing. But when it came time to shoot her, the wad almost knocked her out. The blast threw her against the wall and there was blood over everything so that she thought for a moment she was really dead. Henry McGee surprised her all the time. He had slapped her for his pleasure and she had not intended that. He was not always cruel to her and that was part of his surprises. He had three million dollars already gone from a bank in Hong Kong to a bank in Singapore. Perhaps the pain could be endured if it did not come very often.

Henry moved restlessly around the room. He was naked. He picked up the bottle of Glenfiddich Single Malt on the coffee table and poured some more of it into the glass he had been using. He looked at her on the bed, huddled in sheets.

"You liked that joke, all right," he said.

"I did the right thing."

"You did exactly right. He's trussed up like a present and when they get him tomorrow morning—and they get the other one I'm sending them—half of this is going to be over, honey."

"I don't understand everything."

"You're not supposed to." He sipped the whiskey straight. "You're supposed to fuck and once in a while put a hit on someone for me and fuck some more and look presentable. First thing we get to Hong Kong, I'm getting you some clothes. You'll clean up nice."

"Do you like to hurt me?"

"I don't even think about it," he said. It was the truth and she saw it was. That made it worse. "Who are you sending to who?"

"You wanna know? I got me a genuine U.S. spy tied up in the cabin and I got me a genuine Soviet spy coming up to see him. The pair of them, a matched pair. Who do you think I'm sending them to?"

"What do we do?"

"What we do is have ourselves a good night in the sack. I got a few more ounces of juice left in me, girl. And tomorrow, we start making our peace with the other side."

"I don't understand."

"Bless you, Narvak, you really don't. I could explain it to you if I wanted to hear myself talk."

"Let me have a glass of whiskey too."

"Sure." He poured her a stiff drink and put in ice and she sipped at it to burn her tongue and to make Henry think of talking. He was very large and he had hurt her. She wasn't even there when he was on top of her, using her. She made a sound when he was inside her, to let him know that she existed. Noah was so much softer, gentler. She could tell Noah to do things in a way to give her pleasure. Poor Noah; he wouldn't understand anything at first, and when he finally did, it would be too late.

"I decided dancing on a hot roof ain't as much fun as it used to be. Maybe I just need a rest. So we got some setups and some trails to put out and some reports to file. If you're going to screw things up, make sure there's a lot of trails so they don't know which one to follow. You don't understand, do you, girl? Noah is in Fairbanks now, getting ready to congratulate himself and the ULU people's movement for blowing up the white man's oil line. He'll do it too and get the martyrdom he wants so bad. And Koolie. Well, your brother is going down to Seattle now and wait for his mythical fifty thousand dollars, and when the G-men get him, he's gonna figure it was Noah double-crossed him at first, and when he gets around to figuring about me, well, shit, girl, we're going to be sleeping on satin sheets in Tahiti."

"Will they hurt him?"

"Sure. Hurt both of them. You think the G plays any fairer than any other side? This isn't beanbag, honey."

"He said he'd kill himself if he had to go back to prison. He hated prison. He said it was all the time and the time never moved for you."

"He ever poke you, girl?"

She stared at Henry McGee and thought about the three million dollars.

"Maybe. I don't know. It gets so cold."

"Damn. You'd rub up against a gatepost to get rid of the itch, wouldn't you?"

"Please," she said. She was never a person to ask or plead. She saw the change in Henry's body again and she reached out her right hand to touch him the way he wanted to be touched. She tried not to think of her brother or Noah or the man they had left in the cabin or about anything in the world except three million dollars.

TWENTY-TWO

The Man
from Dutch Harbor

Skeeter took him out. It was nearly eight in the evening before they cleared the island and were flying north across Bristol Bay in the Bering Sea. Dutch Harbor on Unalaska Island in the Aleutians was covered in clouds. A storm was building against the rim of islands that stretched up until they paralleled Kodiak Island and then the Alaska Peninsula. The sun was setting in Thursday across the Bering Sea and they were flying against the clock on Wednesday. The sun would take a couple more hours to set.

Skeeter was retired navy whose last posting had been the naval air station near Dutch Harbor. He pretended not to know anything about Pierce except that he was a good cribbage player and he had to go to Anchorage a lot on business. Pierce was a friend and you pretended to believe a lot of things your friend said.

Pierce had received the fill on computers that were linked

by satellite to the second bedroom of the small house that Pierce rented on the hill above Dutch Harbor. The house was secure; it was a station house and a drop and there were people who came and went on the arc of the Aleutians down into the sunny depths of Pacific Asia.

Pierce might have been a former policeman as he told everyone. He was large and calm and his eyes betrayed an edge of madness, just as the eyes of all policemen do in time. His eyes had seen too much. They were baby blue and he had blond hair and a neat little mustache of the kind policemen like to grow. He had a policeman's hands and he wore very good clothes. He wore a tie now and a sports coat and a leather coat with a Thinsulate lining. The sun made the Far East look red and it blinded Pierce for a moment as he adjusted his seat.

They had finally paid attention to his reports on the business of Otis Dobbins and the ULU raids on the pipeline. Hanley had talked to him by phone on the double scrambler and had told him about November, about Denisov, about the possible identity of the woman headed north with Denisov. November had not reported home in more than two days. Something very bad was happening, Hanley had said. Pierce knew it because Hanley was worried enough to breach the security of another agent's operation.

"How long is it going to be this time?" Skeeter said.

"I can't say. Maybe a day or two, whatever it turns out to be."

"I brought along a rifle."

"I don't think we need a rifle."

"You brought along a gun."

"I did."

"I got the horse killer on me," Skeeter said in his laconic way. He meant the .45 Colt automatic that had been standard military issue since the days of cavalry when a gun big enough to bring down a horse was preferred. He was from Georgia by way of Athens and he had country good looks, including freckles. He had done two straight tours off the coast of Vietnam in his time and never talked about it. He understood silences as much as Pierce did.

Pierce brushed his mustache and looked down. The twin-engine Cessna was powerful and made a lot of noise. His feet were cold. The mountains and glaciers glittered in the last rays of the long evening of sun. The peninsula's Kvichak Bay was below, still dotted with floating ice broken from the glaciers. The plane was headed north by northeast now, up past Homer, coming in on Merrill Field on the east side of Anchorage.

The radio broke into chatter from time to time as they passed control posts and took a fix on Anchorage. It would be twilight when they landed, but they would still have an hour to get across town to the international airport where the big Delta jet from Los Angeles would be landing.

"Who are we looking for?"

Pierce thought about it for a moment. He owed Skeeter some information, even though they had given him almost nothing. It was the way things were in Washington. They liked to send you out blind, as though the secrets they didn't tell you made them more in control of you. He reached into the pocket of his sports coat. The computer printout had been done by laser but it was still a crude depiction of Ivan Ilyich Denisov, late of the Committee for State Security (KGB) of the Soviet Union. The shades of black and white were not subtle and the face looked flat in front view and profile.

Skeeter took a long look at the face. "What is he?"

"Someone we know who has no business in Alaska.

He's with a woman we don't know. I'm supposed to get a photo of her and we're supposed to baby-sit them."

"What do you want me to do?"

"Play it by ear," Pierce said in a laconic way. "Just get over by the Wien Air counter because Delta will debark out of gate seven and you watch for the man. If they split up, you take the woman and contact me through our friend at the Sheraton."

The assistant desk clerk at the high-rise Sheraton on Fifth Avenue—a woman named Sheila Merritt—was the very unofficial drop for messages between Pierce, Skeeter and others, who paid her a decent retainer for the service. Sheila Merritt was a loyal employee of the hotel and she enjoyed the spy game she was asked to play. She had been a radar operator during her four years in the U.S. Air Force when she had been first approached by R Section.

"Your people got this covered, know even what gate Delta is coming in."

Pierce made a little sound that might not have been meant to be agreement. He thought very little of the intelligence of intelligence. He was a better man than this Dutch Harbor posting, despite its strategic importance, but he did not insist on his superiority. Alaska was a good place for him because, in sixteen years in Section, he had grown very tired of the world and its people and the stupidity of life in a modern society. He sometimes went into the mountains for days with a rifle and pack and the small survival tent and he would watch the grizzlies in the forest. He would hunt rabbits and cook them over a frugal fire and let the cold and stillness and aloneness fill him with contentment. The forest was full of secrets and he knew he walked in places where man had never walked before. When he came out of the wilderness after four or five or six days, he felt very good and he would sit with Skeeter and some of the others and play cribbage all night and drink whiskey and not talk about the forest or the thoughts he had there.

"This isn't a dangerous game right now," Pierce suddenly said to Skeeter. Skeeter was a friend and he had to tell a friend a little more than he would have told anyone else. "Just keep alert and don't go inside."

"Don't go inside what?"

"If they split up, just keep your distance from her, whoever she is. If she books a bush plane, just get the number and we can follow it up later, don't go off chasing her."

"Might be a pretty girl," Skeeter said. "You probably already know if she's pretty or not."

"She's pretty," Pierce said. "They want a line on her as fast as they can get it. There's a red-eye to Seattle at 12:10 A.M. and I want the film on it. They'll have it by the morning—"

"What's the name of this guy?"

"You don't want to know that," Pierce said. They were over the Chugach Mountains and falling down the other side to the lights of Anchorage, laid out on a long, rectangular grid between the Knik and Turnagain arms of Cook Inlet. They approached from the east and the ground came up quickly and it was dark finally, though that peculiar blue and purple darkness the North wears when the long days come.

Merrill Field, just west of the Northway Mall and Humana Hospital, was laid out in a long L south of the Glenn Highway, which led up to Palmer. The Cessna bumped down with the precision Skeeter used to bring down Phantom jets on heaving aircraft carriers. They had sixty-one minutes and they did not say another word to each other because now it was all operations.

Denisov spotted Skeeter almost right away and he tightened his grip on Alexa's left arm as they shuffled with the other passengers through the gate. The exhausting trip was marked on the pale faces of the passengers, on their wrinkled clothes, in their glazed eyes. They formed a weary, straggling line that wound its way to the baggage claims area.

He slowed her and they fell behind the other travelers moving ahead into the large concourse.

He saw the second watcher a moment later, coming toward the gate as though looking to meet someone. The second one was better than the first, Denisov thought. He memorized the face: blond, wide, mustache, blue eyes, even teeth in a wide face.

He kissed Alexa and she understood. He held her and said: "Go to the Sheraton Hotel by cab and book four rooms if possible and get all the keys and wait in the bar."

"Is there such a hotel?"

"I read this in the magazine in the plane," he said. "You'll be followed."

He wanted to see which one.

She broke away from him and went past the Wien Air counter and the first watcher peeled off and began an exaggerated saunter behind her to the front doors, where the taxis waited. It was a large clean airport exactly like every other airport in the northern hemisphere. The second one turned to her as she went to the door, and lit a cigarette with an old-fashioned Zippo lighter.

He was merely staring at a very pretty woman with long legs encased in tight black trousers. Of course he was.

Denisov had not seen the camera trick used for years and he wondered that it was still so obvious. What would all the spies do when the world gave up cigarette smoking? How would they be able to take their photographs then?

Denisov waited for her bag and his at the carrousel. The carrousel began to circle slowly and the bags came pouring down the chute from the luggage cart and the bags went round and round. He picked his two bags and turned and saw the watcher on the other side of the baggage claim area, still smoking his cigarette. What a very dull business it must be, Denisov thought with sympathy for the other man. He had been a watcher as well, and the long, numbing hours were hardly worth it. Like the poor fat man in Santa Barbara who watched him leave the apartment building with Alexa and who followed him all the way down the crowded freeways to LAX. The world was full of dull existences, even the world of intelligence. Nothing ever happened and then it did and it was over in a moment.

He had to see November in Nome at 11:00 A.M. in the Polaris Hotel. He wondered who this watcher might be. It was a problem and he had to have an answer right away, even if it was the wrong one. Nome would be too small a place to lose two watchers.

He realized then he had decided to kill this one.

The thought came on him so suddenly that it startled him. But it was obvious, wasn't it?

This one must be Soviet, he thought. He would kill this one and it would give him a little time to understand November's game and a little more time to decide on which world he would stay in.

The other one would wait at the Sheraton Hotel and Alexa would be in the bar. He would call Alexa in a little while and she would merely lose the second watcher, who would then become confused and try to contact the first man and would waste much time doing this. The second one would probably not have to die. He and Alexa would leave tonight for Nome, wherever Nome was and however they could get there.

He had never been in Anchorage and he wondered how you killed a man in this city. He supposed it was the way you did it in the other cities except there must be different rules.

The Walther PPK was in the bag he had checked through because the checked bags are never X-rayed or passed through a metal detector. He opened his bag in the back of the cab that picked him up.

"I would like to go to a place where there is drink and women," he said very carefully.

The cabdriver looked at him. "There's a nice place on Northern Lights Boulevard," he said. "You know Anchorage?"

"I have never been here," Denisov said. "But in every city, there is a place to drink in the company of women."

"They're nice-looking girls," the cabdriver said, pulling the flag and ending the commercial. The Chevrolet Celebrity galloped up to speed and fled north and east up Spenard Road to Northern Lights Boulevard and then due east across the south side of the city.

He saw the second cab pull behind him. Would the watcher tell the driver too much or too little? Cabdrivers all were the same; they wished to break the monotony of their lives by pretending to be something else. Policemen or spies or something else.

"You sound like a Russian," the cabdriver said. "You fly in from Russia?"

"I am Polish actually," Denisov said in his ponderous way. "I am living in Chicago."

"Down in Chicago, never been there. You come up on business?"

It was either professional or amateur nosiness. Perhaps the cabdriver was the third watcher. Denisov thought about this.

"I am to business. Ball bearings. Not for now, though. A little fun." His face was sad and his voice was heavy because he thought about killing a man. It was strictly business and there were things you had to do in this trade. "I am here to have fun now. With women."

"You in ball bearings, I hope you got the equipment with you. I mean, I hope you brought up samples." The driver laughed and Denisov smiled in puzzlement. It must have been a joke, he decided.

"Beautiful women in Alaska and they ain't shy. I never met a shy woman lasted up here," the cabdriver said. "Think you're gonna like Alaska, want to come back up inside even when you're not here on business. We like people because we ain't got a lot of them. Hope you have yourself a good time." He said it in such an open way that Denisov thought he must either be very good or just an amateur after all.

The Arctic Circle Lounge was set back from the road in a separate low building isolated by a huge parking lot that was not very full. Denisov studied the parking lot. It was dark enough and he noticed that the second cab pulled into a Wendy's down the street. So the watcher would walk back across the lot.

Denisov took ten dollars from his wallet and tipped the driver and got a cheery good night as he stepped toward the door. The cab pulled away to the boulevard and turned east, back toward the airport.

Denisov stepped to the side of the door, into the shadows. There were no windows on this side of the building. It looked as though it had been constructed for long winter nights. It was now truly dark in the city and a cold wind blew up from the southwest. Denisov opened his bag and took out the pistol and checked the safety and put it in the pocket of his overcoat. He waited without expression in the shadows. He could hear the thumping beat of the music from inside. Perhaps they had a band. A car pulled into the lot, the lights sweeping the semidarkness, and parked. A man and a woman got out, slammed the doors, and the man said something and the woman laughed. She wore white pants and a down jacket and her hair was lovely, Denisov thought. He felt the pistol in his pocket.

They went into the place and the music was suddenly deafening.

The door slammed shut.

He saw the watcher on the sidewalk beyond the parking lot. The watcher was large and looked like a policeman.

Denisov thought about the problem again. Perhaps there was some other solution. Except everything was a matter of time.

He could not go back to Moscow, he had known it from the beginning, but he had to find a way to escape from Moscow permanently. He had been betrayed in Section and Moscow had known that Devereaux would call on him. Would Devereaux be part of his betrayal? It was so complex that he could think of nothing else; it was like thinking of God as a child. The thought of God had overwhelmed him for weeks after his *busha* had told him about the universe and the way God had made every thing. He had been seven and had never heard of God before, except when his father had cursed. His *busha* was very old and had a little mustache and always wore a kerchief on her balding head. The immensity of God gave him nightmares. God pried and poked at every secret in his mind. God knew even at the moment Denisov would know. God knew when Denisov would die. God would give Denisov eternal life, either in heaven or in hell. In hell, he would burn for eternity. God would know, God would judge, God would be in every empty room, God would know and know and know and it was so complex to think about this simple thing that Denisov had cried until the morning came when he found his relief: He could not stop believing in God but he could believe something just as good, something that gave him relief. God knew, but God did not care.

He must do simple things, step by step.

The blond man walked into the parking lot, between a row of cars.

God knows, Denisov thought and fitted his finger around the trigger.

The blond man was very large in the shoulders and he walked in the way of a policeman, putting down each foot squarely as though walking on ice or staking out a new territory in such a way that it could not be taken back.

God knows, his *busha* told him.

He made his eyes cold. He was not a saint and he had never been one. He had the body of a peasant and a mind that loved the music of Gilbert and Sullivan. He had not wanted to be recognized that morning on a foggy street in Santa Barbara.

It was not his fault.

And it was not the fault of the blond watcher either. They did as they had to do because God had known they would do these things from the beginning of time.

The blond man saw him in the darkness. He was good, he was nearly as good as Denisov. They were six feet apart and Denisov felt the pistol in his pocket.

"You spotted us," the blond man said.

"I'm sorry," Denisov said, because he was.

The blond man understood. He did not make a move. He stood in the dim light cast by the changing neon of the Arctic Circle Lounge sign above the building.

"I can see that now," the blond man said.

"You are Soviet," Denisov said in careful Russian.

The eyes of the other man narrowed. "ULU," he said. "You're the link, aren't you? To ULU?"

The shot caught him high in the chest and smashed his breastbone and drove stakes of bone into his heart. He fell back hard and cracked his skull on the asphalt of the parking lot. Denisov dropped the pistol into his pocket and pulled the body to the shadows. He opened the pockets of the dead man.

He found the gray card without any numbers on it that looked exactly like an unstamped credit card.

"Damn," he said in English.

He did not understand: This one was from Section and now a way was closed to him that had not been closed a moment before. He had made the wrong choice. He had shut off a way of escape and he could not wish the blond man back to life. "Damn," he said again in English. He opened all the pockets and found the usual things and the laser printer depiction of him. He took the lighter out of another pocket and removed the tiny disc of film. At least they still would not know about Alexa.

He had killed the wrong man.

And he wondered, as a child might, if God had always known this. Or if God cared.

TWENTY-THREE

Flight and Capture

Kools said, "Why do they need to know how we do it?"

Noah said, "It doesn't matter. I made out the report."

Kools had a gym bag packed with an extra pair of jeans, underwear and socks. He had the ticket for Seattle via Anchorage. He had everything he needed. "I don't understand what happened."

"They found the suitcase."

"How the fuck they gonna find a suitcase on the line? They looking for a suitcase? Somebody drop their suitcase halfway to Barrow? Come on, Noah."

Sure, Noah was worried too. He looked it. He had intense eyes and he liked to stare you down with his superiority. But it was getting to him.

"The only three people knew about that suitcase was

you and me and the old man," Kools said again. He had said this off and on for two hours. They had been waiting in the apartment in Fairbanks. The saloons were all open and night was just settling in for a brief nap before the sun would rise on Thursday at 2:10 A.M.

"I told you you were crazy with that kind of talk," Noah said. He stared at Kools and fondled his light beard in imitation of some professor or another. Kools knew he was doing his you're-only-a-dumb-fucking-Eskimo look. It usually didn't bother him any more than it bothered him when Noah poked his sister. But he wasn't getting away with it now because Noah was scared too and the fright showed in his eyes, even when he was being superior.

Kools was supposed to be halfway to Seattle but he had stuck around, he wanted to see it blow. He had never seen an atomic bomb go off before. They were in Fairbanks and the bomb was supposed to go off 150 miles to the north and they both figured they would see the blast from Fairbanks.

Except there hadn't been any bomb. Not a word on radio or television.

Their apartment building was a three-story wood-frame on the south side of the street. There was the smell of a storm in the air and the clouds had gathered all evening to make it possible. They could hear the other apartments through the thin walls. They heard toilets flush and televisions blare and the sound of a child demanding its rights.

"We got to get out of here," Kools said. He had said that before as well. He had no great affection for Noah, but there was something going on and he did not want to run away to Seattle alone.

"If nothing happened, why do we have to run away?"

Noah asked. "We make out a report the way we always do and we wait for contact. The old man said he would contact us on Friday."

"The old man said that when we thought we were putting a bomb on the pipeline. The old man said a lot of things."

Noah bit his lip. He felt the way Kools talked. He couldn't figure out what was going on, except it was wrong. It had never been like this before. Every previous bombing had gone off like clockwork. The training in Siberia, all of it had been directed to this moment. And now what?

Below them, a woman's voice told the whining child to shut up. The child continued to whine. The woman repeated it. Someone turned on a radio and there was the thumping sound of heavy guitars coming through the walls from someone's stereo.

Kools wore his light jacket, jeans, black sweatshirt. A cigarette dangled from his mouth. He was ready to go, he had been ready to go. He looked down at Noah sitting on the one straight chair by the table off the kitchen. Noah wasn't going—fuck Noah, let him hold the bag. Yet Kools did not make a move. He really wanted to see it the way Noah saw it, see it cool.

"The old man wouldn't screw us, there was something wrong with the device," Noah finally said. It was the first time he had tried out this thought. Kools turned it over in his mind. It had a shape to it at least.

"You don't need to be a brain surgeon to arm the thing," Kools said.

"We didn't screw up. That isn't what I said. I said there has to be something wrong with it. Like you said, they didn't find the suitcase, they had to know what to look for to find it and that would've meant the old man or someone crossed us. So if it wasn't that, then there has to be something wrong with the device."

"Or maybe the clock stopped," Kools said. He meant it as a joke.

"Or maybe the clock stopped," Noah said with approval. "Lots of things. It was under freezing out there, maybe something happened to the clock or something."

"It was a quartz clock, it had one of those batteries," Kools said. Noah was such a cheerful Charlie, he thought. Noah tried to see the bright side of things.

"Something happened to the device itself," Noah said. He was convincing himself.

The door splintered as soon as he had finished the words.

The man with the sledgehammer stepped back and two others with Uzi submachine guns entered and covered the room.

Kools just stared at the muzzles, he didn't even see the men.

"Hit the floor and spread them," one of the men said.

Noah got up and raised his hand as though asking permission to go to the bathroom. "Look—" he began.

The second man slapped him across the face with the muzzle of the gun.

Kools heard Noah's teeth crack. He was on the floor and he was spreading them.

A moment later, he heard Noah's body hit the floor as well and he heard the sobs.

Kools felt the hands on his body and he took it easy, put on the prisoner mode, just took it one step at a time. He thought about doing time again. He thought he couldn't stand to do time again. Noah didn't know, never had done time, didn't know what time was like. Time never stopped but it never seemed to get started either. They could tell you, just like that, two years or six years or eighteen months and then the goons led you to the corridor behind the courtroom and you were gone, man, you didn't even exist for the straights in the courtroom anymore, you were just Mr. Six Years or Mr. Ten to Life or Mr. Asshole.

Kools was thinking about time when he felt the cuffs go on his wrists behind his back. They were cold and tight and cut off the circulation and his hands were already beginning to feel numb. They pulled him up to his feet by the hair. They were really going to play rough, these guys weren't state cops.

"I got rights," Noah said. Kools winced: Man, don't tell them nothing. You think you're talking to your public defender? You think these guys are from the ACLU?

The second one shoved the muzzle of the Uzi very hard into Noah's belly and Noah gagged and started to retch on himself.

"Ain't he beautiful," said the one with the sledgehammer.

"Which one of you is Arthur Wakely?"

Arthur Wakely for Christ's sake, Kools thought. He almost smiled at that except these guys didn't want smiles.

"I am," Noah said.

Arthur Wakely, for Christ's sake.

"And that makes you Henry Yin'ik, doesn't it, asshole?"

Kools waited because they were just fucking around now. If they wanted to beat you up, they'd beat you up, there wasn't anything you could do about it.

The guy with the sledge put it down and smacked Henry Kools Yin'ik in the face with a hand nearly as large as the head of the hammer. Kools felt the bone breaking in his nose because it had broken once before, in the prison at Palmer.

"You two assholes are in the deepest shit of your lives," the first one said. Kools tried to look at them but he kept seeing the Uzis instead of the faces behind them. "A couple of fucking terrorists, you guys don't terrify me, you want me to be terrified?"

Kools blinked at the speaker. He liked to talk tough, which meant he probably wasn't that tough. The second one, who said nothing, he was just staring at Kools the way guys in prison do that ten-yard stare.

"We under arrest?" Noah said. Kools blinked. Noah was incredible. Kools didn't realize until this minute what a stone asshole Noah was.

"Notes," said the second one.

"Jesus Christ, they even write it out for us," the first one said, picking up Noah's report. The one with the sledge opened the bag on the easy chair and saw the ticket to Seattle. "I guess this is the one we were supposed to be able to pick up in Seattle," the sledgehammer said.

"You ain't never going to see Seattle," the first one, the mouthy one, said to Kools.

Kools said nothing. His nose was broken and he could taste the blood on his lips. He thought about tomorrow. There would be oatmeal for breakfast, always had fucking oatmeal for breakfast or corn flakes or, big fucking deal, pancakes. He got to the point inside of craving meat so bad that he could dream about caribou. He could actually dream about killing a caribou and skinning it with an *ulu* and scraping down the meat and shoving it in his mouth still hot from the body of the dead deer. They called them Eskimos because it was some French word for eaters of raw meat. Kools could dream about eating meat in prison.

"This one is a space cadet," said the first one. They were looking at Kools.

The second one said, "No, that's the inside stare. He's just doing time. He's doing time now, we just picked him up. He'll be a good boy, won't you, Henry?"

Kools nodded.

The first one smiled. "Well, we better get them the fuck out of here if we want to have any time with them."

Kools picked that up. He knew Noah wouldn't get it but Kools let himself think about it and he felt a surge of hope. These guys weren't cops at all. These guys didn't have any right to do what they had been doing.

Kools thought about it and it was better than thinking about time.

TWENTY-FOUR

To Build a Fire

Devereaux awoke frequently. When he turned his head, he felt dizzy and he knew it was a concussion. He did not know how bad it was. There was dried blood on his lips and under his nose. He must have bled from the concussion. He thought of the girl in the blood-splattered blouse and he felt the ropes cutting his wrists and ankles.

He would fall back into unconsciousness then. He would dream that he was tied up to the legs of a sleeping shelf inside a cabin in the wilds of the Alaskan bush. It was an absurd dream.

He awoke again and it was evening but he could not see because the cabin did not have any windows. This time he could feel his head hurt and he thought he might be better and that he might be able to hang on to consciousness.

It was very cold.

He blinked and he thought about the cold that must have begun creeping into his body while he was unconscious. He was sure he had not been cold before, the other times he awoke.

He turned his head and felt dizzy. He looked across the room at the kerosene heater in the middle of the floor. The heater was off.

Did Henry McGee intend this? Henry McGee said he had intended everything, even the false trails, even the killing of poor old Otis Dobbins merely to signal R Section that Henry McGee was still alive and still playing tricks on them. Henry had wanted Devereaux to come after him. But did Henry have him tied up and then intend that the heat would be shut off and Devereaux would freeze to death?

It was just May in Alaska and Devereaux was in a cabin a hundred miles from the Arctic Circle. The wind blew constantly off the shallow Bering Sea. The days were bitter and damp. There was a lot of rain and it froze you to the bone when it seeped through your clothes. There was great, wild beauty all around but the reminder of winter was always there, even when the sun shone twenty-two hours a day.

The heater had kicked off. The cabin was losing its store of heat through the walls.

Devereaux wore the same trousers and sweater he had worn that morning when Narvak picked him up at the Nugget Inn. How long ago was it? A day or a week?

Devereaux felt a wave of nausea and then cold sweat on his forehead. He began to shiver and he realized the cold was really inside his body now and that it was seeping into the bones, pouring itself into him carefully and slowly. When the bones were all cold, they would squeeze the last warmth of the rest of the body. He might be unconscious then.

He could not believe that Henry intended for him to freeze to death.

He pulled again at the ropes around his wrists. The ropes bit into flesh when he pulled against them. He could scream if he wanted but there was no one to hear it.

He tried to get leverage but he was tied down flat on his back on the shelf. The ropes were not tight but they left no slack. He shivered again and turned his head and expected the wave of dizziness and then finally threw up. There was nothing in his stomach and the spittle ran onto the floor.

The girl wasn't really dead, he had been so shocked by the noise of the scatter-gun blast and the blood on her face . . . but it had been just a trick. Why did Henry tell him everything he had told him?

Unless he was dead.

They had noted a peculiarity in the 201 file on Henry McGee, something Devereaux had put in after the first interrogations of the man who had come across the ice from Siberia.

Devereaux had been fascinated by Henry McGee's elaborate stories and his endless talk. Devereaux came from the world of silence and Henry McGee was exactly the opposite. He seemed to have no secrets, no insight. He told stories on the surface, almost like folk tales, in which the lucky peasant or the unhappy farmer's wife is merely described as lucky or unhappy and then the story unfolds without any characterization. Henry McGee answered every question. Henry McGee had no secrets. Henry McGee was completely open.

Devereaux had written: Is anyone without secrets?

It was such a cryptic observation that it had been scrutinized at the highest levels inside R Section. Admiral Galloway, then the head of Section, had finally answered Devereaux's question by ignoring it. The notation had not been included in the final report on the interrogation of Henry McGee, and McGee had been carefully programmed and recruited into R Section. He had been a double agent all along. Or had he been? Perhaps nothing had happened "all along" but Henry McGee merely invented details moment by moment, including his own life's script.

Devereaux felt the hard wood beneath him. He stared at the rafters. The cabin smelled of damp now as the cold seeped across the spaces vacated by warmth.

He could see his breath. He coughed once, as an experiment, and the sound startled him.

He tried to flex his arms against the ropes. He flexed first his right arm and then his left. The ropes strained and held.

He exhausted himself for a moment. He let himself relax, even at the risk of accelerating the cold seeping into his body. He felt the cold on his tongue and in his throat.

Denisov. There were photographs of Denisov in Zurich and there is no doubt that the other man in the photographs would turn out to be a Soviet agent. Why would Henry McGee have told him these things? Because he knew that Devereaux had turned Denisov seven years before, knew that Devereaux had made contacts with Denisov over the years. How much did Henry McGee and the Soviets know? Was Section so breached that its secrets were worthless? Was this Henry's message?

Devereaux could bring a lot of doubt back to Section. If he lived.

Henry had not thought about the heater breaking down. Would it take a day for Devereaux to die? Or two days? What would it be like, to die of the cold?

He tried to remember the Jack London story about the man dying because he could not build a fire. The man goes through stages of confidence, panic, then despair and finally acceptance of death by cold. Would Devereaux accept death?

Devereaux thought about Rita Macklin because he did not want to accept death just yet. He remembered her in little vignettes because they had already lived through so many pieces of their lives that the vignettes were the most shining things he could remember. He could never remember her except she was pretty, except she was staring at him with her lovely and deep green eyes, except that she lay naked in bed with him and they had just made love. He remembered her on the boat on Lac Leman below the sloping terraces of Lausanne. They were sailing in the fresh breeze and her wild red hair was blowing. She broke his heart every day he was with her. Nearly every day he was away from her. He had fallen in love with her when he was certain he was incapable of loving any creature in the world.

Then he thought of her frown that afternoon when the telephone rang in the hallway of the town house and she knew what it was. He had felt her frown like a hurt. She had not understood. Section held him in a way that he could not escape. Like ropes binding his limbs in a cabin near the Arctic Circle. Like death creeping up on him in the cold seeping through the walls.

Two weeks, Rita. Or three. Just a little matter and then he would return.

He pulled at the ropes again and they held again and he

wondered if he was really going to die. The possibility seemed more a certainty now. He thought he could hear his heart beating.

He tried again against the ropes and they held his body down.

He thought about the trail of Henry McGee. The absurdity of everything Henry supposed. Was it possible Denisov was dealing in secrets from Silicon Valley and selling them to the Soviets? Espionage had become such a lackadaisical enterprise that all sorts of people were attracted to it now for the most mundane reasons. Sell us that microchip and we will give you the down payment on a new Chevrolet Beretta with red racing stripes.

Was Denisov stupid enough to let the Soviets know he was alive and living in California?

Henry McGee told his folk tales incessantly and there were so many of them that his logic was never questioned. The time passed too breathlessly to question anything.

Devereaux suddenly and quite inexplicably felt angry. Again he strained against the ropes holding down his body and he willed himself to be free of them. The moment went on and on. He could hear his heart beating. He wanted to be free or for his heart to burst. He pushed his body up and he knew the ropes would break at any moment. He was very angry and it turned his pain into an act of will.

The ropes held.

The moment ended. Devereaux felt himself collapsing. He knew he was blacking out again and he blinked to clear his vision. He felt as weak as a baby. He had no more strength. He tried to see Rita Macklin and he could not see her. He remembered that she smelled of flowers. She always smelled of flowers to him and her breath was sweet against his cheek, but he could not see her. He saw her in mind. She turned to him and the telephone was ringing. He should not answer the phone. He reached for the phone and she was frowning at him and he knew he should not pick up the phone but he could not stop his hand. The telephone was ringing and he had to answer it, it was a matter of his life. She said, "Don't." She told him she did not love him. She sold the house. She went away one morning on the bus and never came back. She left him. He reached for the telephone to stop the ringing.

He was falling into blackness now.

He felt the cold and he felt the blackness and he knew he was dying. He did not accept it. He struggled to open his eyes but he could not do it. He had no more pain. A curious peace was spreading in a warm pool across his body. He was becoming warm again. It meant he was dying. He was smiling and he did not want to smile but the pain was all gone and the pool was warm and it was all around him and there were flowers and the sweet breath of the wind and he was very small, perhaps only a baby, perhaps he was not even born. In a part of his mind he knew he was dying, but his body insisted that he was merely being born.

TWENTY-FIVE

Consider the Source

Patricia Heath had the usual perversions of the powerful. Power begat power and became its own end so often that it was the only factor she looked for in her other pleasures.

Sex was one of her pleasures.

In Washington, sex is usually about power. It is a way to relax for the powerful. It is a game that allows the frustrations of gaining power in real life to be put aside for a time.

Patricia Heath took lovers and her husband knew this and it did not matter to her that he knew it. In fact, it made it rather better for her. Her husband was an attorney and he liked power but not as much as she did. People said that she wore the pants in their family. It was quite true, like most clichés.

"Do you like being rich?" she asked her lover.

She had spent all day with Malcolm Crowder and considered him as a lover and finally decided he would spend the night with her. She knew that men were easy and that Terry would just have to understand. That was part of the fun of it, to think of arranging this while Terry would certainly have to know what was going on. Terry had a thirty-year-old body and a certain charm and a nice chin but Patricia Heath had all the experience in the world and experience always won out over mere beauty in sex.

"Do you ever think you might be a monster?" Malcolm said to her. He was quite serious. He had taken her in the straightforward, manly fashion at first and then he saw, to his horror, that she might be insatiable. In fact, he began to enjoy it in the second hour, doing the things she wanted him to do.

"I don't think about it, no," Patricia said. "Monsters shouldn't try to define themselves." She was smiling at him. He was naked and she was naked and the bed was a mess. They were in the master bedroom of her house and she had a commanding view of the shallow still waters of Turnagain Arm. Her husband was in Washington and she thought she might leave the bed the way it was for her maid to find or perhaps for her husband to find when he came home. Patricia knew she enjoyed little cruelties but thought that was normal enough.

"You are a monster," Malcolm said. "A very lovely monster. I don't know why we didn't do this years ago."

"We didn't have the opportunity. We were drawn together by our love of money."

"I always knew that about you," he said.

"You didn't know anything. Put your mouth here," she said.

"You are a monster," he said.

"Yes. Yes." She said nothing for a time and she held herself against him. "Yes," she said at last.

The telephone rang and it was the brief moment before dawn at 2:30 in the morning. She picked up the phone and didn't speak for a while. Then she cupped her hand around the receiver and said something and put the phone down.

"It was the security people," she said. "They found the two of them in the apartment building in Fairbanks the way our friend said we would find one of them. Apparently, the other one stuck around to watch the bomb go off."

"It would have gone off."

Patricia sat down at her dressing table and began to brush her hair. Her body was pale, like marble, and Malcolm was watching her. Even when she wanted to pleasure herself, she involved her lovers to such an extent that they almost forgot their own desire. It was very clever of her, almost instinctive.

"The problem is what we do now," she said.

"That's no problem. We can turn them over to the FBI—"

"That is a problem, Mal," she said. No one called him Mal. "You don't think things through, you never did, that's why I did a gotcha on you eleven years ago."

"Don't bring that up."

"I won't." She stopped brushing her hair and and looked at him. She was smiling and her eyes shone with pleasure. "You're very good, Mal. You must make Terry very happy. What's she like? Do you think she's better than I am?"

"Come on, Patricia. Come back in bed."

"You have to tell me first."

"You're very good," he said.

"That's not good enough."

"I never made love to anyone like you."

"You know what I would like right now?"

He nodded and got out of bed and went to her. They didn't talk again for a long time and the position was absurd but when people have sex, they really don't look at themselves from a distance.

"We have to decide about this," she said after a very long time. They were standing by the bedroom window, naked, looking down at the sunlight on the water. The pines on the hillside stretched to the top of the ridge and there was an immense sense of loneliness in the scene.

"There's no way the FBI will trace our money to us," he said. "I can fly down to Hong Kong tomorrow and get it. In cash."

"Should I trust you to get my share as well?" Patricia said.

He put his arm around her. "Can't we be friends?"

"Of course we can, Mal. I like you now, I like the way you handle yourself." She smiled. "The problem is these two. They link back to us. We got a message from the man about a bomb and we handled it ourselves. Do you think the FBI is going to believe this? They'll start checking accounts and they'll go over us like I don't know what. Do you have anything to hide?"

He smirked and made a bad pun.

Men were really children sometimes, she thought. She turned from the window and put on her nightgown. It was sheer and black and, like everything she owned, designed to enhance her beauty and give her pleasure.

"The security people are private but that doesn't mean they won't wonder why we don't turn these people over to the FBI. I've been thinking about it but we're caught in a box of sorts. I thought about having them killed," she said, going into the bathroom to brush her teeth. She brushed her teeth six or seven times a day.

"What?"

Malcolm Crowder stared at the open door of the bathroom. "What did you say?"

But she had the electric toothbrush in her mouth and Gleem was scrubbing her teeth. Her teeth were perfect. She had bitten Malcolm on his chest early in the evening.

"I really think we have to put a story together," she said at last, coming back into the bedroom.

"All right. What kind of a story?"

"The people in Chicago and Dallas know they paid the blackmail and they want some results, so the easiest thing is for them to make the decisions. We were only peripherally involved," she said. "You got the note, you got the demands, you considered the danger. After all, the FBI doesn't know about the other attempts on the pipeline."

"We have tried to handle it."

"The problem is, the only illegal thing we've done is not notify the police when we saw a crime," she said.

"That and siphoning off a million bucks from the blackmail money," he said.

"Nobody knows about that, Mal," she said in a very low voice. "Nobody is going to know about it. Let the money sit in Hong Kong, we're not in a hurry, are we? Turn this over to the people in Chicago and Dallas and let them decide. They haven't been inclined to go running to the Justice Department before, why should they now? Publicity is the thing that could hurt the pipeline; not even an atomic bomb could hurt it as much. The publicity is the thing and now we've got the two little shits who wanted to blow up the line, so we should just handle it normally. I'm not going to be involved, Mal, and I suggest you don't get involved. Just turn it over to whoever you turn it over to in Chicago or in Dallas and let them figure out what to do.''

"I could turn it over to Clay Ashley in Chicago," Mal said, thinking of the large man in the expensive suits who worked in a marble tower on Wacker Drive. "Clay Ashley would take care of it and he would tell the others just enough to convince them the problem was handled.''

"Good. You talk to Clay Ashley. That puts us once removed from doing it ourselves.''

"I don't think I could kill them. I think Clay Ashley could, if he looked at it logically.''

"Will he do that? Look at it logically?''

"I think so. I don't know about the whole bunch in Chicago and Dallas, but Clay Ashley can look at things logically.''

"An atom bomb on the pipeline. You think they'd want to admit the possibility of such a thing?'' Patricia Heath said. "Wake up, Mal.''

He made a look of annoyance. He was naked and she wasn't. He didn't like that. A moment before, they had been chums.

"So we do what you suggest. We kill them," he said.

"I never said that. You might have thought I said that but I never said that. If I had said something like that, I might be involved in whatever happened next and I'm not involved, I told you. When you talked to this man, this man who got in touch with you, when you talked to him, you told him you would need a couple of chumps to give to the people in Chicago and Dallas. He came through for you. You got the chumps and he got three million and everyone is happy. Even Chicago will be happy when they have a couple of live bodies in exchange for the money.''

"Just turn it over," Malcolm said, thinking about it.

She went over to him and she put her hand on him. She did it the way she did it with all her lovers. They liked it, every one of them. They might not have known they would like it but they all did finally. It was the power that came out of her in those moments. Power was wet and warm and it rushed into them like a drug because of the power of her touch.

"God, Patricia," he said. His voice was soft because it was all the voice he could muster. He took a step back and she held him with one hand and stared into his eyes.

"Just turn it over to your people," she said. "They'll know what to do with the chumps. The chumps have been cut loose, it was part of the deal and the other party kept the deal. You won't have any more bombings on the pipeline. I think the two chumps did all the heavy lifting, and this guy, whoever he was, just sat back and was setting up the deal. There isn't any power-to-the-people group behind this. Just a couple of chumps and a guy who knows where to get an atom bomb.''

"I can't get involved in killing," Malcolm said.

"Be quiet, Mal. I want you to do it again, the way you did it before.''

When she touched him, it was as though she were opening him. Terry was a good lay but this was a lot more. He kissed her slowly. She let herself be kissed. She knew she did not have to touch him anymore.

TWENTY-SIX

The Partner
of Henry McGee

Nels Nelsen took the turnoff just after dawn. It was ten minutes after one in the morning. The clouds were heavy on the white hills and the wind from the gray sea was full of threats.

He was talking to himself, he had been talking to himself in the truck for two hours. He talked about what a fool he was and what a fool Henry McGee was and what a fool the government man was. Everyone in the whole blessed world was a fool. It was foolishness for the government man to go off with that young girl. He wanted a piece of ass and no doubt he was safe and happy sitting in a cabin somewhere with the lovely bit of girl between his legs. It was just such foolishness for a fool like Nels Nelsen from Norway to be out looking for him. The man could take care of himself.

There wasn't any smoke coming from the chimney in the cabin set at the end of the trail. The cabin did not have any windows. Nels stopped the pickup truck and turned off the engine and sat a moment, thinking about what he would do next. Then he lifted the Winchester off the gun rack behind the bench seat and got out. Nels had his rifle cocked when he pushed open the door.

He saw the form on the bed. There was no light and no heat and the room was almost damp with cold. His breath came out in puffs.

Nels went to the center of the room and looked at the stove and then at the form of the man on the sleeping ledge.

He went to the man and touched his bloodied face. The eyes were closed. The face was cold. He touched his chest. He felt nothing.

He thought the government man was dead.

He put his hand around the man's wrist—and felt the rope tied around it. He cut the rope quickly. He felt the wrist for a moment. The wrist and hand were cold. He rubbed at the white skin to see if he could redden it.

He piled furs on the body of the man at last. He began to search in the cabin for fuel. He found the kerosene behind the meat cache. He brought it to the stove and poured it in and relit the stove. It took a long time for the warmth to come back into the windowless square of a room.

Devereaux opened his eyes. Nels sat next to him with a cup of coffee in his hands. Nels wore gloves and Devereaux felt very cold beneath the heavy weight of the furs.

"Drink some coffee, get yourself warmed. I got some whiskey for later, when you get your temperature up a ways, but it's no good right now. I thought you was dead."

Devereaux did not speak. He sipped at the scalding cup

of coffee in the chipped ceramic mug. The cold was so deep inside him that it would never come out. It was in the marrow of his bones. He was too cold to even shiver beneath the furs. His feet felt like slabs of ice; his fingers were turning red with the beginning of frostbite. Nels stared at him. Devereaux wanted to speak to the old trapper but the words were stuck in his throat. He drank more of the coffee, feeling it turn cold inside him as soon as he swallowed it.

"I went around looking for you. I asked at all the saloons. I was in the Wet Pussy when the night bartender came in and he said he saw you with the native girl going up the Teller Road.

"It was Narvak what had picked you up at the dock the day before and I thought it was kind of funny that you went off with her. I thought it was funny you had asked me how long I knew her, like you were suspicious of her. Then I thought maybe you went off to knock off a piece, she was a nice pretty thing. And then I thought about it some more and it didn't seem right. Too much coincidence, her hanging on me one day and then on you and coming back for you. I don't know; it seemed like too much coincidence."

He paused, thinking about it: "So I came up the road looking for you. Got to Teller and started back. I just been looking without knowing even what I was looking for except I knew you didn't make it to Teller."

Devereaux stared at the whiskey-bright face of the old trapper. Nels Nelsen had been part of it from the beginning but he wasn't part of it at all. Nels Nelsen had had the misfortune to be lonely one afternoon in Anchorage and he had fallen in with another old-timer named Otis Dobbins, who went by the name of Henry McGee. Just a couple of lost souls in the world who found each other and yet they were nothing but characters told in a continuing story by the real Henry McGee. Had Henry foreseen this? That the heater would go out and Devereaux would freeze to death? Or that Nels Nelsen would follow him and find him before he died?

Devereaux forced down the thought as though it might be good for him.

"The girl was no good then," Nels said. "I thought she was doing me a favor, going down to the dock that day to pick you up. Except it wasn't a favor, was it? She was in it after you."

"She was in it," he said.

"What happened?"

"I believed in what I saw," Devereaux said.

Nels stared at him.

It was warmer in the room and now he felt like shivering beneath the furs. "How did you start the heater?"

"It was just out of fuel," Nels said.

"You could see that?"

"There's a gauge on it. Anyone can see it."

"Then Henry McGee knew," Devereaux said. He saw the heater, saw the gauge, knew the heater would kick off finally and Devereaux would freeze to death. Was it that simple? But these were all Henry McGee's stories and Devereaux was just a character in them. Perhaps it was his time to die; perhaps he was needed for another chapter. It was up to Henry McGee, wasn't it? "I wonder if he knew about you."

"Henry McGee? You mean the man you're looking for, the man I thought was my partner?"

"The real Henry McGee," Devereaux said. He felt sick and still cold but there was an urgency to things now. He tried to sit up and the dizziness seized him a moment and he nearly blacked out.

"Looks like they beat you up."

"Hit my head. Concussion. I'm just a little dizzy," Devereaux said. He sat still on the bed a moment. The dizziness passed and a momentary feeling of nausea passed with it. He had suffered concussions twice before; he knew the symptoms. You could ignore the symptoms as long as you didn't move your head too fast or upset your balance by reaching for something beneath you or behind you and twisting for it. "I've got to get into Nome. What time is it?"

"Six in the morning," Nels said. "Just sit a while and collect yourself. I'll give you some whiskey if you want."

"Yes," Devereaux said.

The whiskey burned its way down his throat. He felt flush and warm, the false warmth of alcohol.

"I've got to get to a phone," Devereaux said.

"Maybe you just ought to rest a little. I can make some beans, I found cans by the stove."

"I'm twenty hours behind Henry McGee," Devereaux said.

"It was him? The same you told me about?"

"It was him."

"I don't understand it. Why would my old friend take his name? And why would he get himself kilt?"

Devereaux looked at him. "I don't know now. I thought I knew but I don't know. Henry had to get out of here so he had to go to the airport unless he had someone waiting for him. Then I'm never going to be able to find him."

Devereaux pushed himself up from the bed of furs and felt dizzy again. This time, he held on to the ledge until the dizziness passed. He stood up uncertainly and felt dizzy yet again. It was a bad concussion, worse than he could remember having before.

He sat down suddenly. Nels started toward him but Devereaux waved him away. He was exhausted by cold and pain; it had happened before. He would wait a moment for whatever reserve of strength he had to come up.

It was not supposed to be physically demanding or even threatening in the field. Perfectly capable agents past their primes continued to function. Men who ate too well or smoked too much or drank too much or who loathed exercise or had heart murmurs or bad vision all carried on. Now and then, an agent disappeared; now and then, an agent was killed. These were the accidents of the trade. Devereaux had run into more than his share of them: Perhaps Devereaux had run outside the perimeters too often to expect the sedentary life of the intelligence agent. He had spent four years in Vietnam in the most dangerous part of the trade and the death of war all around him had hardened him in a way that an easier, softer career in R Section would not have hardened him.

He felt stronger. He got up again and this time shrugged into his parka.

"Are you going to be all right?" Nels said. He held the rifle in his hand.

Devereaux looked at the rifle and at Nels and did not say anything. He opened the cabin door, went through the winter entryway and outside. Morning was gray, the hills were gray, the tundra was gray, all of nature had lost its colors. He could smell the sea. The Siberian clouds crossed the sea and smothered the peninsula on the American side.

Devereaux said, "Did you look around the cabin?"

"No. What would I look for?"

"The man it belonged to. Or the woman."

"I don't know," Nels said. "It's a nice cabin."

"If you don't miss having a view," Devereaux said and started around the cabin. They found the owner behind the cabin, on the rise of land that led to a dry cut through the tundra. The man might have been a trapper like Nels by the way he was dressed. His face was gone.

"Kilt," Nels said. "This is just a horrible thing, isn't it?"

Devereaux said nothing. He turned back toward the pickup truck. Nels Nelsen got in on the driver's side and they started down the gravel road toward Nome. Forty minutes later, Devereaux saw the battered old Thunderbird in the parking lot of the small, neat airport building.

"Park there," Devereaux said, pointing to a place behind the car. Nels stopped the truck but did not turn off the ignition. Devereaux opened his door. "Wait," he said. He climbed down from the gray GMC truck and shut the door and went around the car. He opened the door. Did Henry want to leave him a clue? He went through the glove compartment and found a package of cigarettes and a book of matches carrying the advertisement of the Captain Cook Hotel in Anchorage. There was nothing else in the car except the keys to the ignition.

He closed the door of the Thunderbird and walked across the lot to the airport building. They had flown out but they could be anywhere in the world. Devereaux was doing the dogged things now that he had done from the beginning. He had no idea that he would ever run across Henry McGee again—unless Henry planned it. He pushed open the door to the terminal. It was small and quiet and there were posters on the wall celebrating the annual Iditarod dogsled race from Anchorage to Nome.

Devereaux felt a sudden chill when he saw the other man. Life was out of context again.

Denisov took a step, decided something, took another step. "You told me to meet at the hotel. I did not expect this."

Devereaux stared at him. A sense of dizziness not related to his concussion came over him in waves. Denisov was real, that was really his voice with the stuttering Russian accent, but there was nothing real about this meeting. He had existed yesterday in a series of photographs that captured him exchanging packages with a Soviet courier in Zurich. Henry McGee's photographs, Henry McGee's story about Denisov. Denisov was part of another scenario in Devereaux's past and Henry McGee had casually lifted him into this milieu; would it turn out that everything in the world was connected to everything else? Denisov was in Santa Barbara, in a defector's exile, watched and guarded by the government. Now he was at the edge of the Arctic Circle in the last place on earth Devereaux would have expected to find him.

"I did not expect you at all."

Denisov let his eyes grow wider behind the rimless glasses. "Is so?"

"Why are you here?"

"I have a message from Armistice Day, the same as the other messages. I am to meet you here, in this city, at eleven hundred hours today."

"I sent no message," Devereaux said. His eyes were steady. Henry McGee had arranged this story. It was the concussion but he felt very disoriented, outside himself, staring at his own body and trying to guess what words he would say next.

"Is so?" Denisov saw the truth of it in the sick thing

at the edge of the gray eyes. The eyes betrayed nothing but Denisov knew. He thought then of the dead blond man in the parking lot in Anchorage.

The two men stood in the middle of the airport staring at each other exactly like the enemies they had once been. They had been enemies so long that it was nearly as good as friendship. They knew each other—or thought they did.

"What can this be, then?" Denisov said at last. His voice had lost its edge. Everything in his voice was flat, almost at the end of its rope.

"Tell me, Russian," Devereaux said. It was the standard technique, they both understood that. You answered no questions but proposed your own.

"I do not understand this," Denisov said. He again thought of the dead man in the parking lot on Northern Lights Boulevard. He had killed that man, an agent of R Section. Devereaux would know that in time. What would Devereaux do then? He thought of the man in Santa Barbara who had walked out of the fog that morning and identified him. The world had fallen off its axis that morning and had been plunging and bucking down through the spiral of the galaxies ever since. Denisov shook his head and muttered something in Russian and stood absolutely still.

"This is a setup," Devereaux said in a very quiet voice. "You understand that."

"Of course," Denisov said. "But for whom?"

"For me, for you." He thought of the photographs. He thought of Henry's game in "killing" the girl called Narvak. He thought of all of Henry's stories. He began to understand a little more. "We're part of a scenario."

"I do not know this," Denisov said. His voice was completely lost in its flatness.

They were silent another moment. The small terminal was not very crowded and everyone else seemed interested in their own business. A woman with Alaska Air was dressed in a native costume consisting of beads and furs. She held a manifest list in a clipboard and seemed to be looking for someone.

"This trap," Denisov said. He stopped. Did it matter if he told the truth? "Alexa is also here. We are found in the program. How is this so, Devereaux, that we are found in the program? She is threatened, I am compromised. We are running, we are trying to decide where we must run."

"I don't know what you're talking about—"

The girl had just arrived at the Alaska Airlines counter and was opening up for the morning passage to Anchorage. She stared at the two strangers in the middle of the sparse terminal.

"Where is she?"

"It is dangerous. I have hidden her."

"Where?"

"It is too much in danger to tell you this," Denisov said.

"Try to make some sense—"

"Is this your desire?" Denisov said. "To make me run for you again, like the time in Zurich? You betray me to Moscow, is that this game?" And Denisov felt for the pistol in his coat. The bush pilot had been given too much money to bring Denisov here; the trail was wide and he only had a few hours before the chasers from R Section would be after him. They would find out about the airplane chartered to Nome, about the identity of the passenger. They would check the files and they would know that Denisov had committed murder in the United States. Worse, he had killed an agent of Section. Devereaux did not know this yet—or had he set it all in motion?

It was absurd, Denisov thought in desperation. He was trapped here. If he killed Devereaux, he was trapped. In any case, he was trapped in Alaska. Perhaps that was the choice—he had to go back to Moscow after all. The man called Karpov in the fog in Santa Barbara had been right after all.

An immense sadness came over him. It was as thick as fog and as gentle. He could not struggle against this thing. He released the grip of the pistol and shrugged, as though to himself.

Devereaux watched him. He knew that face, he knew that look. They had matched each other in Vietnam and in the wider theater of Southeast Asia and out on the rim of Asia. He knew this Russian and yet he was still puzzled by him because he could not get behind the Slavic stoicism.

"What did the message say?"

"A place called the Polaris Hotel at eleven hundred hours."

"It impelled you," Devereaux said. "And you brought Alexa."

"It is more than that," Denisov said. "If I tell you, then you will know why I must come. If you do not know what I am to tell you, then you are correct—this is a set against us, against you and me as well. And if you know these things I will tell you, it is merely a set against me."

"A setup," Devereaux said.

Denisov shrugged.

"You have to tell me, Russian," Devereaux said. "This is a matter of timing and we don't have a lot of it."

"I tell nothing," Denisov said.

"Why did you come here? How were you compromised?"

Denisov stared at him for a long moment.

"Let's go to the Polaris Hotel, then," Devereaux said at last.

"You think someone is there?"

"Unless you make this up," Devereaux said.

The two men walked out of the terminal to the pickup truck where Nels Nelsen sat with the rifle across his lap. Devereaux opened the door. Denisov stared at the rifle. Devereaux picked it up and shoved the muzzle against Denisov's burly chest. The truck was to the right of the terminal building and there was no one around.

"Are you to kill me?" Denisov said.

Devereaux reached into the Russian's pocket and removed the pistol. He dropped the rifle back onto Nels' lap. He unsnapped the safety on the automatic. He stared at Denisov the whole time. The action took less than five seconds.

"Why did you come here?"

"The message."

"Who compromised you in the program?"

"Is man named Karpov. But it is not him; he is messenger."

"What did Karpov tell you?"

"Nothing."

"I'm not going to fuck with you, Russian. I'll kill you where you stand."

Denisov looked at the gray man with gray eyes. "I am to see you here. You will want to go to . . . you will want to go to Soviet Union."

"Siberia?"

"Yes."

"Karpov told you."

"Yes."

"You will take me."

"I have no choice."

"Why Alexa?"

Denisov began to tell him. Devereaux listened and he held the pistol. A taxi from Nome pulled up at the airport and two natives got out and paid and shuffled into the terminal with their bags. The wind was blowing very softly and steadily, a lingering howl across the tundra flatness.

"Are you so naive? Why let yourself be blackmailed? They'll kill you on the other side."

"Who am I to speak to? To you? To the program which lets this happen to me?"

Devereaux thought about it for a moment. "All right," he said.

Denisov thought about the dead man in Anchorage. There was no way out, no hope, no chance of turning back. He said nothing.

"You meet someone in Nome, then you pick me up at the cabin, then we go across. That has to be the rest of Henry's story. That's not what this is about, just what this part is about," Devereaux said. He was connecting it in mind. It was a crossword puzzle but each word had to fit exactly so and in exactly the right sequence of time.

"I have to make a call," Devereaux said. He looked at Nels. "Turn on the motor, Nels, it's getting cooler. Get in. I'll be back in a moment."

"What do we do?" Denisov said in a dull voice.

But there wasn't time to answer, not if Devereaux had figured things out in the proper sequence. There was just time to do.

TWENTY-SEVEN

The Solution

"Where are we going?" Noah said. He was pulling at his little beard as though it might get him an answer.

"Shut up," Ernie said. That was the name of the first one. The second man stayed in the cabin along with the man who had opened the apartment door with a sledgehammer. They had talked in the cabin and they had both been slapped around until a radiophone call came. The radiophone was in the second room of the cabin and Kools and Noah could not understand what was being said. After the call, everything was different. The men had not touched them again. The cabin got quiet after the call and Kools knew they were waiting for something to happen. He was afraid of what was going to happen.

Then they had heard the helicopter land on the level ground at the foot of the forested hill, and the first one, Ernie, had taken them outside, his rifle held on their backs.

The cabin was the only habitation on a lake north of Fairbanks. The countryside was full of mountains and the shining faces of glacier passes that never melted. The immensity of the Alaskan countryside diminished human dimensions; the chopper sat on the ground like a child's toy, waiting to be played with. Kools looked around at the mountains and the blue sky and he could not get rid of the feeling of something bad about to happen.

"We got rights," Noah tried again. Noah didn't get it. Kools looked at him with the superiority of the lifer regarding the new fish. Noah knew all about bombs and explosives and he had the Russian contacts in the first place and he fucked Narvak and he patronized Kools and the old man and he seemed to know every step before you took it. But Kools had realized since the men broke down the door of the apartment in Fairbanks that Noah was a baby, that Noah didn't understand a damned thing, and that the whole action with ULU and setting off bombs on the pipeline had been a kind of game to him, a violent childhood carried into middle age. Kools was disgusted with Noah. The fool wasn't even doing it for money.

"We got rights," Noah repeated.

Ernie said he was getting tired of reminding him. He hit him in the back with the rifle butt this time.

They were in handcuffs. The bracelets were tight across their wrists and their arms were twisted behind their backs.

Kools reached the open door of the helicopter first and put one foot on the ledge but he couldn't make it up without help because his hands were behind his back. Ernie pushed his butt and Kools stumbled inside the chopper and sat down hard on the bench. Noah was next. Noah looked very scared by everything. Kools was thinking about what these guys were going to do to them. He had decided a couple of hours ago that they were going to kill them. It wasn't anything they said, just the way they had looked at them after the radiophone call.

Kools was working on the bracelet on his left wrist. He was skinny and the bracelet was tight but not as tight as it had been when they took them in the apartment in Fairbanks.

Ernie got into the helicopter. The pilot was a big guy with a beard and a cap that bore the name of an oil company.

They lifted abruptly and made a dizzy turn and the cabin was below and then it was gone, hidden by the white glacier on the mountainside. It was a beautiful morning, full of sunlight on the tundra and on the hills.

Ernie smiled at Noah. "You first, honey," Ernie said. He reached behind Noah and unlocked the bracelets and Noah rubbed his wrists for a moment and stared at Ernie. Ernie was about 250 pounds and he had hands like bear's paws.

Kools pushed at the bracelet behind his back.

Noah said he didn't believe it. The trouble was, it didn't matter if he believed it or not.

Ernie opened the hatch.

The helicopter chopped at the air and the violent, turbulent sound deafened everyone inside the eggshell frame.

Noah started screaming at him. Noah said a lot of things and even included a prayer in what he said. Ernie listened to him for a moment and his small eyes kept smiling. Kools watched Ernie's eyes and rubbed his wrist against the steel bracelet behind his back. Noah kept screaming as though anyone could hear him above the roar of the chopper blades. Ernie decided it was time, and besides, it was getting cold in the chopper. Ernie grabbed Noah by the face hair and pulled him across the narrow cabin of the copter and shoved him out the hatch.

The rush of wind nearly drowned out the long, falling scream.

"Next," Ernie said, reaching behind Kools to unfasten the bracelets.

Kools kicked him in the groin the moment the bracelets were off. The thing was, Kools had been a good prisoner and answered questions when spoken to and kept quiet the rest of the time and Ernie was in such good humor that it had not occurred to him until the last moment that Kools would do something like this.

Kools stared at him like a prisoner with those prisoner eyes that don't have a trace of mercy in them.

Ernie stared back with eyes that were not smiling because Ernie was stumbling back through the hatch. A strong gust of wind and the sudden loss of 250 pounds on that side of the copter temporarily upset everything. The pilot held on to the controls as Ernie went screaming out the door. He fell a thousand feet before he was speared by the top of a fir tree.

Kools climbed behind the pilot and wrapped the dangling bracelet around his neck.

"I don't want to die," Kools said. "And you don't want to die."

"That's right," the pilot said.

"What's your name?"

"Bill."

"Well, Bill, what do you say?"

"I say the hell with it. Where do you want to go?"

"Where can you take me?"

"I got about ninety minutes of flying time in the tanks," Bill said.

"Why don't you take me to Anchorage?"

"Sure," Bill said.

"Why don't you find someplace to set down where there aren't a lot of people," Kools said.

"Sure."

"You and me walk into town and you can tell them what happened, just the way it happened," Kools said.

"You wouldn't kill me." Bill said it cool but just on this side of hysteria. He was already wheeling the copter south toward the Denali Mountains.

"No," Kools said. "I didn't have that in mind at all."

"I just take orders," Bill said.

"I understand," Kools said. "I don't want no trouble."

"We're two guys don't want no trouble," Bill said. He tried a smile and twisted in his seat so that Kools could see it. Kools was looking through him, all the way to Seattle.

TWENTY-EIGHT

The Senator's Choice

"Who are you?" she said in the darkness.

"The man who opened the account in Hong Kong," Henry McGee said.

Patricia Heath thought she must not act afraid. The maid would come in the afternoon to clean the house. It was midmorning. If he came to rob her, he could do it; he could even rape her if he had to. The thing was not to be afraid.

Henry McGee told her to sit down.

They were in the darkness of the bedroom. She sat down at her dressing table. He walked over to her. He did not have a weapon.

"You fucked Malcolm all night, I saw him leaving. You are quite a surprise to me, even for all I know about you," Henry McGee said.

"What do you know about me?"

"I know you and Mal got those two terrorists killed off.

I know you and Mal found the bomb and it was a real bomb, wasn't it? And I know you and Mal think you got a million waiting for you in a bank in Hong Kong. I know a lot about you, Pat. You're a fine-looking woman.''

"What do you want?"

"Not what you think," Henry McGee said. He smiled at her and touched her chin and lifted her face. "Fine-looking woman."

"What do you want?" she said. The black nightgown clung to her and her breasts formed themselves against the silky material that barely covered them.

"Someone has to be the chump," he said.

"That's why we got those two," she said.

"But Mal got his tit in a wringer. He's got the contact with the oil people, the pipeline crowd. They musta decided to waste the two chumps I set up for this. Mal is out there on a limb like a fucking monkey. I know you don't want to be out on that same limb. I knew you'd waste them. You don't want this to go to the Justice Department. Not the stuff about the pipeline bombings and this blackmail and how you and Mal got a piece of the action for your part in it. Even the people behind Mal wouldn't like to know they were not only paying me off but you were skimming on the side."

"I don't know what you want," she said in the same cold low voice. The voice always worked in Washington. It marked her as a woman not to be trifled with. She would lay it out like that in a hearing room or even in the secret committee hearings on intelligence matters and everyone would admire her command of herself. She looked at Henry McGee to see if it was working on him.

"I want you to know what the FBI will know at 1:00

P.M. so that they won't surprise you when they come to see you this afternoon," Henry said.

She shivered then. She couldn't help it. She thought about what a fool Mal was. Why had she let herself be tempted by the money? It wasn't so much the money but it was dealing with someone like Mal. Mal was an asshole, she had always known he was an asshole, anything he touched would turn out like this.

"I don't know why anyone is coming to see me."

"Honey, get smart." He slapped her face. No one had ever slapped her face. It made her eyes tear and that made her angry and she almost forgot herself for a moment. Henry waited to see if she would get control of herself. It was one of his little tests. Every scenario had three or four possibilities.

She stayed calm.

"All right, Pattie, this is part of it, a massive conspiracy by the various oil companies and certain broker organizations to keep secret the details of a series of sabotages on the pipeline.

"Do you like that for starters? Senators are good at getting in a rage when there are secrets they want to know. I bet you give good rage when you have to. Lots of indignation in it. Is that right, Pattie?"

Patricia Heath did not know what to say. This madman was talking to her in the darkness of her own bedroom. She was all alone and she didn't know what he wanted her to say.

Henry said, "The information came to you about the pipeline bombings two days ago at your office in Anchorage. It was the usual anonymous shit, you can work out the details yourself of how you got it. Just make sure you don't change your story with the telling of it. You're going to have to tell a lot of people. Invoke confidentiality. Hint that it was a disgruntled employee of the pipeline. Do any damned thing you want. After you got the information, you set out, alone, to find out the truth behind the allegations. You are a very brave woman, Pattie, and you should be commended."

For the first time, she thought he wasn't going to hurt her. He stood close to where she was seated and he kept the grin on his face.

She put her hand on the sheaf of papers.

"You did not involve your staff in this because of the serious, secret nature of the allegations. Allegations of rip-offs by former Senator Malcolm Chowderhead. Allegations of a massive cover-up of sabotage on a vital national resource. And it all involved a secret organization not authorized to operate in the United States, called R Section. Right now there is an agent in Nome making a deal with a known Soviet double agent to transfer security plans of the pipeline to the Soviets for their use in case of war—"

"What are you talking about?"

He slapped her face again very hard. She broke this time and made a fist and hit him hard in the chest. He slapped her face again. She was sitting on the backless bench and she nearly fell over.

"Don't hit me," she said.

"Then pay attention, Pattie, I ain't got all day."

"Who are you?"

"Pattie, you know how much I collected on you? All that stuff you had as attorney general when you should've gone after Malcolm instead of just taking his seat in the Senate? You're a bad girl, Pattie, just as bad as Mal, maybe a little worse. You know you could go to jail for what you did? You know that?"

"I didn't do anything," she said.

"Exactly. And you should have," Henry McGee said. He continued:

"Now let me explain what you're going to do now and what you're going to do tomorrow and what you're going to be doing for quite a few months. I'll be watching you, Pattie, and if you fuck up, it'll all come back down on your head. You think it's easy on a woman to do time? Even if they give you a country-club prison, it isn't easy, not for someone who's had power and money and men. No men, Pattie, unless you want to get in a prostie ring, which all the best women's prisons have. Well, I'm just saying all this to throw a good scare into you so you'll think about it when you have a weak moment."

"What do I have to do?"

"Turn in Mal, for one thing. I wish you hadn't've fucked his brains out. I didn't figure on that because you two were such enemies, but those things happen. I just want you to fuck him in a different way a week from now when he's already cornered. That's when you'll come up with the information about the bank account in Hong Kong. Mal is going to hold the bag on that one. A million in cash."

"He's going to say I was in on it."

"No, he's not. Not at first. Then when they find the money, they're going to go after him. The only ones who could have leaked this stuff about the terrorism on the pipeline was either Mal or the terrorists or both. See, everyone has got to not trust Chowderhead, that's for starters. Then everyone has got to trust all your bona fide information. You'll be the toast of the *Washington Post*, Pattie. Especially as a ranking member of the Senate Select

Oversight Committee on Terrorism and Intelligence. You're going to be the 1980s' version of Frank Church, only you're going to do to R Section what Church did in the seventies to the CIA. You understand?''

"Who are you with?"

"The fucking CIA, didn't I just make that clear?" Henry McGee said.

"Is that why you know everything about me?"

"Of course, Pattie. We didn't forget what was done to us in the 1970s and we got a long memory. You weren't on the hit squad then so we gave you a pass. But Mal went along with cutting our balls off back in the bad old Vietnam days, so Mal, we don't waste any sympathy on him. You getting the picture?"

"You're going after Mal—"

"No, Pattie. He's just a little part of it. We're going after R Section. R Section has been playing fast and loose for a long time. For example, this is bona fide, do you know they have perverted the Witness Protection Program?''

It was all going so fast. She sat in her black nightgown on the bench by her dressing table and she listened to the raspy voice in the half darkness and she was absorbing it all.

Henry McGee explained about the program and how a Soviet agent protected by the program was used illegally in Alaska and elsewhere to continue funneling information to his former masters in Moscow. About a mole inside R Section named November. About the use of agents named Denisov and Alexa to courier information to Zurich and Berlin and trade with KGB for simple money. About Malcolm Crowder's part in the conspiracy and how he and the R Section agent blackmailed the oil conglomerates to stop the terrorism on the pipeline. It was terribly complicated, the kind of story that comes out leak by leak by leak, day after day after day in the pages of prominent newspapers. The story was too complicated to make up; because it was so complicated, it must be true. Patricia Heath saw how it must be true and the CIA agent carefully led her through the scenario, pointing out pitfalls.

They got an atomic device from East Germany in trade for blueprints for a new computer system under development in a think tank in Palo Alto, California. The accounts in Hong Kong Bank of Commerce belonged to Denisov and Devereaux and Malcolm Crowder and each account contained exactly 1.33 million—the way they had split the money.

Henry McGee went over and over the material again. He had photographs of the rogue agent and of the Soviet double agent who had compromised the Witness Protection Program. It was a stunning scandal and Patricia Heath saw how clever the CIA had been to trust her with the details of it. The CIA must not be involved in leaking any of these details to a reporter; the world would not soon believe another Deep Throat. She was a senator, a respected political leader with White House ambitions. She was respected by both NOW and the Moral Majority. Of course, she would be believed because this terrible business had involved her home state of Alaska.

"Malcolm will want to involve me," she said at one point.

"Malcolm is a Chowderhead as you knew at one time," Henry said. He was grinning and his teeth were bright in the darkness of the room. "He will make all sorts of accusations before it's over but it really doesn't matter. That's his name on the account in Hong Kong. Those were his bombings of the line that were covered up. Hell, he just killed the last two boys could start to refute the whole story, you both saw to that.''

"Is this the way it is? Is this the way it always is in espionage?"

"This is intelligence," Henry said. "There isn't espionage and all that spy stuff. There's just one side and the other and a lot of underoccupied people figuring out their private scams. Denisov is almost a millionaire on his own, not to mention the money he just took in on this last scam. R Section is a corrupt, vicious component in the intelligence community. Open their files, air their linen, make yourself a name.''

She looked at him. "And CIA is on my side."

"Absolutely," he said. "That's what I've been trying to tell you."

TWENTY-NINE

Change of Luck

After they landed, Kools put the cuffs on the pilot and smashed the instrument panel with the rifle butt. Bill looked sad about that but happy about not being killed. Bill had a wallet full of credit cards as well as six hundred in cash.

"You gonna take all my money?"

"Sure," Kools said.

"And the credit cards?"

"Sure," Kools said. "What the fuck you care about credit cards? The only people get screwed is the card company. It isn't like it was your money."

"Well, I guess you're right but I wish you'd leave my driver's license and the pilot's license. That's a pain in the ass to get replaced."

Kools thought about that and took out the two licenses and shoved them in Bill's jacket.

"That's decent of you," Bill said.

"Hey, it wasn't your fault," Kools said. They might have shaken hands on it if Bill hadn't been wearing handcuffs.

Kools finally hitched a ride from a tractor-trailer truck hauling lumber down the Glenn Highway from Palmer. The driver let him off by the Northland Mall and Kools took a cab to Anchorage International on the other side of town.

He bought the ticket to Seattle with the green American Express card.

He was moving like a sleepwalker. He held the ticket in his hand with the American Express card. He looked at a couple of city cops in the crowded terminal and he thought they were staring at him. He went into the bar and ordered a screwdriver and he drank it like it was plain orange juice. He ordered another one. The plane left at noon and there was absolutely no way he was going to make it. He always got caught. Like robbing that gas station. Everyone robs gas stations. Gas stations are put out there to be robbed and they never catch anyone but Kools got caught and did some serious time. Now what was going to happen to fuck up getting away this time?

He thought about the look on Noah's face when he was getting pulled by the beard out the hatch of the chopper. It made him dizzy just to think about it, about Noah falling all that way down. Noah did not believe it, as though that had anything to do with getting it. Kools thought about the Russians and the women on the other side and how they had played at this Mickey Mouse stuff about explosives and how to arm the bombs and it was all just a dream, like most of his life had been.

The Delta Airlines plane left at noon and Kools was

absolutely amazed to be on it, amazed to be alive, amazed to be getting out of it. He tried not to think of Noah or whatever happened to his sister. He was just out of it.

He ordered rare steak for lunch but it was overcooked anyway.

THIRTY
The Stories

Hanley got the call at noon. He had decided not to go to Sianis' place for lunch after all. A straight-up martini and a well-done cheeseburger were part of his serene routine when Section was running on automatic pilot. That was no longer the case.

Stories were coming out of Alaska about a bomb on the oil pipeline. The stories seemed to confirm the earlier reports of the agent from Dutch Harbor. There had been something there and Section had ignored it. The first report came out of a Fairbanks radio station; the Associated Press in Anchorage had been asked to look into the allegation.

The name *Alaska* alerted Hanley. He had had two agents there and one of them had been found dead shortly after 5:00 A.M. Washington time in the parking lot of a disco lounge in Anchorage. His name had been Pierce and he had been a good man. He had gone to Alaska trailing a defected Soviet agent and a woman companion. The Soviet agent had been defected by Devereaux, the second R Section agent in Alaska. It was all connected, it had to be, connected to Pierce and Devereaux and ULU terrorism. All connected to Henry McGee. Hanley felt very afraid when he thought about Henry McGee.

"What does it mean?" Mrs. Neumann had demanded. She was a large woman with a raspy voice and a homespun manner. She had accidentally become head of Section because of politics she was not part of. Hanley had seniority in service. He did not resent her, even when she asked rude questions.

Hanley sat in the large red leather chair at the corner of the desk in Mrs. Neumann's office. The room was a standard, dull government office but it conveyed touches of Mrs. Neumann so that, unlike Hanley's office, there was a sense it was occupied by a real human being. On the wall behind the desk was a homespun needlepoint design that had been given to her years before when she ran Computer Analysis division: "Garbage In—Garbage Out."

"I don't know what it means," Hanley said. "I have the feeling of being battered suddenly. Four weeks ago, I put November on the matter of Henry McGee. My mistake was in not telling him everything Pierce filed with us, about the pipeline bombings Pierce had looked into. I didn't think it was relevant to looking for Henry McGee. I didn't expect anything, but suddenly everything is happening and none of it makes sense. Who killed Pierce in Anchorage? What earthly reason was there to kill him? It had to be Denisov or the other one, the woman he was with. Why haven't we heard from November in more than thirty-six hours? The ship he was on tied up at Deadhorse this morning and that man Holmes said Devereaux left the ship at Nome. Where is he? And the wire services are reporting rumors of a bombing on the Alaska pipeline—''

"It's always connected, isn't it?'' Mrs. Neumann said. She stared at Hanley's eyes and expected to find an answer in them.

"We have to get all the files together,'' she said to herself. "Henry McGee, Devereaux, Denisov, all of them. And we contact FBI now about the mess in the San Francisco office—''

"Mrs. Neumann.'' His voice was sharp. "We do not tattle to the Justice Department.''

"This is not our matter,'' she said. "This is domestic and you know our charter and the charter of the FBI. The Witness Protection Program is a useful tool for us but it is under the aegis of the Justice Department, not Section. We tell them about Miss O'Hare, the leaks, we cooperate—''

"The FBI will shit all over us.'' The vulgarism was startling because Hanley rarely indulged in them. Mrs. Neumann's face filled with clouds of anger.

"We run by the rules.''

"There are no rules.''

"We run by the rules,'' she repeated. "What if this all blows up against us and we have no place to hide because we have broken all the rules?''

"The rules are what you make up after the game is over to justify what you've done,'' Hanley said. "The FBI is under no urgency in this. If we give them information that the program is compromised, their urgency is in proving our allegation is not true. The name of intelligence is cover-up when the wrong people know the wrong things.''

"We have a dead agent in Anchorage," she said. "The FBI has liaison with local police and—"

"What was the agent doing in Anchorage? That's what the FBI will want to know first. What do we explain? Do we give them Denisov? And how many others? Or just open our personnel files to the Hoovers?"

She said nothing. Hanley let the silence work on her.

"The final paranoia," Hanley said.

"What are you talking about?"

"I have been thinking about this in terms of paranoia. The life of counterintelligence is wrapped in paranoia. We must lead the other side to mistrust its own information about us; we must plant false information for them. They, in turn, must make us distrust ourselves. Why did we believe in Henry McGee in the first place? The initial interviews were made by Devereaux when McGee led his people across the ice bridge from Siberia. Why did we believe in him sufficiently to draw him into Section?"

Hanley looked at her, looked at the needlepoint behind her desk. He was staring into his own thoughts and he was seeing nothing in the office.

Finally, he went on: "Devereaux questioned him and then we put others on it. In time, we were convinced of his bona fides. He had enough stories, enough real information. We could act on what he said. Every story was buttressed by a real event. Only Devereaux ever raised any suspicion about him. He did not believe in Henry McGee. It turned out that Devereaux was right. It was noted in his 201 file when Henry disappeared back behind the curtain five years ago. That was the reason I put Devereaux on the trail when the name of McGee resurfaced this spring."

"You're just rattling on," Mrs. Neumann said. "What are you really thinking about?"

"About how everything suddenly falls, everything was dependent on everything else. Henry McGee barks at the hounds and off we go, chasing him over the fields, and all of a sudden we lose a Soviet client, we have a dead agent in Anchorage, our second agent has gone radio-dead on us, and you want to call in the FBI. They would tear us apart, Mrs. Neumann. Pierce had his reports on rumors of bombings on the pipeline; he had done some research on this supposed terrorist organization. Now anonymous callers are reaching radio stations in Alaska with rumors to fit Pierce's facts. Is everything connected? If it is, God help Section, because it is going to look as though we were in this thing from the beginning."

"You're indulging in professional paranoia," she said.

"You have to. The trap is being set, you can see that yourself, Mrs. Neumann. But it's not a trap for one of our men, it's bigger than that. I think all of Section is in danger."

"That's impossible."

"Our files," he said. "We have Henry McGee's stories as bona fide facts in our files. Our files were compromised by this man, our agents compromised. Remember the double agent we thought we ran in East Berlin three years ago? Who was running whom? I used Comp An to search through every operation Monday touched, going back fifteen years. Comp An then correlated the scenarios with the scenario pool. Do you know what I got back this morning?"

Mrs. Neumann waited. The room was very quiet even though official Washington snarled its way through another perpetual morning traffic jam outside the windows of their solid old building. The city was full of quiet rooms where people even more powerful than the head of R Section sat in judgment. In Washington, all the places without power were full of noise; the reality of power required intense quietness.

"Henry McGee. A planted story about a planted spy fifteen years ago. Somehow bona fided by an East German agent we thought we turned seven years ago. Years passed and the stories that we questioned at the beginning take on the mustiness of being true. They must be true, they've been around so long."

"Like the search for the mole in CIA," she said, her voice taking on a sad timbre.

"Two defectors say that a Soviet mole exists inside CIA and CIA begins to tear itself apart in the 1970s to find him."

"Because the head of counterintelligence, Angleton, is convinced the mole exists—"

"And is accused in his turn of being the mole—"

"And the Church committee destroys the Langley firm's ability to perform counterintelligence—"

Hanley finished it: "Because the directors of CIA finally agree to slash counterintelligence and make public the most secret secrets, the ones the Langley people called 'the family jewels.' "

They did not continue the story. They knew it. Everyone in counterintelligence knew it. The questions lingered long after the fact, long after Angleton was forcibly retired, long after the mole theory was discounted.

Had there been a mole in CIA after all?

How high had the mole risen?

Was the mole behind the destruction of CIA counterintelligence for nearly a decade?

The retired spies who lived on Florida's west coast and in southern California below Los Angeles still argued the question because it was an endless question and each conclusive answer to it led to another question.

"Is that the nightmare we face now?" Mrs. Neumann said.

"We are this close," Hanley said, holding up his thumb and forefinger. "Involve FBI and you involve Justice finally and then Congress. It all seems rather small, but if our confidence is cracked—if we give away our own family jewels—then R Section will turn itself inside out looking for its own moles and we will cease to function anymore as a counterintelligence operation."

"Counterintelligence was not originally part of our charter."

" 'Who will spy upon the spies?' " Hanley quoted. It was the rhetorical question of John Kennedy, who had pushed for R Section in the first place, when he felt betrayed twice by Langley's secretive incompetence.

Mrs. Neumann sighed then and dropped her hand heavily on the padded arm of her chair. The computer screen on her desk was blank, save for a single blinking cursor waiting for her instructions. She looked at Hanley. "It is all in the stories," she said. "There were too many stories."

"Too many," Hanley said. "He kept them all straight, and years later, this agent or that would blunder into our arms and another gem of bona fides would be handed to us. We would have Henry McGee's story buried in files and this new story that proved Henry was telling the truth. Or Henry proved the new man was telling the truth. And sometimes it was the truth and just as often not. We are wounded, Mrs. Neumann, I should have seen it more clearly when I sent November after him. We are wounded and we don't even feel the pain of it yet. November is part of the trap being set for us, a trap without edges to it yet. I don't even know if it has snapped on us.''

"It was all the stories,'' she repeated.

"Too many damned stories,'' Hanley said.

THIRTY-ONE

The Price of Silence

The trap snapped three hours later.

The senator from Alaska was on the phone all night after the Friday edition of the *Washington Post* hit the street Thursday late afternoon. Patricia Heath called in her press secretary to field the calls and issue a prepared statement.

Patricia Heath was glowing with that peculiar sheen that comes over the face and eyes of a politician who suddenly is at the center of all attention. It was as good as sex. Even better. The news media was so compliant and never demanded satisfaction in return. It worshiped power. She handled it well. She wore a little, black dress of the kind always called "a little black dress" and enough makeup to make her look good on the television cameras at the press conference held at 11:00 P.M. outside her Georgetown home.

The first story did not sandbag Malcolm Crowder. That would come in a day or two. But for the first time, the name of R Section was spoken of in the press.

What was R Section anyway?

Few files existed in the newspaper offices of the country and a check of the federal directory revealed only this obscure "crop reporting and international agricultural estimation" service stuck in the dreary bowels of the two old Department of Agriculture buildings on Fourteenth Street, Northwest.

The absence of information about R Section made it all the more fascinating. And yes, there was a connection between a man named Pierce from Dutch Harbor, Alaska, found shot to death outside a disco in Anchorage and the R Section manipulation of information about a series of terrorist attacks on the precious Alaska pipeline. Everything had been kept secret up to now.

It was the act of secrecy in government that fascinated the press.

The man from ABC camped on the doorstep until Patricia agreed to talk to him. He said R Section was spying on its own citizens. Patricia did not disagree with him, although that was not part of the story. The story had very careful limits and the dark-faced man had made her go over the story again and again until she understood those limits.

Patricia Heath said to ABC that secrecy in government, especially in an open society, could not be tolerated.

The press got the quote exactly right.

Denisov went to the Polaris Hotel and asked for Mr. Schwenck and they said they had never heard of the man.

He walked out of the hotel and went to the corner of Front Street, which paralleled the rocky coastline. Nome was quiet in the midday glaze of clouds.

Behind the storefronts on Front Street, the Bering Sea stretched out before him to the Soviet Union. A milepost sign on the street said it was less than 190 miles to Siberia.

Like all Muscovites, Denisov had always thought of the vast waste of Siberia in terms of east and north and now he was standing at the western edge of the world and the thought of Siberia "over there" made him almost dizzy. He was this close to home; he was too close to home. He thought of the quiet face of the man he had killed in Anchorage and of Alexa's calm acceptance afterward of the fact of murder. None of it seemed quite real anymore, not this place, not the closeness of Siberia, not Devereaux telling him to play it out. He felt disoriented. He had been frightened in Santa Barbara, frightened by the crude blackmail implied in the photographs of Alexa in that hotel room. Yes, he could justify the murder of the agent in Anchorage; he could explain it in reason to himself and to others. But what about the price of R Section's eventual revenge on him?

His face was as dark as the clouds. He walked past the memorial to the Iditarod race and did not see it, saw nothing at all because he was looking for some way out.

And then Karpov was standing in front of him, his hand on the single parking meter in the entire bush country of Alaska. Karpov was the meet. Karpov had identified him in Santa Barbara; Karpov had known the code between Devereaux and Denisov; Karpov was the next step in the plot. It was true, then, Denisov thought in a rush of black feelings: Everything was arranged and there was no reason to struggle against it anymore. He almost felt release.

At the moment Denisov met Karpov, the red phone in Hanley's office rang. It was 4:00 P.M. in Washington, five hours later than Alaska.

"I thought you might be terminated as well," Hanley said.

"What happened?" Devereaux asked.

"Denisov is in Alaska. He finished one of ours in Anchorage last night. Where are you?"

"It doesn't matter," Devereaux said. "I'm getting closer to Henry McGee."

"Henry McGee is not important anymore," Hanley said. "A very bad thing has happened, it's much more important." He told him about the breaking story of sabotage on the Alaska pipeline and the way R Section's name was now being connected with the cover-up.

"I'm not interested in politics or public relations," Devereaux said.

"Damnit, you're an agent," Hanley hissed. "I want you to drop McGee now and find out where Denisov is and—"

"He's in Nome, I'll be seeing him in a little while," Devereaux said.

"I don't understand—"

"With what you've just told me, I begin to see what Henry McGee intends to do," Devereaux said. His voice was calm and it made Hanley nervous. "Henry McGee was behind that sabotage, Henry McGee gives this Alaska senator the story, Henry mentions R Section. . . ." It was as though he was talking to himself. "I want you to put a guard on Rita Macklin and Philippe. And on my Aunt Melvina in Chicago."

"Why? Why on earth should I do that?"

"Because Henry threatened them—"

"You saw Henry McGee?"

"I don't have any time, Hanley," Devereaux said.

"You saw Henry McGee?" Hanley repeated, his voice echoing back inside his receiver so that the question seemed idiotic to him as soon as he asked it.

"Will you do it?"

"Yes. But what about Denisov and this—"

"Denisov is working on the next step of Henry's plot," Devereaux said.

"Denisov is a killer," Hanley said.

"And an arms dealer. But I need him at the moment."

"You can't trust him."

"I never did," Devereaux said. "The trouble with going after Henry McGee the way we did is that we arranged to always be behind him. That's the way he wanted it. It's time to stop following him. I have to run ahead and wait for him."

"When will you get him?"

Devereaux paused and smiled into the telephone. Nels Nelsen was outside the airport building, waiting in the truck, the rifle still across his lap. He had driven Denisov into town from the cabin and now he would drive Devereaux back to the cabin. "Hopefully, before he gets us."

"Us? Did you say us?"

"Us," Devereaux said. "As in Section." And Devereaux began to tell him a fantastic story about a storyteller and about spies and about all the things that must be done to make the ending change.

THIRTY-TWO
Enemies

Denisov sat in the car next to Karpov as they moved up the road toward Teller. The endless sunlight depressed Denisov; Karpov depressed him. The Jeep they had rented in the town was made for winter, with heavy tires and a growling engine and the slight whine of four-wheel drive.

"The matter is arranged for you to conduct November into Big Diomede," Karpov said for the sixth time. He said it over and over, like a child. He had insisted on dinner in Nome at the Nugget Inn, he had insisted on bragging a little to Denisov. He had never mentioned Alexa and it became clear after a while that he was a very small cog in the larger machine. He did not know about Alexa and he was quite certain that the Section agent named November would be waiting for them.

"And do we fly over?"

"Arranged," Karpov smiled, watching the road. "Do you like to travel by submarine?"

"Of course. It is convenient, picturesque and very comfortable," Denisov said.

"We meet the others after we pick up our friend, November."

"I do not understand why he is important in this."

"He is important because we say so," Karpov said. "Just as you are important."

Denisov tried to think of the Soviet Union just beyond that bank of clouds over the water. When he was at the big red-stone train station in Helsinki, he was already home in Moscow because the buildings and the people reminded him of Russia just across the border less than a hundred miles away. Russia revealed its presence by degrees in Europe as you moved east to meet the country; you were involved in Russia long before you reached the Soviet border. But this was so different. This was abrupt. Here was Alaska, a strange, half-savage country with glittering cities and deep and endless isolation, so close to another strange, half-savage country of pine forests and immense rivers and Asiatic people who were only Soviet citizens, not Russians at all. Denisov felt very lost at that moment, abandoned between two worlds.

Karpov glanced at him once and frowned. "What are you thinking, Ivan Ilyich?"

Denisov gazed at the gentle tundra turning green and the white mountains in the distance and the expanse of shifting sea.

"I am thinking of Gilbert and Sullivan," Denisov said at last. He turned to Karpov. "Comrade, what does this mean? Why must this American agent and I be taken back to the Soviet Union? Will we ever know?''

"That is not for me to say.''

The car turned at the rough track and climbed up to the summit where the windowless cabin stood framed against the gray sky.

Denisov got out beside Karpov and they walked up to the cabin.

The heater was on and the room was a little too warm against the day. There was dried blood on one wall. They saw the figure of the man on the sleeping shelf. Karpov had the pistol out now and was crossing the room ahead of Denisov. He pointed the pistol at the figure on the shelf.

Devereaux stared at Karpov. He was bound by ropes to the shelf. Nels Nelsen had retied him and thought the American agent was completely mad, as mad as the Russian he had taken to Nome, as mad as the world had been since the day his partner got himself shot. Nels Nelsen thought how good it would be to lose himself again in the sanity of solitude in the bush.

Karpov spoke Russian now. He ordered Denisov to cut the rope and then retie Devereaux's hands behind his back.

Denisov took out the small penknife and worked at the ropes and cut them. He stared into Devereaux's face while he worked. Devereaux stared at him with gray eyes, exactly like the eyes of the wolf. Neither man revealed anything.

Devereaux stood up, staggered, nearly fell.

"You are comfortable?'' Karpov said to the American agent.

Devereaux stared at him.

Karpov could barely contain his glee. "This is the end of November," he said. "Not the end of November but perhaps a new beginning for you and for your agency. You have betrayed your country, November, you have betrayed its security and its security programs. You have been a terrorist in your own country and you and Denisov have amassed a fortune together by working against your own country."

Denisov stared at Karpov as he once had examined stamps. He had been a collector as a child and turned the stamps over and looked at the colors and fitted them in a book. When he became a man, he stopped collecting stamps and examining them. It was the only pleasure of being an agent: examining people.

Karpov could not keep still. He danced around the room as he talked. And then he shoved the pistol in Devereaux's belly and said it was time to go.

"Where do we go?" Devereaux said. He took a step and staggered again. The concussion brought no pain now, only this sense of walking very carefully on a rope thirty feet above the ground.

"There is a place where we will be picked up," Karpov said.

The road was not heavily traveled, although a truck boomed along behind them from time to time and pulled ahead, spraying gravel. The day would last forever. The clouds parted over the sea and let sunlight fall on the gray water and turn it to blue.

The wind never ceased. It was not uncomfortable but it never ceased.

Denisov sat in the front with Karpov; Devereaux on the backseat. Karpov had thrown a blanket over him.

The car swung along the lonely, uninhabited countryside. They saw a bear once and they saw dogs or wolves and they saw a beautiful herd of caribou grazing.

Karpov began to hum the lush romantic bars of "Moscow Nights." Denisov had been forced to join in, not in voice but in thought, because it did remind him of Moscow, of the Kremlin and Red Square and the houses on the hill and the children skating in Gorky Park and so many other things. In that moment, he suddenly was removed from Alaska and Siberia and the great emptiness of the Arctic, even the emptiness of his quiet existence in Santa Barbara. He was home again in that moment because he could feel the sense of Moscow in him.

The Jeep was off the road again, this time whining over the unmarked tundra toward the coastline. The clouds still obscured the sun.

They reached the edge of the continent and got out of the car. The little silver raft was coming toward the shore.

Devereaux said to Denisov, "What do you intend to do?"

"We go to Soviet Union," Denisov said in flat English. "This is the only way."

There were two men on the raft with automatic weapons. They helped Devereaux aboard but did not untie him. The raft was large, made for the open sea, and the men pushed off with short paddles. The car sat on the shore, headlamps staring at Siberia beyond the horizon line.

The submarine surfaced suddenly in the shallow water of a secluded rock harbor off the rugged coast. It broke the waterline with a shock and the water fell away from the conning tower and then it was there, not massive and not too small, already alive with sailors coming out of the hatch.

THIRTY-THREE

The Peril

Bob Wagner met the man who liked peanuts and beer in the Fairmont Hotel bar again. Pell said they had good peanuts. Pell said he was picking up the check anyway, even if Wagner called the meeting.

"I got to cover my ass," Bob Wagner said. He was very pale and he had been drinking awhile even though it was only eleven in the morning. He had the abused look that men get when they know they don't have a chance anymore but they still have to go through the motions.

"Have a drink," Pell said in his thin voice. His eyes were narrow and he was staring through Wagner's head at a point six feet behind.

"Karen. She's gone crazy. She's burrowing into files that are like six years old. I know she's making all kinds of file checks. Like a busy beaver."

"You got a problem, huh?"

"She's on my case. She's like an FBI guy. You can

see she's spying on me. That business down in Santa Barbara, it set her off, whatever it was."

"Whatever it was," Pell agreed.

"You got to get me out of this."

"Or what?"

"Everything I know—" began the threat.

Pell waited, peanuts in hand. "The fuck you know? You know shit. You know me? You know my number? You know anything about anything? This is real stuff in the real world, Bobby, and you are just stumbling around like a second-grade kid finding out what urinals are for. The trouble with you guys is you like the action but you can't take the heat. You wanta turn State's? Turn State's. Confess your bleeding heart out. You know what they do to you? Put you inside one of those max places where all you do all day is lift weights to make your muscles big so that the cons leave your ass alone. You wanta be a fish?"

"I don't wanta be nothing. I don't wanta be involved."

"You sap. You never were. I told you. Let her look through her files. What's she gonna find?"

"I don't know."

Pell made a face and said nothing.

"They're after me," Bob Wagner sputtered as the barman brought up a Stoly on the rocks. He was thinking now what he had thought before he called Pell. They were going to make him the patsy in this thing. Wagner had thought about it all the way to work. He had decided he was going to kill Karen O'Hare because he had to. He stopped in the Chinese bar on Powell Street at eight in the morning and drank until ten and then he called Pell. He was thinking about how they were all working in this thing to put Wagner in the bag and it wasn't going to be that way. He really had to face up to it: He really just had to kill Karen O'Hare because he couldn't talk Pell into doing it.

He thought about Karen dead and the thought didn't frighten him as much as going to jail did.

Pell studied his peanuts as though they might foretell the future. Then he ate one. "You got anything more to tell me?" he said.

"No," Wagner said. He knew it was hopeless with Pell, that he was going to have to stop Karen himself.

"Don't forget to stop by the bathroom again."

"I'm not wired," Wagner said.

"Yeah, sure, I know. But I think my friend likes you."

THIRTY-FOUR

Fifteen Minutes of Fame

Malcolm Crowder sat beneath the moose antlers in the den, the wood-paneled room with the heavy books on heavy shelves, and watched his life go before his eyes on "ABC World News Tonight" with Peter Jennings. His life was also passing before his eyes on the smaller Zenith with Tom Brokaw and it had already passed before his eyes with Dan Rather. It was hard to drown three times in one day.

The dirty bitch.

Malcolm was taking it all in like body blows from a street fighter, which is what Patricia Heath was. She was very good on television and the story was not a television story, so it was all the more impressive. When a congressman or senator starts accusing a semisecret government agency of being involved in the cover-up of one of its agents who was really a secret arms supplier to terrorists who intended to blow up the Alaska oil pipeline—well, it was the sort of thing that TV anchormen cannot talk about without their eyes glazing over. Usually. But Patricia Heath was a nice package and she talked short and clear, so she was worth letting the cameras linger on for more than the usual ten seconds.

She was waving papers around, she was shocking the world; there was an inset graphic showing that morning's *Washington Post* front page, just to make sure everyone understood the story was important. It was hard to tell sometimes on TV news.

And there was a map of Alaska and a suitcase and FBI agents arresting security guards and the body of a terrorist found in a secluded area north of Fairbanks. Blackmail paid to terrorists, said the television set. Terrorists set up by a government intelligence agent who had already defected, along with a Soviet former defector who, it was now believed, had actually been a Russian double agent all along. The secret agency was called R Section and the name was on every newsman's lips. Nobody really understood the whole story but everyone understood that it was important because Bob Woodward had been assigned to investigate it for the *Post* and Seymour Hersh was doing the same thing for the *Times*.

The dirty bitch was putting it all on him after all he had done for her.

Malcolm Crowder had the same feeling now that he had had the day she showed him the papers in Juneau and told him that he wasn't a senator anymore. The only other time he had felt that way was flying through the storm in the little plane in 1955, bringing the vaccine up to the North Slope. He had been scared in that plane, he had seen death scratching at the cockpit windows. Damn, he thought suddenly, very sad for the young man he had once been.

He saw the logic as he watched his life slip away. It was too small a catch, what the terrorist on the telephone had left him. Two punk kids in a rooming house in Fairbanks. It just wasn't enough. Whoever the man was, he had needed a bigger fish to muddy up the conspiracy. He had needed Malcolm Crowder and now Patricia Heath was skinning him with a big knife.

The story was so complicated—like Watergate or Wedtech—that everyone was trying to find a handle for it so that the news media would not have to reexplain it day after day. The *Post* tried "Pipelinegate" and *The New York Times* tried "Alaskagate" and neither term was very satisfactory.

But at the heart of it was Malcolm Crowder's checking account in a Hong Kong bank, how he had hushed up terrorism on the pipeline, and now the disappearance of an American espionage agent and a Soviet defector who had worked on the terrorism on the line. They had provided an atomic device. And there was a dead American agent in Anchorage and there were reports of a mysterious dark-haired woman who acted in pornographic movies and was used by all three men for sex and for other duties.

The editor of the *National Enquirer* told his men he would pay a hundred thousand dollars for photographs of the woman, whoever she was. *Playboy* was already planning a tasteful spread of photographs of the woman, whenever she was found, wearing swim suits and bared only to the breast.

The FBI was ordered by Justice to begin an audit of its San Francisco office of the Witness Protection Program and was alerted to the possibility that an unauthorized federal intelligence agency called R Section had contained traitors and terrorists on its staff.

Patricia Heath had everything: glamour and guts, a sense of righteousness and pride in her home state.

Who was the missing American agent?

Who was the missing Soviet defector?

The questions were not to be answered, not today or tomorrow. The story was unfolding; the story was dribbling its way into the consciousness of Americans one fact at a time, the way it is always done. When the story was finished—in a week or a month—it would go on but not in the public eye. There would be congressional investigations and long tedious reports sent to the president and the National Security Council, and heads would roll quietly out of the quiet rooms of power in Washington.

But tonight was Malcolm Crowder's fifteen minutes of fame.

THIRTY-FIVE

Rita Macklin

Again, he came. It was exactly like the last time. It was the middle of the day and there was the messenger at the door. The last time was in Switzerland, in Lausanne, in the little apartment they had shared on the Place de la Concorde Suisse, which means "Square of Swiss Peace."

Rita Macklin opened the door of the town house on Rhode Island Avenue, Northwest, and did not cry or speak because, unlike the first time, she expected him.

David Mason was an intelligence officer with R Section. He was now thirty-four years old and he had been two years younger the first time he had come to Rita Macklin to tell her that Devereaux had disappeared on an assignment. That had been in Switzerland; now the same scene was to be played again on a quiet street in Washington.

She had heard the breaking story about Alaska and the pipeline and a bent agent in intelligence who had played terrorist for profit. She was a journalist. She had called her old sources and friends to find out the story behind the mad story being peddled by the senator from Alaska. And all the while, she had a bad feeling that it would all involve Devereaux and there would be a call in the night.

Hanley had called her and told her a very little, only that he had to send around a man to "baby-sit" her for a few days and would she cooperate?

"Where is he?" she had said to Hanley.

"I can't reveal—"

"It's about this Alaska business? This pipeline sabotage?"

"I cannot reveal—"

"Spook stuff," she said.

"I beg your pardon?"

"I'm sick of it."

"Miss Macklin," Hanley had said.

"I won't go through this again," she said. She thought of the times she had thought him dead. You can't do it over and over, she had thought. You can't have that much pain all the time. There was screaming going on in her head. She said, "I won't go through this again." But she would go through it again and again and again, she thought. It would never end until one of them was dead.

And now David Mason had come.

"Is this intended irony?" she said to him. She had very mixed feelings about David Mason. David Mason was in love with her, she knew that, and it was part of the pain and the humor of it that he would again be sent to comfort her and protect her.

"Intended by Hanley, I suppose," he said. He had grown in the two years in Section. There was a tiredness to his eyes and a glittering sort of hardness as well. He had not seen it all yet, just some. Hanley had told him so little that he might as well not have come to her. But she compelled him even more than Hanley's order.

She was in her thirties, tall, with striking red hair and green eyes. She was very good at what she did, which was to be a journalist and to know part of her life was always a secret pool. The secret pool was Devereaux. They loved each other. Everything he was, she was not; everything she believed in, he disbelieved. So they did not speak of these things to each other but swam in the secret pool at night, when it was dark and when no one could see them.

She let him in and led him to the living room.

The room reflected her. It was spare and bright and full of books. He sat on the couch in the uneasy way of visitors.

"You want coffee?" she said. "Did I ask you last time you came to tell me bad news?"

"I don't have bad news," he said. "There was a threat made against you."

"How do you know?"

"I was told—"

"By Hanley? Do you believe Hanley?"

Her voice was hard. She stared right through him.

"I was told," he repeated.

"Tell Hanley I don't want to be protected. Not by you."

"He sent me because I—I knew you."

"God, I hate you all."

"Rita," he tried again.

"And him," she said. Her voice was very calm now but just as hard. "I'm not going through this over and over again. There are other things. Like children and vacations in Yellowstone Park and things like that. I'm not going through this again."

David Mason stared at her and did not speak. It was as though he understood she was talking only to herself.

"Is he alive or dead? Tell me that," she said.

"I don't know," he said.

"Lie to me," she said. "I really want him dead this time. I want him dead and that makes an end of it. I won't be pushed around anymore."

"I don't know," David Mason said.

"Do you want to comfort me? Put your arms around me and hold me while I cry?" Rita said. "Well, I won't cry anymore."

"Rita," he said. "Don't say all these things."

"It's finished," she said. "It is going to hurt a long time but it's finished. Women are built to take hurt but I don't want it anymore, not every goddamn time he packs his bag and puts a pistol in it and says nothing about the job or where he's going or when he'll be back. Spies can't talk about it and I can't stand it, not anymore."

David just stared because she really didn't want him to say anything.

"I'm not kidding," she said and this time she seemed to see him. "I don't need a baby-sitter and I don't need him, not anymore. I don't need you. I can find a man when I need one and he can be a lawyer or lumberjack and I don't care, I don't need you people, any of you."

And David saw that now she was not crying.

THIRTY-SIX

One Little Detail Missing

Henry McGee liked what he saw in the lobby of the Olympic Hotel in Seattle, liked the way she wore a dress, liked the pseudo-shy attitude that still had sophistication to it. The girl would play well just about anywhere, which was important to Henry McGee. He might take her to Tahiti with him if she worked out.

Her name was Mai-Lin. She was known to the boys down in the public market and in some of the fancy joints down on Alaska Way and some of the old-time joints too. She was a nice girl and she spoke nice to people. She wore those shiny dresses that make boys working in the fish market dream. She was a hooker but a high-class hooker and Henry tried her out.

When he was finished, he told the girl he wanted an arrangement.

The girl said no.

He explained things to her.

When that was over, she went along with the arrangement.

Mai-Lin or whatever her real name was was not a problem. Just about every problem was cleaned up now, with Devereaux on his way to Siberia, with every connection wiped clean three times with ammonia, with R Section wringing its hands. One agent can destroy an intelligence section if he knows how to go about it. The trouble with counterintelligence was in the methodology called HUMINT, short for "human intelligence," as opposed to the machine intelligence picked up from SIGINT or PHOTINT. Counterintelligence had to rely on machines, and when it used people, they were always vulnerable. People made stories.

Poor Narvak. She was having such a good time that she didn't understand that a man travels best who travels alone, and when it comes down to it, a piece of tail is just a piece of tail. Henry McGee had genuinely admired that girl and not just for her body. She had manipulated the two chumps, she had killed the old trapper named Dobbins, she had even fooled Devereaux that time. A girl like that would have had a future if it wasn't for the fact that she was a comeback, that she was such a real link to Henry McGee. Not even seventeen yet and now she was very asleep in the trunk of a car at Anchorage International Airport. Henry had regretted that for about thirty seconds.

Pell said to Henry McGee: "They only found one."

"I can read a fucking newspaper," Henry McGee said. The two men were sitting in the suite. Mai-Lin was in the bedroom, sleeping. Henry had kept her up all night. He had worked out an arrangement with her to stay in his suite for a few days.

Pell said, "You got any nuts, any peanuts, to go with the beer?"

"Do I look like a restaurant?"

"All right," Pell said. "I took the plane up, all they got on airplanes anymore is these goddam honey-roasted nuts. I hate it. I want to eat candy, I'd eat candy."

"What about the other one? They missed him, didn't they? They fucked it up, didn't they?"

"Kools made it to Seattle."

"I didn't expect that."

"Ernie Bushman didn't expect it. He got a tree stuck through him."

"Don't give me names I don't need."

"The one gets iced, Ernie reaches for the other and he kicks Ernie out of the copter. Makes Bill Bradley land him in Anchorage, steals his wallet. We trace the credit card and he uses it for a plane to Seattle. Paid for a night at the Pacific Plaza Hotel."

"Kools. I would have had to bet on Kools. Boy had some common sense to him, saw the main chance."

"So what you want to do?"

"The problem is we don't leave details behind. You got a way to ice Kools?"

"Are you insulting me or what?"

"Is Kools around?"

"Three-legged alligators are always around."

"Do it," Henry McGee said.

"Anything special?"

"Just do it."

"You care about Wagner?"

"The geek in San Francisco? No, he's not connected to me."

"The only way he gets caught is if that little girl on his

case down there really finds something, but I don't think there's anything to find. I think the only way he gets hung is if he hangs himself.''

"Couldn't care less."

"You need anything while you're in Seattle?"

"Not at all. Just some rest and relax. Got a couple more calls to make in the next couple of days and then I go away."

"Mr. Anthony said for me to say to you that we appreciate the stuff."

"It's good stuff all right, never use it myself but I know good cocaine," Henry McGee said. He was all smiles with Pell. But he was thinking about details.

THIRTY-SEVEN

Kools Again

Peewee was thinking about Kools again just when he came into the bar. The place was full of smoke and music. Couple of the girls were shaking their tails by the big juke and there was rain on the small front windows. Peewee felt good, as good as he ever felt; didn't even think about his nose or the way he looked when he tried out a smile. Mai-Lin even wanted to feel sorry for him after she saw him and how bad he looked; that had been the only good thing. What the hell, he had a buddy now, that's what it was about; the man was straight with him, Peewee be straight to the man. Guy had come down from Alaska where Peewee always wanted to go. Guy was cool, had some bread on him, bought Peewee drinks. Kools and him were tight now, been buddies for three, four days. Kools all right, Peewee thought.

"You all right, my man," Peewee said to Kools in the

middle of his thought. Kools picked up a Rainier beer and tried it and looked around.

Kools stared through him for a moment and then softened. What the hell, wasn't Peewee. Just thinking about what he was going to jump into the next time.

Seattle had been edgy the first day and he thought he had made a mistake staying at the Pacific Plaza and maybe made a mistake charging the trip down, but what the hell, it would take them a month to figure out the charges and he'd be long gone by then.

"What's rolling tonight, my man?" Peewee said. Peewee was always talking that way, talking sort of hip and it annoyed Kools, who didn't like to talk very much at all. Kools thought there was something of the chump in Peewee but Peewee had some guts at least, had stuck a few, had a face that looked like it had been hit by a brick wall.

"Everything," Kools said. It meant nothing was happening. Kools felt the jitters again and poured more Rainier down his throat. He held the neck of the bottle the way some boys hold the necks of their girlfriends.

"We score, first of the month, always money in Seattle on the first of the month," Peewee said.

"You think like that, you think small."

"First of the month, I gotta man take welfare checks, all he can get, runs a grocery by East Side—"

"Thing is, you get time for the big business as much as the small business," Kools said.

"You're talking."

"I know," Kools said. Peewee was dumb. "We need to score, man, at least I know I do. I ain't gonna be working in no fish market, smell like a fish." Peewee did smell a little and he knew it. He washed his cut hands all the time but it was still there, the slightly rotting odor of the trade.

"What's on your mind?" Peewee said. His voice was quiet against the noise of the bar. The place was full. There were office workers cutting loose and office girls looking at losers. There was a desperate sort of gaiety to it all, to the noise and the loud laughs and the music up too loud and to the rain coming down so hard against the windows. The rain was part of it too.

"I don't know, I keep seeing money around in this city and I got to be able to get it. Make one solid score and get out. Was in a place today with money. Get me someplace warm, go down south a while around L.A. You know L.A.?"

"I never been," Peewee said.

"L.A. is good, man," Kools said. He had never been there. "L.A. is just like Hollywood, like you think about when you're cold sitting in the church hall, watching the movies of these big women with big breasts, watching these sissy guys kiss them up in the movies, that's what L.A. is like but it's not like that. It's like down and dirty and you can have everything you want, so it really is like the movie, if you can see what I mean. I mean, when you're sitting in fifty below and some Baptist shows you a movie about this pretty valley and this girl with big bazoos—"

Peewee waited and Kools finished. Peewee couldn't understand about looking for something, that L.A. to Kools had been like the Promised Land when he first found it and he saw it just that way, no matter if there were boys dressed like girls on Hollywood Boulevard, selling their filthy fannies. Kools had been cold and he never wanted to be cold again. Never wanted to think about the sound his partner Noah made screaming out of the copter or the dark old man on the submarine with his crazy stories.

"What you wanna do?" Peewee said.

"Get us some of those white uniforms. Those uniforms that the kitchen help wears. I been over to this big hotel, I was watching, I see the way it is. You ever do a hotel?"

"No, man, I was never in that action."

"It's easier than you know. You get this cart, you roll it up and down the corridors. You look for the room. You knock on the door. Work it about seven at night, make it Friday night when the tourists out touring. You knock on the door. Someone's home, you say you got the wrong room, you go down the hall. You knock on the door and when they don't answer, you go in."

"Those doors are locked."

"Locks don't mean shit," Kools said. "Besides, I do the outside and you do the inside. You go in and you find the stuff to look for. Look under the mattress all the time, you be surprised how many times they put the wallet under the mattress. Purse. Jewels. Watches. Keep it small, we want to travel. You game for this? I gotta be opening doors. It takes forty minutes tops. We hit two floors and then we don't get greedy."

Peewee put it in his mind and turned it over. It was big time, just the way he knew Kools was big time. Kools had that big-time look about him.

Peewee thought about the way things were and about Mai-Lin turning those pity eyes on him. Shit, didn't do any good. Mai-Lin was out of his league but he loved her anyway, she was kind. Peewee told Kools about Mai-Lin, pretty Chinese girl or whatever she was.

Kools pretended to listen while he sketched out the plan in his head. He needed Peewee but he'd cut loose from Peewee as soon as they knocked over the hotel. Big hotel down the street that was real glittery and full of money.

THIRTY-EIGHT

A Man with Two Countries Has None

The submarine suddenly began to dive. It was very quick for such a big thing in the water. The inlets filled with water, the buoyancy tanks took on weight, the thing began to shake and sink.

The two sailors saw it at the same time and they began to shout in Russian. Denisov understood the words and looked at Devereaux and decided.

Rather, the submarine had decided everything and he felt the same helpless feeling now he had that day in Santa Barbara.

He took out his pistol and said four words in Russian and everyone in the dinghy raft understood.

The submarine shuddered down beneath the waters of the gray sea. Now everyone could see the American frigate that was coming around the spit from Norton Sound.

"Did you plan this?"

Devereaux stared at Denisov. "Perhaps Henry McGee's

stories aren't the only interesting ones." Before the frigate appeared, Devereaux had begun to think Hanley had failed him.

"I wanted you to know—" Denisov began. But it was no good. They were too skilled at this game of lie and counterlie to ever believe each other.

Devereaux said, "Have him untie me."

Denisov spoke to Karpov. He had to say it twice. Karpov's mouth was open. The sailors were still shouting at the submarine but they were watching the gun in Denisov's hand. All that was left of the submarine now were the waves washing roughly against the dinghy. The fat craft went up and down and everyone had to hold on. Denisov held the pistol on the other men.

"Have you decided?" Devereaux said.

"You arranged this thing, this other thing?"

"I told you I never trusted you," Devereaux said.

They had planned finding Devereaux in the cabin; Denisov had not understood it all. Until the moment he saw the frigate, Denisov had decided nothing. He agreed to the plan proposed by Devereaux because Devereaux had the say of his life and death in the United States then; nothing had changed.

The frigate was immense and it loomed closer to the shore. The submarine was completely gone.

Karpov said, "They have abandoned me."

Denisov said, "Untie him."

"You don't know who you are talking to," Karpov said.

"Welcome to America," Denisov said in perfect English. It was exactly what Devereaux had said to him seven years ago on the beach in Florida.

Devereaux rubbed his wrists a moment later and stared

at the large Russian he had known so many years. Denisov still had the gun; perhaps Denisov still did not see he had no choice.

"What must we do?" Denisov said.

"Try to do the right thing," Devereaux said.

"Will it be safe for me?"

"What choice do you have?"

"To kill you."

"That would not be the right thing; you tried that once and it was wrong." Said in the same flat voice, without inflection and without irony.

"Do not trust," Karpov broke in.

"Shut up," Denisov said. Then, to Devereaux: "Take the automatic weapon."

The sailors took a long time to row back to shore. They saw the foreign land and thought of many things: Their ship and mates, their wives and homes, the sound of Russian, the smell of the countryside.

The sailors were a problem, Devereaux thought. He had not expected it to come this far.

He had expected Denisov to cross him, especially after Hanley told him of the murder of Pierce in Anchorage.

"The sailors will have to get back on their own," he said. "You tell them the way. How far are we from Nome?"

"Fifteen miles," Denisov said.

"Tell them the way and the distance and hope they make it. Tell them to walk fast. The weather isn't so bad and maybe someone will pick them up."

"They might freeze if the weather turns bad," Denisov said.

Devereaux said nothing.

Denisov told them and the weapons were thrown in the

dinghy and it was shoved offshore and it floated across the waves with violent bobbing. The frigate had turned in the water and it was tracking the submarine.

"What about me?" Karpov said.

Devereaux looked at him and said nothing. He took Denisov's pistol and fired once at the dinghy. The craft had several air compartments and Devereaux had to fire two more times. The shots were muted in the vastness of the countryside.

The three men got in the car then and drove to Nome. The sailors, still cursing the submarine, began to walk south toward the Teller Road.

THIRTY-NINE

Persuasion

"Where is Henry McGee?" Devereaux said.

"I don't know," Karpov said.

"Who knows?"

"I don't know."

"Who knows?"

"I don't know."

After that, Devereaux said nothing.

The plane landed at Merrill Field fifty minutes later and the three men got out. A car was waiting and the driver took them to the hotel.

Section had rented six suites on the eighth floor, three on each side of the suite where Alexa waited.

Denisov had refused to betray Alexa's hiding place in Anchorage. Devereaux had smiled at that. "She's going to have a long wait for you, then," he had said.

Denisov had betrayed Alexa then, after he thought about it.

Karpov was reasonably afraid but he knew American methodology in interrogation. It was not violent, did not use physical force to compel answers.

He blanched when he saw Alexa, dressed in black, standing in the hotel room. He wore handcuffs now, like any federal prisoner, and he wondered what Alexa was doing here.

"What must I do?" she said in perfect English to Devereaux.

"Find out where we have to go," Devereaux said. "Can you do it in fifteen minutes?"

"Perhaps," she said. "Maybe a little longer."

"We'll be at the airport."

"Then what about him? I mean, if I have to kill him after?"

"You decide," Devereaux said.

Karpov spoke in Russian to Alexa. She did not change expression. Her face was white, her dark eyes were deep pools without any focus in them at all, without any threat or any pity.

"Take him into the bathroom."

She had him kneel at the edge of the tub filled with cold water.

"I don't know anything," Karpov said in Russian. Devereaux and Denisov opened the door and walked out.

She said to Karpov, "Where is Henry McGee?"

"I don't know," he said.

She put his head in the icy water and held him under for a minute. She pulled his head out.

"My God," he gasped.

"Where is Henry McGee?" she asked in the same toneless voice.

"I am a messenger—"

She drowned him for a minute again.

There was pain through his body now and the cold water was in his mouth and nose and ears and it rubbed at his eyes. He did not know cold could be so painful.

"Where is Henry McGee?"

"The Americans do not torture spies—"

"I am Russian," she said.

Devereaux listened at the pay phone a moment and then replaced the receiver.

He nodded at Denisov and they crossed to the Delta Airlines counter.

"Did she kill him?" Denisov said.

"I didn't ask," Devereaux said, taking out his American Express card.

FORTY

Sea City Friday Night

Kools was in room 614 of the big, square-block Olympic Hotel. It was a nice room. That was the first part of the plan, to actually be in the hotel so they could have a place to divide up the swag. The second part was to order room service. He ordered a bacon, lettuce and tomato sandwich with steak fries and Heineken beer. The boy brought it up and Kools signed for it, and while he was doing this, he talked to the boy about the hotel and about the people who were in it.

When the boy left, Kools ate the sandwich. He took out the tomato because he didn't like tomatoes.

He was eating the fries when Peewee came in. Peewee had cleaned up some, washed good, tried not to smell like fish. His face looked bad but a lot of people have smashed-in noses. Like Kools, who had gotten his nose busted twice.

They started working it after Kools finished the fries and after Peewee and he changed into the right clothes. Clothes had cost $200 from a couple of dudes who worked in the hotel. Everything was for sale and now it was payday night.

It was 7:01 P.M. when they knocked at the first door and got no answer.

Henry McGee picked up the phone after the second ring.

"The matter is aborted," said the voice. That was all.

Henry put the receiver down. His eyes went flat for a moment, thinking about the plan, thinking about what could have gone wrong.

He was naked and Mai-Lin was on the bed, crying.

"Shut the fuck up," Henry McGee said in a very soft voice.

"You hurt me," Mai-Lin said.

"Shut the fuck up," Henry McGee said. He was thinking of the story, how it was going to come out. He was figuring out his own comebacks.

He got up from the bed and went to his shirt on the chair and took out the slip of paper with all the numbers written on it.

He dialed a number.

"I got to have transportation," he said.

"A brown Toyota sedan will be on the Pike Street entrance in thirty minutes, license 3H487," the voice said. The voices at these numbers always sounded the same.

"Where are you going?" Mai-Lin said. She had stopped crying but Henry had really hurt her. What had hurt her was not the kinky stuff but the fact that he didn't care if he hurt her or not. That was new to her. When some of the others had wanted to hurt her—not that she was into that—they were always very nice about it and sorry afterward.

Henry put on his shirt and trousers.

"Where are you going?"

He stared at Mai-Lin. Was she a comeback? But she didn't know anything about this operation, nothing at all. Except if they came back to the hotel, she was always working the hotel. He could have lost her on Tahiti, it wouldn't have mattered then.

On the other hand, what was the percentage? He could kill her really soft, just put a pillow over her face and push it down until she was dead. He didn't get any kicks from that, he liked life too much to get kicks from that.

What had gone wrong?

Devereaux.

Henry McGee smiled at the thought and Mai-Lin thought more than ever that he was crazy. She was starting to get very afraid of him because she had been in the suite for three days and that was scary in itself. She wanted to go out, take a walk down Pike Street, go jogging on Alaska Way alongside the docks and the big ships. She wanted to get out of here.

Henry went over to the bed and bent over and gave Mai-Lin a nice gentle kiss.

Mai-Lin tried to tongue him but he pulled away.

He reached in his pocket and took out four $100 bills and dropped them on the bed.

"Sleep tonight, honey," he said.

He had decided not to kill her. He was so lost in his own thoughts that he didn't know that Peewee had knocked at the front door of their suite or that Kools and Peewee had opened the door and come inside. Henry turned to the bedroom door and he saw Kools standing there, just staring at him.

Bob Wagner was drunk and unhappy. Karen O'Hare was trying to smile. They were in Spagoli's, the week's newest sensational restaurant according to the San Francisco news media. There was always a new and improved restaurant being touted in the city and the crowds were always enormous once the name was whispered in Herb Caen's column. The restaurants were invariably Italian in nature, had something to do with vegetarianism or fresh fish, and everyone ate fifteen-dollar-a-plate spaghetti and said they were very satisfied with it.

This one was on Broadway, toward the wharf. It was Friday night and crowded.

Karen O'Hare was watching him because this was crazy.

He plunged ahead. "I really want to get on the right foot with you, I want you to know that you and I should not be fighting."

"I'm not fighting," she said. She had said it six or seven times in the past two hours. The spaghetti, she thought, was dreadful, especially the green sauce.

Since he was going to kill her, he wanted to apologize with a nice meal in a nice restaurant. He wanted her to like him.

He had a .32 because his house was in a neighborhood where burglary was not infrequent. He had never been burglarized, though his car had been broken into twice. He knew how to shoot a pistol but he had never shot anyone.

He was going to kill Karen O'Hare, he thought. The thought was absolutely amazing to him.

"Eat your spaghetti," he said and smiled. "Drink some more wine."

When they were finished with the meal and the wine, she thought she knew what it was. She had an instinct and it usually was right. He was going to make a pass at her. It was going to be an office romance, that's how he was going to win her over, she thought.

Bob Wagner thought it would be best in her neighborhood. She lived in a creepy neighborhood and anything could happen in a place like that. He would make it happen when he drove her home.

She insisted she didn't need to be driven home. He insisted it was on his way to his own house. It was.

The streets were dark and it was raining again and he pulled up to her block. She lived at the end of the block. He stopped the car and turned to her.

"Look, don't do this," she said, reaching into her purse. "You're a married man."

"I hate to do this," he said.

"Don't then," she said.

"I don't want to kill you, believe me."

"Kill?" she said.

She processed the word and then brought it back up on the screen: "Kill?"

He had the pistol in his hand.

He squeezed the trigger once.

Nothing happened.

He looked at the gun in his hand.

She didn't scream at all. She pulled the squirt gun out of her purse.

"It's the safety," he said to himself. Then he saw the squirt gun.

"What are you going to do with that?" he said.

"I carry it for protection," she said.

"A squirt gun?" He unclicked the safety.

She squeezed the squirt-gun trigger three times and three stinging sprays of ammonia caught him in both eyes. He couldn't see a thing then but he heard the sounds of his own screams.

Kools said, "Motherfucker."

Peewee said, "Mai-Lin."

Henry McGee said nothing. Then he took a step toward the door and grabbed Kools by the shoulder and pulled him into the room.

Peewee stared at Mai-Lin. He had imagined what she would look like naked and here she was. She looked really good. He stood in the doorway and stared at Mai-Lin. There was surprise on his face and a little pain. She was in a bed naked for this man who had her price when all Peewee ever had for her was himself.

Kools crashed against the light stand and hit his head on the edge of the window ledge. Henry McGee roared up behind him and Kools felt the movement and ducked and McGee swung against the window. The safety window held without cracking.

Henry turned again and swung but Kools was very fast, much faster than Henry expected. The old man stopped a moment, catching his breath, figuring on the move.

"You motherfucker," Kools said and he was on his feet still, waiting, arms out, waiting for the old man, the crazy old bastard who had tried to get him killed.

Henry pulled the knife. The knife was curved, with the handle on top, and Peewee stared at the knife in the hand of the old dark man.

Same fucking knife, Peewee thought. *Ulu* knife.

All the thoughts were the same, all the frustrations were the same. He remembered the spring night in the soft rain standing beneath the stairs that led up to the public market, waiting for the crazy old seaman to come down the stairs. Was pretty then. And the seaman had this crazy knife, crazy enough to cut the back of his hand.

Henry McGee brought the knife down and Kools danced back the way Peewee had not been able to do that spring night four weeks ago.

Mai-Lin screamed and tried to pull a cover over her breasts.

The room was small, and the action was too large for it, like the court of a pro basketball game. Another piece of furniture crashed. Henry snarled something and Kools smiled.

Kools smiled: "Fucking old man, I grew up using that knife. You the big ULU, you shit."

And Kools had a knife, a straight knife, the kind he knew how to use and not an old Eskimo woman's knife used to clean out caribou hides.

Henry turned and Peewee had his knife out as well, the knife he had not used since four weeks ago. They had the edge, the two of them, and they knew it. Peewee saw the old dark man knew it too.

Henry backed up and Kools came to him and Peewee moved to the side wearing his bellboy's uniform with a big blade in his hand. It was ridiculous, exactly like grown men in shorts crowding each other under a basket, trying to block and tip the ball. Except this wasn't a game and the room smelled full of fear as well. No one wanted to move for a second.

"Put it down."

The voice was very quiet, nearly as powerful as the

pistol in the gray-eyed man's hand. Peewee saw it, saw the gray-eyed man. It was making him crazy, this was the sonofabitch smashed his face. This was making him absolutely crazy.

Henry saw it too but he smiled and said, "They drop theirs, I drop mine. I don't go in for knife fighting."

"This is for you to do," Denisov said to Peewee and he had a gun too.

Guns and knives.

Kools saw the way it was. He dropped his knife and Henry made a move toward him. Devereaux hit him very hard in the face with the muzzle of the pistol and Henry looked surprised for a moment. Then he dropped his *ulu* on the soft carpet and it didn't make a sound.

"You didn't have to do that," Henry McGee said. "You didn't have to hit me in the face." There was blood on his lips and on the bright even teeth in that dark face.

"You should hit him in the face again," Mai-Lin said in a thin voice that hissed now. "You should cut his balls off."

Devereaux looked at her.

"I been here three days," Mai-Lin said. "He hurt me. I wanna make charges. I got a suit here."

Devereaux waited for someone else.

"That's Mai-Lin," Peewee said. "She works here."

Devereaux stared at him. "What does she do, leave the chocolate mints on the pillows?"

"Hey, man."

"Put the knife down," Devereaux said.

"You the police?" Peewee said. "I put the knife down, you smash up my face again."

Devereaux recognized him then. He almost smiled. "Put the knife down, kid. I won't hurt you."

Peewee believed him then, though he could not explain why. He put the knife down carefully on the carpet and then stood up.

"You work the hotel?" Devereaux said.

"No, man. This was a scam, him and me, my buddy Kools—"

Devereaux turned at the name and looked at Kools as though he knew who he was.

"Shut up, Peewee," Kools said.

"We were robbing rooms," Peewee said because he trusted this guy with gray eyes now, he trusted him to see the way it was.

Mai-Lin said, "I got to get out of here."

Denisov had a smaller pistol. He stared at her and she did not move off the bed.

"Kools," Devereaux said.

"I ain't done nothing," he said.

"You know this man," Devereaux said.

Everything was said very softly, almost as prayers.

"I know him, I maybe seen him around."

"You worked for him," Devereaux said.

Very softly still, the words turning over like clumps of spring earth full of worms.

"You know about this, I want to see my attorney."

"Take her out of here, Peewee," Devereaux said. "You didn't see anything and she didn't see anything."

Peewee nodded then. He went over and picked up Mai-Lin's silky little dress, pretty thing that he had imagined her without sometimes. He gave it to her and she looked up at him and didn't say anything. She carried the dress with naked dignity to the bathroom and put it on. She came back and paused a moment to pick up the $400 in hundreds on the bed.

Peewee said, "I take you home, Mai-Lin."

She stared at his broken, punk's face. "OK," she said.

"You be all right," Peewee said, trying to make his voice bigger for her. His eyes were shining and she started to smile at him the way she smiled at the boys in the fish market but she stopped. She took his hand instead and let him lead her out of the suite.

"Very nice," Henry McGee said as they walked out of the room. "I like that story. I like love stories. That boy is in love with her, ain't he? I like the sentimental touch. You got a sentimental side?"

"On the floor, flat, spread them," Devereaux said.

Kools and Henry McGee got down. The carpet was soft against Kools' cheek. He couldn't figure this one out, not like the other time in Fairbanks.

And then he was being picked up by the hair and it hurt. He struggled to his knees between Henry McGee on the floor and the gray-eyed man with the gun and the look of death on his drawn face.

"He killed Narvak."

Kools went very cold. He looked at Devereaux to see the truth in the wolf eyes.

"Put two shots in her, just the way she killed Otis Dobbins. She was in the trunk of a rental Dodge at Anchorage International."

Kools thought about the little girl. She was his sister and he remembered her as a collection of faces seen at various ages and the smell of her as they slept beneath the furs. Why did Henry have to kill her when she never did nothing to him?

Kools blinked and felt a tear. He never cried, not for himself, not for anyone or anything. It was just thinking of Narvak dead. It wasn't fair for Henry to kill her. She wasn't even seventeen.

"You knew all about his plans," Devereaux said to Kools.

"Sure. Not as much as him. But I was in on it. Went to Siberia three times."

"Good," Devereaux said. "As long as you understand—you talk to us, it's all right."

"Shut the fuck up," said Henry McGee. "This guy don't know nothing, you just shut up, he ain't gonna do you any favors."

"You killed her," Kools said. "Motherfucker."

"Shut the fuck up," Henry said.

FORTY-ONE

The Next Story

Henry McGee told them everything in excruciating detail. He sat at a table with the tape recorder running and started from the beginning. The only thing he denied was having any part in the murders of an oil pipeline security worker and a terrorist code-named Noah. And, of course, he knew nothing about the murder of the agent from Dutch Harbor in the parking lot of the Arctic Circle Lounge in Anchorage.

Across from Seattle International is a boulevard full of motels. They were in two rooms of one of the motels. Kools was eating and waiting, the handcuffs very tight now and no question of breaking out of them. The cuffs were around his ankles, which made it easier to eat but hard to run.

Henry McGee only held back on one thing—penetration of the Witness Protection Program. But it was the part Devereaux really needed.

Devereaux insisted. In the eerie bedtable-size light of the hotel room, Devereaux's face was just as wintry as it had been by the gray Bering Sea light in Nome. Henry McGee said, for the third time, that he was not a killer.

"You got that boy confused in there, Devereaux. I just tell my stories. The girl was alive; maybe he killed her."

"He didn't kill his sister," Devereaux said.

"He fucked her. He might have. Incest they call it."

"Don't dance me—"

Up until now, it had been easy enough, but for some reason, Henry had now decided to play. It was still an urgent matter. Section was the prize and it was being destroyed hour by hour in Washington.

In one part of the methodology developed over fifty years of intelligence interrogation, there is the school that says all interrogation must be nonadversarial, no coercing of answers through infliction of pain. This school argues that all information gained from hostile sources is suspect, and that information gained from hostile sources through infliction of pain is even more suspect because the hostile source will lie with a real, immediate purpose—to stop the pain.

The principle is ignored at times in war zones, in cases where inept interrogators let themselves go, in cases where time is a factor.

Devereaux thought time was a factor.

He explained this to Henry McGee.

"I see," Henry said. He sat and thought about it a moment. "I can take pain for a while."

Devereaux shook his head and hit Henry McGee in the face. He broke his nose and one of the perfect teeth in his mouth. Henry's mouth was filled with blood and his nose bled and he went over backward onto the soft blue carpet of the motel room. The television set was on and there was a rerun of an old "Baa Baa Black Sheep" program.

Devereaux picked Henry up by the hair. Henry's hands were cuffed in front of him and he tried to raise his arms. Devereaux slapped him on the right ear with an open palm and then on the left ear. Then he hit Henry again in the mouth. Then he began to slap him, left and right, across the face. When he thought Henry really felt the pain, he put him down in the chair again. The tape recorder had been running. Devereaux backed it up to the place where he considered the various theories of interrogation.

The blood dried on Henry's shirt.

Devereaux asked a question.

Henry said, "We didn't make the discovery of a weak link in the program. A certain figure in organized crime in San Francisco put a certain guy in Witness on the wire. The guy in the witness program was vulnerable, the usual shit, I don't remember if it was gambling or women. So this crime guy offered a trade-out through our consulate in San Francisco. Nobody knew what to do with it. It was rattling around inside the committee for six months. Russians just got no imagination when it comes to positive counter, you know that."

Devereaux said nothing.

"We gave the guy dope. Best stuff. Cocaine. Lots of it. I got my plan approved."

"What was the plan?"

"I know you know now. You want a name? Heartland. We called it Heartland. First I got to get Denisov on the move, off the dime, and I get two names from the people in San Francisco. Alexa and Denisov, complete with code names, addresses. We knocked over Denisov's apartment three months ago, came across a book that had the code in which you and him corresponded and he was William Schwenck and you were Armistice Day." Henry grinned with a broken, bleeding mouth. "That's cute. I liked that code, you could make a story with a code like that."

"And why Alexa?"

"To scare Denisov. She wasn't important. The important thing was to get Denisov to do what we wanted him to do. That would tie him in with you and the whole thing would be so much more plausible. Alexa didn't matter."

"Women aren't very important to you, Henry."

"Can't live with them, can't live without them."

"You killed Narvak."

"Look. I am helping you some because I want to stay in one piece until I can talk to someone in reasonable power so they can start making a trade with Moscow."

"What have you got that we want?"

"We've always got someone. If we don't have someone, we'll snatch someone, like that professor that time doing his two-week holiday in Red Square."

"Who is the mob figure in San Francisco?"

"I never met him."

"Who is he?"

"I never met him," Henry said.

Devereaux hit him on the ears with open palms. The blows were hard and they started the ringing again in his ears.

"You could make me deaf."

"We'll get you a hearing aid."

"The contact is Pell. Rudy Pell. He works for someone called Mr. Anthony, whoever the fuck Mr. Anthony is, if that's more than a name. And the guy in the office is Wagner."

"Keep talking."

"We spring Denisov and he links up with you while you're on my trail in Alaska. And then, at the same time, we're winding up ULU. The windup is an atomic device."

"Would you have blown up the line?"

"Sure," Henry McGee said. He smiled. "You know you can't bluff in this business, you either do a thing or they call you on it. It would have worked either way. It was best working through Malcolm Chowderhead and the cunt senator. Not blowing up the pipeline. Story fits more logically like that. But if it had to be the other way, it would have worked too. We do our homework, that's one thing Russian intelligence is about. We knew about Patricia Heath, knew her right down to the size of her panties. And everyone knew about Malcolm Chowderhead."

"She knows."

"She knows some. She was going to do it for a half million at first. Now we pinned all that on Chowderhead so she's out a half million but she's getting ten million dollars worth of publicity and power. She might really make it as the next woman president, you know. All she has to do is keep tearing R Section apart, looking for the mole who set off the agent to become a terrorist, who defected to the Soviet Union with another well-known former Soviet agent named Denisov. You see how each part fits nice against the other part? Like a piece of carpentry, piece of cabinetmaking. They don't teach much about cabinetmaking anymore. Not in wood, not in intelligence. Everything is so damned sloppy."

Devereaux stared at him for a long time.

"I would be baited into going to Alaska because I was assigned to find Henry McGee," Devereaux said. "And it would all be very logical, the crooked intelligence agent and the defector named Denisov, who was really a double agent.''

Henry smiled again.

Then he spoke: ''Who was the mole, then? The one who let me run free as a terrorist? Who helped me penetrate the witness program and spring Denisov to the Soviet Union? Who blackmailed the pipeline?''

Henry McGee smiled at that. ''Who runs counterintelligence?'' he asked. ''Who is the director of Operations?''

Hanley.

The trap was set not only to tear apart the counterintelligence life of R Section but the head of Operations. Let Congress start rooting for a mole that did not exist and it would not be stopped until everything was in shreds and R Section had no secrets left for anyone.

The thing had worked for a while in the Marine Corps when a nest of ''traitors'' was found in the U.S. Marine Corps staff at the American embassy in Moscow. Except it turned out there was only a single traitor and he had given away few secrets. One marine had cast suspicion on the whole corps and embassies from Moscow to Mexico City had worked for more than a year under expensive, clumsy alert that their security staffs might be traitors. It could be done just that easily in a paranoid world and Devereaux knew it. Henry McGee would have finally planted some evidence with Patricia Heath to show her that the mole inside Section was the director of Operations. It was all a lie but it was buttressed by so much truth that the bigger lie would be believed.

''Can I make you one last offer?''

Devereaux blinked. Then he refocused on the man in chains at the table beside him.

"I can go up to three million dollars. Just give me twelve hours. You almost didn't catch me the way it was."

"Where will you get the money?"

"Delivered here in two hours."

"Is it that easy?"

Henry smiled. "Money is always the easy part. The guys who don't have it think it's hard but that makes it easier on the guys who do."

"But, Henry, I need you."

"You got the tapes—"

"What did I do? Turn my head and you knocked me out? Did I let you use the bathroom and you escaped through the transom? Do they still have transoms in bathrooms?"

"You could become head of Operations yourself, you could work it such a way that the mole, Hanley, was trying to frame you and—"

"You have good stories, Henry. Hanley isn't a mole. You make everyone want to follow your trail."

"Three million—"

"Watch television for a while, Henry, I have to make some telephone calls."

"I'm disappointed in you," Henry McGee said.

Devereaux stared at him. "Not disappointed, Henry. Surprised by the ending. Because you didn't write it."

FORTY-TWO

The Trade-offs

Waverly from FBI and Hanley from R Section and Captain T. C. Neal from the Office of Naval Intelligence shared a table in a glass room inside R Section. The room was a totally clear glass chamber with a clear table and clear bench seats located in a conventionally soundproofed room. The clear room, as it was called, was used for the most secret conversations and proved to the three occupants that each of them could be certain of speaking without being picked up by an enemy electronic receiver because the glass produced almost no vibrations from their voices.

Captain Neal said the submarine was Soviet T-class and was outfitted with the new Japanese turbines. Once the navy cruiser had adjusted the radio sonar beams to the new and subtle sounds, it could follow it easily. The chance encounter with the submarine off the Seward Peninsula was a coup for the navy. And yes, in the most secret of reports, the navy would acknowledge the work in the matter by R Section.

The trade-offs with the FBI went nearly as smoothly.

Waverly said, "Special agents in San Francisco arrested Robert Wilson Wagner and, with the cooperation of Mr. Wagner and the work done by Karen Elizabeth O'Hare in the office of the Witness Relocation Program, we have managed to penetrate into the organization of Alberto Spiloggi Antonius, alias Mr. Anthony, a major supplier of narcotics in the northern California area. We have made a number of arrests, including Mr. Wagner's contact, Rudolph Edward Pell."

Hanley closed his eyes for a moment. It was always like this dealing with any level of the FBI above the rank of field agent. They all still talked like J. Edgar Hoover and they always insisted on using middle names, even in quiet conversations. They sounded like public relations announcements.

"And the murders," Hanley prodded in a quiet voice.

"Yes," Waverly said. "We accept your work there."

It was a relief. The murders were very important because that was the province of the FBI and that was the deal with Devereaux. Denisov would get off for the murder of Pierce. It was the only way to keep the whole matter secret, including the capture of Henry McGee. Henry McGee could still cut either way with Section because he had been a Soviet agent inside Section for a decade before he went back across. How could he be revealed to Congress, to the FBI, without tearing Section apart?

Hanley said, "Then you're satisfied."

"You had information on a pipeline conspiracy of terror

for nearly a year without revealing it to the proper authority. In this case, us," Waverly said in that ball-bearing voice. He wore a dark suit and a blue television shirt and a rep tie.

"And you didn't have the information," Hanley said. "The matter cuts both ways. You accuse us and you accuse yourself. Accept the deal: We were working together on the matter and the terrorists killed Pierce in Anchorage, a crime you have solved. We were sister agencies, cooperating with each other."

Waverly looked at the navy captain and looked at Hanley. "All right," he said.

"Now the matter of Henry McGee."

"The matter of Henry McGee," Waverly said.

"A spy in the United States," Hanley said.

"A Soviet agent. Exactly like Karpov."

"Dropped by a Soviet submarine on the Seward Peninsula," agreed Captain Neal.

"Detected by the American navy," agreed Hanley.

"A spy ring broken up with valuable overseas help from R Section and the combined special forces of R Section and the FBI cooperating in the United States," Waverly concluded in his long-winded way.

The three of them stared at each other. No one wavered. The story was good and it held water. It was the kind of story that is better than the real thing sometimes. Especially when agencies want to get out of something.

"Is everything buttoned up then?" Waverly said.

"I think so," Hanley said.

"The Office of Naval Intelligence is satisfied, especially with the results. We knew they'd been testing that goddamn sub but we couldn't get a handle on the frequency of the turbines. It was going to take us another eighteen months.''

"Then we're agreed," Hanley said.

The three men stared at each other for a moment.

"Agreed," they all said, almost with one voice.

FORTY-THREE

Making Her Understand

There were no secrets in the middle of the Alaskan spring night. The sun shone down on the eternal glaciers in the panhandle and on the white mountains across the Brooks Range that led down slowly to the North Slope, where all the oil was buried beneath the Arctic Sea.

The sun slowly moved around the top of the world in the position of three o'clock in the sky. The world was bathed in eternal afternoon. The clouds and winds conspired across the top of the Soviet Union, across Alaska and the Northwest Territories and Labrador in the east of Canada, across the little bit of water to the top of frozen Greenland and the top of Scandinavia, where Norway and Sweden and Finland and the Soviet Union meet again.

The tourists were in Alaska now, picking through the souvenirs shops on Fourth Avenue in Anchorage or watching the islands from the blue Marine Highway ferries from Seattle to Haines. The tourists flew into the bush by private

carriers from Merrill Field or went by trains up to Fairbanks
from the First Avenue station. They climbed the mountains
in the Chugach; they rode on the rickety old buses down
gravel trails through Denali, past the grizzlies and caribou
grazing, until they could see the slouched shoulders of
Mount McKinley, glittering with snow.

The country was too large and it was full of illusions
that were incomprehensible and the tourists came in this
season to find something. They saw the bush, they saw
the valley full of smoking springs, they saw mountains
and fierce seas like the ones off Kodiak Island. It was too
much to understand, what this country was. It was the
savage place left in the heart and because it was so savage,
the people who came to Alaska in this season thought they
saw it as pure and good, as they imagined they had once
been or could be again.

The man came in the morning when the house was silent
and when the sun was already full of strength on the glittering shallow waters of Turnagain Arm. The hillsides
were full of green firs and the thin roads full of campers
going to some new place.

She opened the door for him because she expected
him.

He was an anonymous man in a light, soiled coat with
the pasty look of the traveler.

"I don't really understand this," Senator Heath said in
her not-to-be-trifled-with voice.

Devereaux said nothing.

"We can sit here," she indicated the living room of the
pretty house.

He went into the kitchen instead and sat down at the
kitchen bar. The bar top was made of a single piece of

walnut. Patricia Heath was dressed in slacks and a light cotton sweater and she frowned because he had chosen the place.

She sat down.

He told her the truth, from the beginning. He told her where the truth came from. He told her the proofs of the truth that were in R Section. He told her about Henry McGee and the native called Kools and about the pipeline deal approved by a man in Chicago named Clay Ashley, who had paid blackmail and had ordered the death of two saboteurs.

"Who are you?" she said at one point.

"The agent terrorist," he said. "The agent who supposedly went to Russia. By the way, Mr. Denisov is in Santa Barbara. A woman named Alexa is in Los Angeles. There was no porn ring, no terrorism by an agent of the government."

"You'll have to prove it," she said, just beginning to be afraid.

He stared at her.

"The plot was by a Soviet agent named Henry McGee directed against an intelligence department of the government," he began again. "And you were an unwitting part of it."

"You can't prove it."

"We can prove it. Believe that if you are going to believe in anything."

"What about Crowder?"

"We have to leave that part of the story alone. Someone has to swing for being a bad boy. We are just not interested in going after a bad girl. That's you, Senator. You were a bad girl."

She thought about it.

If she could get away with it, scot free, why go on? They had things on people, these intelligence agencies. "But he told me he was CIA," she said. "The man who came to see me."

"I'm Santa Claus," Devereaux said. "Do you want to see my sleigh?"

"He wasn't," she said, putting on a dull voice and a blank face. "CIA, I mean. It's very confusing."

"He wasn't."

"Where is he?"

"In federal custody. He was arraigned this morning."

"What do you want?"

"Drop it," Devereaux said.

"All of it? How can I do it?"

"Convene a closed-door session of your committee. A man named Hanley will testify."

"Will you testify?"

"I don't exist," Devereaux said.

"You . . ." She didn't know what to say.

"I'm a story invented by Henry McGee. It was part of the conspiracy against the United States and against R Section. He used you to advance disinformation."

"You do exist," she said.

"I'm an illusion," Devereaux said.

"I can't go along with this."

"Do what you want, then. That was the easy approach. The hard approach will be much harder."

"Are you threatening me?"

"You'll be in jail in eighteen months. What Henry knew, we know now. About you, about Malcolm Crowder. About the half-million payout. You can get out of part of it, but not all of it."

"Why give me any break at all," she said.

Devereaux paused. It was the hardest thing to say and the words stuck in his throat for a moment. It had not been his decision. That had been decided in one of those quiet rooms in Washington.

"Because it's for the good of Section," he said.

FORTY-FOUR

The Reluctance of November

"Is it safe now?" Mrs. Neumann asked Hanley.

They sat in the quietest room of all, the secret room in R Section. It was raining in Washington. On the Fourteenth Street Bridge, two cars had decided to run into each other and the traffic was backed up on both sides of the Potomac River for miles. The cursing of horns in the streets was just a low squeak in the room.

Hanley was pleased with himself. He made another tent of his fingers and did not speak for a moment. "It is reasonably safe. The National Security director is not displeased with events. I even think there will be congratulations for Section for a job well done in apprehending two agents from the Opposition."

"Then it's safe enough," she said.

"Safe enough."

There was another long silence in the room. Morning was somber against the windows of the room. Mrs. Neumann thought well of Hanley in the light of morning; he had advised the right thing at the right time, he had taken the right action. The expected bureaucrat, of course, had taken the credit for the various operations that resulted in the arrest of Henry McGee in a Seattle hotel room.

As he had told Devereaux in private: "My neck was on the line if you had failed."

Devereaux replied, "You're very brave, Hanley. I admire you."

Sarcasm, Hanley had thought, but said nothing.

"There is another matter," Hanley began, opening the tent to find the palms of his hands.

"In connection with this?"

"Yes. It's November."

"What about November?" The raspy voice dropped a note to a whisper. Mrs. Neumann admired the agent. Hanley knew this. Hanley decided to risk a few points of credit in the light of the general good feeling in Section at not being torn apart after all.

"He sat in on some initial interrogation of McGee—"

"You mean in Alaska the first time fifteen years ago or now in Maryland?"

The point stung Hanley. He opened his eyes wide and gazed at Mrs. Neumann as if a dragon had entered the room.

"I mean now. The problem is in his reports. I really am disappointed in them."

"How are you disappointed?"

"We have some very good people at the complex in Maryland."

There was a place in the panhandle of western Maryland, in those rugged Appalachian hills and quiet, fog-shrouded valleys thick with trees. It contained a half-dozen buildings of Korean War vintage—two-story, frame, with wooden firestairs—where defectors and sudden witnesses and captured spies were taken for debriefing. The days were long and the nights were quiet in this place. It was removed from the world, the only access a guarded dirt road that ran up a steep hillside. The "good people" were the questioners, the seekers of truth in the answers of the defectors.

"I would suppose so." Mrs. Neumann had learned faint sarcasm as part of her elevation to chief of Section.

"Devereaux has been a nay-sayer. He's going against the grain in the questioning of Henry McGee. Frankly, I think it may be something personal between them, something that happened in Alaska. Devereaux can have a . . . visceral reaction at times," Hanley said.

"The word is well chosen," Mrs. Neumann said in a whisper. "What are you getting at?"

"Henry McGee is a realistic man. He has one hope—cooperate with us for light treatment and wait until he is traded out to the Soviets for someone we want."

"So he cooperates."

"He cooperates. It is wonderful stuff, Mrs. N. The matter of the agent in Berlin is all confirmed. He knows things we still didn't know. He has a wonderful rundown on the bureaucracy inside the Committee for External Observation and Resolution inside the KGB. More updated than the stuff we got seven years ago from Denisov. There is a lot more. Matters we should investigate, particularly in our Pacific desk. He has some pretty damning proofs that our man in Dutch Harbor might not have been all he seemed."

Pierce, the man in Dutch Harbor, had been given a quiet funeral in Arlington National Cemetery. The president had authorized the Distinguished Service Medal to be awarded posthumously. Everything had been done, in records and memory, to enshrine Pierce as a hero of Section who fell in the line of duty.

"What is November in this?"

"Against the grain," Hanley said. He began a frown. Some of the secretaries inside Section thought Mr. Hanley had the cutest frown they had ever seen.

"In what way?"

"He says Henry McGee should not be believed. Not in anything. He says it is all part of the same continuing story. I think November has become paranoid on the subject; I think we should 'retire' him again, give him a rest, let him think about other things. Spend time with his 'woman.' "

"He says this totally?"

"Totally. He says the other questioners are letting the stories get in the way of what the purpose of the stories is. I don't understand that at all. He said 'the facts are getting in the way of the truth.' That's a quote. That doesn't make any sense at all. I think he's positively . . . demented on the subject of Henry McGee."

"He was close to the subject."

"Henry McGee is a gold mine. He helped us shut down Patricia Heath and that Senate investigation. He gave us the traitor in the witness program in San Francisco. He has, in a real sense, helped us cement a better relationship with our sister agency on Pennsylvania Avenue."

"Why not just say 'the FBI'?"

Hanley flushed. He had the jargon all down; it made him part of the great game. He spoke of the "Opposition" and "Competition," the "Langley firm" and the "people at Meade," and it was to make certain to everyone that he was a man who kept secrets.

"The point, Mrs. Neumann, is that November is no good right now, not in connection with Henry McGee. Henry McGee can help us go through our cases, find out where we have made a mistake or miscalculation. The information is valuable."

"Why not take November's viewpoint? Perhaps it is disinformation."

"But it's true. Disinformation cannot be true, that's the point of it."

"Truth is a matter of perspective," she said. She said it in her usual rumble but there was a gentleness to the words. "Perhaps he has the necessary perspective."

"He is obstreperous," Hanley said. "He is an agent, Mrs. Neumann, not a trained professional interrogator. They are different jobs, requiring different skills."

"He has interrogated people," she said. She liked November.

"Mrs. Neumann. I think you owe my judgment some consideration at this point. I know about debriefings. November knows about field operations. I think it would be best to let him take a few weeks of leave."

It was her decision and she felt uncomfortable with it. The problem was that Hanley was not always wrong and November was not always right. She recognized in November the resistance to believe anything told him by any "defector" or "enemy agent." Words were the stuff of lies to November. Words inclined to lie; the truth was usually silent.

She made a slight nod of her head before she agreed to everything Hanley wanted.

"There are no absolute successes or failures," Hanley said.

They were in his bare office three hours later. Devereaux had only been there six times in all his years in Section.

"You're pompous again. It must be going your way, whatever it is."

"It is not a matter of things 'going my way.' It is a matter of perspective. I think you have lost your perspective for whatever personal reasons in the matter you're now involved in."

Devereaux stared at him with contempt. The intelligence agent must be reminded, again and again, that however much he knows of the real world, he must still explain it in dumb-down terms to the clerks back in Washington. Devereaux was tired of explaining things to Hanley because every word was too well chosen: He could not let his words lie for him, even to his advantage.

"You're silent. I think you might agree with me." Hanley tried a little smile.

Devereaux still did not speak.

"Henry McGee is valuable to us in terms of his information."

"Henry McGee is death," Devereaux said. "He has no beginning or end. His truths are constructed of facts and lies. You choose to believe him and you're wrong."

"There are six interrogators—"

"He contradicts Kools over and over—"

"Why do you believe Kools?"

"Because Kools is a loser. Kools cannot help but tell the truth. The only good liars are winners. The losers will begin by telling you what they think you want to hear, and if you're patient, they'll end up turning themselves inside out."

"Henry McGee implicated Pierce in—"

"In what? If you go through the transcript of the debriefings, you won't find a thing."

"There is a lot of truth in what he says," Hanley said.

"Fool me once, shame on you," Devereaux said.

Hanley understood and his eyes became as angry as they ever were. "You're off this, Devereaux. That's what I wanted to tell you. Face to face. You're impeding our progress with McGee, demoralizing some of the others."

Devereaux had known from the moment Hanley called him.

"When Henry McGee played his . . . games fifteen years ago, we were a disorganized bunch. Computer Analysis was in its infancy. The world has changed, Devereaux, and you have not changed with it."

"It's not flat anymore?"

"No. It's not flat anymore. It's got satellites monitoring every square foot of the globe. In ten years or less, we'll train those satellites to look inside houses, not just outside."

"And when will you train them to look into souls?" Devereaux said.

"Have you become a theologian in your middle age besides a paranoid?"

"You need to have more than facts."

"There is nothing more than facts. A thing is or it isn't."

"Henry McGee doesn't believe that."

"He's an extraordinary catch. I don't stint my praise in your capture of McGee and Karpov and this other fellow, the Indian."

"Yup'ik Eskimo," Devereaux said.

"Whatever. You did a good job in a tight spot."

"Don't do this thing," Devereaux said. He never asked, never pleaded.

"It's out of my hands," Hanley said. Meaning, of course, that he had already decided what to do.

"He'll poison you and Section with his stories, and when he's done, you'll trade him to the other side for one of ours," Devereaux said.

"It's out of my hands," he said again.

"Nothing is redeemed, nothing is verified," Devereaux said.

"We know what we're doing," Hanley said.

She had moved out of the town house on Rhode Island Avenue after she was told by David Mason that he was safe and coming back to Washington. That was three weeks ago.

She had left him a letter.

She tried to make the letter very short and to explain to him about the quality of pain and about how she could not be hurt anymore. To explain that every time he went away in the blackness of his trade, she lost him as surely as if he had died. To explain that one cannot bear up under so many little deaths.

She did not speak of love because she loved him; but that was a little pain that would go away after a while. She would find a man when she needed one and she would think about her life—her life—and not his life.

He read the letter the day he returned. The letter was on the little table in the hall of the town house where they always left the mail.

He visited the boy, Philippe, who was living on campus. Philippe knew about Rita, but they did not speak of her.

Devereaux was "put to sleep" again in service and his days were empty.

He did as he had done long ago when he lived alone in a house in the mountains near Front Royal. He worked at small tasks in the house and he read. He went to the bookstore nearly every day and bought more books. He read old books he had on the shelves in the house. He read and the words put him into a different world; the words soaked into him like the vodka he drank, until his self was obliterated by the words and alcohol.

She came to see him after three weeks, when she was certain the pain was bearable.

He took her into the kitchen and they sat down. He offered her a drink.

"What about the house? Do you want it?" she said.

"No."

"Then we should sell it."

"All right," he said.

"Will you do it or should I?"

"It doesn't matter."

"Goddamn it, are you going to mope around here?"

"No," he said.

"What are you going to do?"

"I've been thinking about that."

"Well?"

"It doesn't do any good to tell you."

"You told me nothing. You never told me a thing."

"I couldn't tell you," he said. "About anything."

"You never said you loved me."

Devereaux stared at her then because she knew that was not fair, that he would never speak of something that was so utterly true in him that words defiled it.

"Why did you go back? You love it, you love the trade."

"I hate it," he said.

"You're very good, you must have saved R Section or something—"

"They put me to sleep again."

"Great. Until next time they need you and then you will pack your bag and your gun and go play spy for them."

"I broke a few rules along the way. They don't like it but they tolerate it. They say I owe them a life and I can't argue about it. I told you that once. I tried to get away once. It doesn't work out, Rita. On the other hand, what else could I do?"

"What if I wanted to have children?"

He stared at her face, at the green eyes. "Do you want to have children?"

"Not by you. Not by someone like you."

"What do you want?"

"I just wanted to know about the house."

"All right," he said. "It's your house." He got up and went to the hall closet and opened it. There was a large suitcase and a smaller one. "I was waiting for you," he said.

"You ended it," she said.

"No."

"Damn you, I'm not throwing you out—"

"I have a place. I was moving stuff there. It's all right, Rita." He said it like that, as though he wanted her to understand and not be hurt. He saw that she loved him and that it hurt her. He had thought about her every night and every day since coming back to Washington. He had to let her leave or he would just destroy her; he saw that.

"Dev," she began.

"No," he said. She touched his arm. "The keys are on the table," he said. "All of them."

"I'll never see you again," she suddenly said.

He stared at her. He nearly felt too weak to leave her. He could touch her in the way they touched each other in the secret pool and she would be his again, at least for a little time. And then they would do this again, they would have to hurt each other again. There had to be an end to it and he saw it, saw it in the pain of the letter she had written to him and left on the hallway table.

"Devereaux," she said, exactly as she had always said it.

But now the door was closing behind him and he was on the steps, on the street. She ran to the window and looked at him as he walked down the street with the large suitcase and the hated smaller bag that he packed when he was going out of her life for a while. Except now he wasn't coming back.

FORTY-FIVE

Escape

The message came in the usual way and Henry McGee could not believe it at first.

It appeared in the "personal" columns of the *Washington Post*. As always, it was easy to recognize: an ad, in English, babbling about the true love of a "Henry" for his "Wanda." The Soviet embassy knew the code and—it was thought on that May morning—no one else did.

Henry McGee took the first letter of each word in the advertisement, put them on paper, and then reassembled them, trying to spell out the message in Russian. He had time to do this because it was Saturday afternoon in the compound in western Maryland and no one was working except the security guards. The government of the United States kept decent hours.

"Gate C, four hundred on Sunday."

The message had to be directed to him.

One of the contingencies was always escape. It was more easily done in the United States than in totalitarian states like the Soviet Union or Iran, but it was done, in any case, more often than believed. The governments of the world do not like the world to believe in escape.

He had not expected it. He had expected to be subject to a trade in a year or two. But escape is always possible and there it was, in the *Washington Post*'s Saturday edition. The "guests" of the compound were always permitted all the reading material available, as a way to acclimatize them to life in the United States. Even the reluctant guests like Henry McGee.

All afternoon, in the compound yard, he studied the electrified fence and Gate C, which led to the main dirt road down the mountain and to the highway. The message did not explain how the escape would be made. Perhaps it was up to him; perhaps they would fight their way in for him. But that seemed unlikely. The best escapes were the quietest.

Henry McGee felt restless all day and could not wait for the short spring night to begin.

He awoke at 3:45 A.M. to the beeping alarm on his watch. He silenced it and got out of bed cautiously. There was a night light, just enough to make the room visible for the television monitor on one wall.

The rooms in the barracks were crudely made with plywood. The toilets and showers were in a separate room at the front of the barracks, exactly the same arrangement of such buildings from the beginning of World War II until the early 1960s.

Henry went down the corridor to the permanently lit toilets. The monitors watched him; he wondered if anyone was watching the monitors at this ungodly hour.

He took a pee and washed his hands and face. His face was very light now but the eyes were still black and they still glittered with amusement when he told stories. He told stories all day long; they loved his stories because they seemed so true.

He had known Devereaux did not believe him.

It didn't matter. One day, Devereaux was not there. One of the interrogators he was friendly with had indicated that Devereaux would not be coming back. That made him smile. Devereaux was thrown out of the church because he did not believe Henry McGee.

He went back into his room and wondered what his rescuers would do about the TV monitors.

At 4:00 A.M. Sunday, the power surged and failed.

This happened at times in the uncertain scenery of the mountains. There were small, weak backup generators that clicked on then and provided illumination. But the television monitors were on the main circuit, not the backup circuit, and could not be activated until the power returned, usually a matter of a few minutes.

Henry put on his clothes and walked softly down the creaking hallway to the front door of Barracks 2.

The grounds were dimly lit. Henry moved along the shadow of Barracks 2 until he reached the electrified gate. He wondered if the gate was still electrified.

He moved along the ground until he came to Gate C. Inside, the guard was visible in the light. The place was not so heavily guarded because it was not intended as a prison and because the wild mountains all around were not easy places for one to escape to.

What was he supposed to do? He approached the guard shack and looked in.

The guard had been drugged. His eyes were closed and he was snoring, and when Henry smelled his breath, he caught the chemical odor. Henry took the key from the chain on his belt and turned off the gate. He went to the gate and pushed it open. The gate made a screeching sound of metal against metal. He closed the gate.

Henry crossed to the road and began to trot along the road down the mountain.

He moved easily, his body still trim, his legs and wind strong. He moved as quickly as he felt he could go. His eyes adjusted to the semidarkness of the predawn morning. The woods smelled of fog and damp. He heard animals move in the thickets along the road.

He rounded the second curve and saw the taillights of the waiting car. He ran to the car and opened the door and started in. The interior light was off. He climbed inside.

He felt the pistol against his head.

"Put your hands on the dash."

He put his hands on the dash.

The cuffs fell on his wrists and were locked. The bracelets were very tight.

"Too tight," he said.

"Shut up."

He turned to make sure.

"Why are you doing this?"

"Shut up," Devereaux said again.

The cabin was in the hills outside Hancock, Maryland. The mountains were lush beneath the wet Maryland sun and the valleys were full of the familiar rolling fog that burns off by afternoon.

"What are you going to do?" Henry McGee said.

"Ask you to tell me the truth."

"About what?"

"About you."

"My name is Henry McGee."

Devereaux hit him hard with the billy club on the right arm. He did not break the arm.

"This is stupid, this is crude," Henry said. "You are insulting."

"Tell me the truth."

"You know what your own people believe, you can't get the truth by beating it out of someone."

"Perhaps they're wrong." He hit him again. "The point is, you'll say anything to have me stop this and maybe I'll be able to figure out what is true."

"What do you think is true?"

"You are a lie, from beginning to end. Your true stories are lies with just a few touches of fact."

Henry smiled.

Devereaux hurt him to make the smiling stop. When Henry was in tears because of the pain, Devereaux stopped hitting him. He hit Henry without passion, almost without malice, the way a surgeon causes pain for the good of a patient.

"Yes, it's a lie," Henry said. "Everything is a lie."

"I don't believe you. You have to tell me more than that."

"I just told you what you wanted to hear."

"But it's less than I wanted to hear."

"It's all I can tell you; it's all I have."

"About Pierce."

"That was true."

He hit him.

"That was not true. I made it up. It's a lie."

"How do you make it up?"

"You tell them some of the truth. I can remember everything. I can remember every story, every fact. You use the parts you want. To make the stories."

Devereaux hit him again.

Henry was bleeding but it wasn't serious, just messy. His mouth hurt but his jaw was not broken. Devereaux thought it was important for them to taste their own blood. Devereaux had hurt people like this but always the losers and the dumb ones, the ones who had just one or two facts to tell, not the minds like Henry McGee who would resist until death.

He talked to Henry all morning and into the lush, warm afternoon. Thunderclouds rolled in high from Ohio and when it began to rain, a cooling wind came from the north and west. The rain made everything greener.

"You're gonna kill me," Henry said.

"Yes," Devereaux said. "Maybe I got all I came for and it's time to kill you."

"Jesus Christ," Henry McGee said in Russian.

"Yes," Devereaux said. "Time for tears and prayers. Section never believed you, Henry, they just wanted to see how far the stories would lead. They were interested in the technique."

"The technique?"

"The way to tell the stories to make them believable. You fooled Section once but you know you didn't fool them twice."

"Then why arrange this escape?"

"It's the way things are done. The guard was drugged, the power shut down. No one has to know how you got out, merely that you did. You got out and you were killed as you made your escape. Moscow will not believe this at first but they monitor us the way we monitor them. Believe me, it will be believed and the last of Henry McGee and his stories will be accepted. It's the way we can sanction people, Henry, without sanctioning them, if you see what I mean.''

"You're crazy," Henry said.

Devereaux took the shotgun down from the wall. "Go ahead and pray, Henry. We're a civilized people."

"You won't kill me," Henry said.

Devereaux opened the shotgun, inserted the shells, closed it. He brought it up.

"Look, I want to tell you—"

"But I'm done listening."

"I can tell you the truth."

"You couldn't tell the truth if you were dying. Which is what you are."

Devereaux shot him with both barrels.

Blood splattered Henry's face, his chest, his arms. He was a mass of blood. The force of the blast threw him against the wall. He was completely covered in blood and pain from the force of the blast.

Henry was still alive.

"My God, my God," he said in Russian. "My God," he said in English. "You killed me."

"Yes," Devereaux said.

"I'm dying," Henry McGee said. "Help me. Help me, Devereaux, for the love of God."

"Not love or money."

"You were right, you were right, if I got caught, this was the last backup, I was supposed to give them a couple of stories that were true and give you a lot of things that weren't true about the Committee for External Observation and Resolution, none of that is true, and the stuff about Pierce wasn't true and . . . my God! Get me someone to help me! I can't die like this, I can't die just like this!"

"You were lying when you went after Hanley, to plant a story with that senator that he was a mole."

"Yes, yes, Jesus, yes."

Devereaux smiled at him.

Henry felt this enormous pain and there was warm blood on his arms and chest, his own blood.

"You killed me! I don't want to die! I fooled them all except you! You killed me! I need your help now."

"You're beyond help, Henry. You're dying and you're lying."

"Am I dying then?"

"You're really dying."

Henry McGee groaned. "Why did you have to be so goddamn stubborn? Why do you think it was important to have everything exactly right?"

"Not exactly, Henry. I just wanted the truth."

"So now you got the truth and you can't do anything with it because you still won't believe it." And Henry groaned again.

"I believe it, Henry."

"Jesus, Jesus."

"Remember Narvak?"

Henry closed his eyes and felt the death in him. He said the name of his Savior again.

"Remember when you killed her?"

"Jesus," Henry McGee said and made the sign of the cross in the Orthodox Russian manner.

"The first time?"

And it took a moment.

Henry opened his eyes.

But he felt the pain.

The blood was real.

He stared at the blood on his chest.

Devereaux turned off the tape recorder. "The problem is in the charge. You use too much and you might kill someone. Too little and you don't fool them. You and Narvak used a blood bag but I couldn't count on your cooperation, could I, Henry? You use very little shot but the force of the blast is enough to shock you off your stool, and the blood, well, you got enough shot in you to attract magnets but I doubt you're in such bad shape as you think."

"Then I'm not dying?"

"I'm not a doctor. Only an agent." He went to the telephone and dialed a number and spoke to the emergency service at the other end of the line.

In a little while, they heard the wail of the volunteer rescue ambulance on the hills.

FORTY-SIX

The Truth
of Henry McGee

Henry McGee did not die and was hospitalized for less than two weeks with a number of superficial wounds, as well as several broken ribs.

The inquiry was held in secret and it was decided that security at the complex in Maryland had to be increased. It was also decided that the incident involving an agent named November and a detainee named Henry McGee would be expunged from records. This was decided at the highest level in R Section. It was decided reluctantly but there was no other way.

The tape recording, however, was not destroyed.

Devereaux received a private reprimand of the most severe nature. It was delivered verbally.

Patricia Heath announced her surprising retirement from the Senate on July 14. Two days later, she was indicted on various federal charges by the U.S. attorney at Fairbanks who had received undisputable documents of her involvement in the pipeline blackmail case. He did not reveal the source of the documents and there was much speculation that it was Malcolm Crowder.

Malcolm Crowder, in fact, could not balance a checkbook, let alone accumulate evidence on another human being.

The evidence had arrived anonymously from another source.

FORTY-SEVEN

Exiles

A lexa was surprised to find Roger's older Porsche still in the parking lot at LAX.

She drove to her own place and took a long shower and contemplated her uselessness and loneliness. She thought her life had been a full thing only when she was with the KGB and she killed people for them. She had extracted all the information from Karpov without any feeling at all, even if Karpov had a part in frightening her, humiliating her with those photographs. It was business.

The next day, she was visited by a very young woman who said she was from the Witness Relocation Program.

"We have to relocate you, Alexa," Karen O'Hare said. "The program compromised you. I apologize for that."

Alexa had not offered her coffee, had not even asked her to sit down. Alexa felt serious contempt for someone so young talking this nonsense to her.

"I'm never leaving Los Angeles," Alexa explained. "I am in no danger."

"Three men took you to a motel room and they knew who you were. They took photographs of you to force another member of the program to do what they wanted." Karen said this very hard and flat. Alexa was very willful, it was noted in her 201 file.

"That is past," Alexa said with contempt. "There is no place like Los Angeles."

"There has to be something," Karen said. She envisioned the U.S. as a giant menu. "I thought you would like Seattle."

"Is that where it rains all the time?"

"It doesn't, actually."

"I have friends here."

"It is not so far from here," said Karen.

"I will not go."

"I'm afraid you must. It's a matter of security," Karen said. "And we are still paying you."

Later, Alexa told Roger some things. She made love to him for a long time and then told him about three men who had kidnapped her and taken her to a motel room. They had staged her death in the room after stripping her and making her wear a signboard.

"So what they wanted to do was blackmail another person with the photographs?" Roger said. He was naked and they were in bed, beneath the $240-a-sheet satin covers. Roger had been on an up all day with the makings of a new deal in which Danny DeVito would reprise the Marlon Brando role in *On the Waterfront*. The old movie would be rewritten into a comedy and titled *Waterfront!*

"Yes," Alexa said, making her voice small. "I don't know what to do."

"It's fabulous," Roger said.

"Roger," she began. "I was kidnapped."

"Someone like Kim Basinger, a victim kind but very haughty too, someone for the eighties. Make it sort of like that guy that wrote those stories in Czechoslovakia, make it that she doesn't know what's going on."

"Roger, is this not a terrible thing I have told you that happened to me?"

"It's fabulous," Roger said, meaning every word.

Denisov was going to leave Santa Barbara in a few days for relocation to another place in the country.

He felt nothing about this. He had felt nothing about so many things since the day in Alaska when he had decided at the last moment that he was reconciled to returning to Moscow, that he would betray another man to do it.

He was waiting for the movers and he could not stand sitting in the empty apartment.

Karen O'Hare was the agent who had informed him. She had replaced Wagner, who was now in federal custody because he could not make his bond on all the charges against him.

Denisov put on his light coat and went out of the apartment because the movers would be hours late. He had nothing to do.

He walked in the bright morning sun of midsummer in Santa Barbara. The early fog was already burned away from the hills. He wondered if he would miss this place.

He wondered about Moscow and sometimes he hummed the melody of "Moscow Nights" and felt very sad. The man with two countries has none. He had not wanted to make a decision again, but when it came, he had decided to go home.

They would have killed him probably but he would have been home.

He walked in the slow careful way of a heavy man who watches his steps and sees all around him.

He did not see the other man waiting at the intersection, however. He was trained to see in certain situations but not in this one where he was wrapped in his own thoughts.

It had taken Skeeter a long time. Skeeter followed the trail of the Russian man to Nome and then back to Anchorage and even down to Seattle where it disappeared again. The newspapers had no more accounts of the heavy Russian man who had killed his friend Pierce. The man from Dutch Harbor who wanted solitude, and a few friends, and a little whiskey, and whom Skeeter had grown to love.

Skeeter worked the navy to find the heavy man.

Everyone could be found and it was a matter of careful patience. It was also about delving into the business that Pierce did, about the faxcopy photo of Denisov that Pierce had given him in the airplane above Cook Inlet on the last night of Pierce's life.

"He was a spy," someone told Skeeter. Hell, Skeeter had known that when he flew Pierce to Anchorage.

But he had been a friend as well.

Friendship counted for something and this wasn't about politics or spies or who was doing a cover-up.

This was about a heavy man who got away with killing his friend.

He had the horse killer under his jacket and he was waiting for the man to begin the turn around the block.

He knew just the way the man did things, every day of his life.

Or on this, the last day of his life.

Because Skeeter was a true friend and you had to avenge the death of a friend.

FORTY-EIGHT
The Hurt

Ninety-four days later, in the midst of the humid and suffocating summer in Washington, D.C., they sat in an air-conditioned office off Pennsylvania Avenue and signed papers.

It is the ritual of property transfer. You sign and sign and the papers keep coming and the lawyers have grim faces.

He kept looking at her.

When it was all signed, one of the buyers wanted to shake his hand.

Devereaux looked through him.

That made her smile.

They walked into the bright sunshine.

"What are you going to do?" she said.

"About what?"

"Do you want to fight?"

"No."

"You want to buy me a drink?"

"No," he said.

She looked at him curiously. "You know about Ted?"

"Yes," he said.

"He's very nice."

"I know all about him."

"I don't know if I want you to spy on me."

He said, "It's what I do best."

"Damn you," she said, but she wasn't very angry.

"Marry him," he said.

"You give up easy," she said. She had not intended to say that. It was the dumbest thing in the world she could have said.

He kissed her.

They never made it past the door of room 312 in the Willard Hotel. He helped her unbutton her clothes. It was frantic and silly, almost as if they were teenagers.

They made love standing up, in the hallway leading to the room, made frantic and terrible and warm love. They had clothes on. They opened each other and hurt each other with their rough caresses. When it was done, they made love again.

They slept on a rented bed in a hotel room in the warm night, beneath the stars. They slept as exhausted lovers. Their hands touched. It was just a little time apart. In the morning, when sunlight probed their disarray, they would have to decide something and neither of them wanted to think about it. They merely touched hands and let their bodies sleep, forgetting about the next hurts.

Begun in Nome, Alaska
Finished in Chicago

Please turn the page

for a

Special Bonus Chapter

of

THE MAN WHO
HEARD TOO MUCH

by Bill Granger

A WARNER BOOKS HARDCOVER

loaded, and the *Leo Tolstoy* would sail in the morning for Gdansk, on the Polish north coast.

Viktor Rusinov paused on the passageway and sensed his fear. He stood very still to make his fear subside. He smelled the sea and the city beyond. He heard a church bell toll. He blessed himself with the Orthodox sign of the cross because he was a religious man. The fear was suppressed in that ritual.

There were two political officers assigned to the *Leo Tolstoy*. They were both ashore now, probably gorging themselves at the smorgasbord served at the Opera. The political officers—who were, in fact, members of the Committee for State Security, the KGB —were totally privileged men.

Viktor Rusinov had nourished his rudimentary communist hatred for the upper classes during five years at sea. He hated the KGB men and he hated the captain. He hated every superior officer. He hated people with money, and those who could buy goods in the special stores set aside for foreigners. He hated with the fine, certain passion of the committed Christian. He knew God would destroy his superiors in time (and in a particularly cruel way). He was certain hell awaited them for their sins of having more than Viktor Rusinov. Development of this hatred had not been enough for Viktor; he had decided, in the end, to enjoy the benefits of his superiors in the only way left open to him. But there was risk to it, and that made him afraid.

Viktor came from a small village a hundred miles south of Moscow. He had dreamed always of the sea. He loved the life of it. He loved the company of his fellow seamen. He loved to drink and to fornicate, and he saw nothing in those activities that compromised his religious beliefs. The women he had were not important and did not figure in his complex scheme of good and evil and envy and retribution. He was strong and tall and his eyes were blue. He could have been Swedish or Polish because of his fair complexion.

He was going to slip over the side in a few minutes and disappear into the fog of neutral Stockholm. He had only waited for his father to die, and his father had obliged him two months earlier in a cancer ward. He had no one left and no obligation to return. He saw it that way, in those correct, legal terms.

He would have preferred to defect in New York, but Stockholm was here and now. He had been in New York harbor once but had not been allowed to leave the freighter. The immensity of that city thrilled him as well as the constant rumble—the city noises conspired to create a constant sound like that of a train passing in the distance—and he knew it was his destiny to return there sometime. Stockholm was the first step. Besides, in the last few days the KGB men had spent a lot of time watching him. Now was the time. He knew the location of the American embassy —101 Strandvägen, which was the broad street on the harbor in Norrmalm, the northern sector of the city.

The red flag was limp on the standard at the stern of the ship. The ship was silent, full of a thousand tiny noises that were as comforting as lullabies. The ship rode the slight swell of the harbor, the bulkheads rubbing against the pilings, making soft, purring sounds against the ropes.

He opened the door of the radio room.

Yazimoff was there as he should have been. Yazimoff looked up at Viktor.

"So, it's now?" But not really a question. Yazimoff almost smirked. It was very annoying, and it made the tense knot in Viktor's stomach that much more painful.

Viktor inclined his head without a word. He reached into the pocket of his coat and extracted the wad of rubles, deutsche marks, francs, dollars, and pounds. A lot of money, some of it quite valuable. All he had saved from the liquor trade. Viktor Rusinov, when not counting his resentments and nursing his jealousies, was both a maker and seller of illegal vodka. Nothing had helped his business more than the crackdown on vodka by the Gorbachev government.

Yazimoff stared at the money with reverence. It was quite a lot, more than he had ever seen in his life.

"This," Yazimoff said.

Viktor stared at the handwriting on the paper. It was Yazimoff's. He did not understand the message, but he understood clearly it was in code.

"What is this?"

"Oleg? You know, the fat one? He took the message and he decoded it right away. And he used this."

Viktor took the second sheet of paper. The key. It was covered with numbers arranged in sets of four. Viktor didn't really understand how it worked—but so what? That was someone else's problem. Viktor wanted to defect to the Americans. The coded message and its key would be a gift, to show his good intentions and to make certain the Americans would not send him back.

"Is it worth this?" Viktor asked, holding up the bills.

Yazimoff made a little shrug but held out his hand. He took the roll of bills and put it in his pocket without counting.

Viktor folded the two sheets of paper carefully into a waterproof envelope attached to a chain around his neck. He rebuttoned his shirt.

"The water is cold," Yazimoff said.

"I've swum in colder water," Viktor Rusinov said. He had a tendency to brag about his abilities, including his prowess with women and his gargantuan need for drink. No one on the *Leo Tolstoy* much liked him, but as a bootlegger, he was tolerated.

Viktor closed the hatch to the radio room. It was 1600 hours, and the ship was caught in that curious, sleepy time between the workday and the evening mess. No one was on deck. He went carefully and quietly down the ladders.

When he reached the main deck, he looked over the side. The *Tolstoy* rode low in the oily, dark water. The fog made his skin wet. He wiped at his lips. He would drop off on the seaside and swim around to the end of the pier, where it would be safe to climb up the old ladder to land.

"What are you staring at, Seaman?"

Viktor turned.

The first mate of the watch was on the deck, scarcely six feet from him. It was Doesniov, a particularly loathsome specimen in Viktor's pantheon of hated superior officers. Doesniov was a big, boastful man with a bullying manner. He strutted down the deck to where Viktor stood at the rail.

"Well? What are you staring at? Do you see something in the water, in all this damned fog?"

Viktor felt intimidated, not by Doesniov's size but by his rank. Viktor's intense hatred for those in superior positions did not alter his almost religious respect for rank.

"I thought I heard something—"

"What? Heard a mermaid?"

"Something in the water." He was not a very good liar. But Doesniov looked over the rail. There. He was looking over the rail.

Viktor couldn't move.

Doesniov turned to look at him. "You've been drinking your own stuff, Viktor Ilyich."

"I don't . . ." So Doesniov knew about the illegal liquor trade. Why not? Everyone knew everything. "Look—"

"Are you ill? You look ill."

Viktor felt the color drain from his face. He felt fear and cold. He felt the weight of the documents in the waterproof envelope on the chain around his neck. He could give them back, say it was a mistake—

That was stupid! Yazimoff wouldn't give back his money. What would the two pigs from KGB do? They already suspected him, he was sure of it.

"Look!" Viktor pointed down at the water, as though something had caught his eye.

Doesniov turned. Again, he looked over the rail, his head lower than his shoulders.

Viktor had to do it. God offered him no choice.

Both hands locked into a hammer of flesh. The hammer came down hard on the base of the skull. Doesniov grunted, his chin broke on the rail, and he slid to the wet deck. God offered no choice. There was only this one way and no other.

Viktor slipped out of his wool coat and dropped it over the side.

Not a moment to spare.

He scarcely made a splash when he hit the water.

DON'T MISS THESE EXCITING NOVELS
FROM BESTSELLING AUTHOR,

BILL GRANGER

- ☐ **THE INFANT OF PRAGUE**
  A34-780 ($4.95, USA) ($5.95, Can.)

- ☐ **THERE ARE NO SPIES**
  A34-705 ($3.95, USA) ($4.95, Can.)

- ☐ **HEMINGWAY'S NOTEBOOK**
  A30-284 ($4.50, USA) ($5.95, Can.)

- ☐ **THE EL MURDERS**
  A35-209 ($4.95, USA) ($5.95, Can.)

- ☐ **THE NOVEMBER MAN**
  A32-473 ($4.95, USA) ($5.95, Can.)

- ☐ **PUBLIC MURDERS**
  A34-406 ($3.95, USA) ($4.95, Can.)

- ☐ **NEWSPAPER MURDERS**
  A34-290 ($3.95, USA) ($4.95, Can.)

**Warner Books P.O. Box 690
New York, NY 10019**

Please send me the books I have checked. I enclose a check or money order (not cash), plus 95¢ per order and 95¢ per copy to cover postage and handling.* (Allow 4-6 weeks for delivery.)

___Please send me your free mail order catalog. (If ordering only the catalog, include a large self-addressed, stamped envelope.)

Name _____

Address _____

City _____ State _____ Zip _____

*New York and California residents add applicable sales tax.

411